PASSIONATE PRAISE FOR
THE NOVELS OF DELIA PARR

"Few writers are on par with Delia Parr when it comes to scribing fresh and interesting historical romance."

—Affaire de Coeur

SUNRISE

"Always one to break the rules and craft an intelligent, thought-provoking romance, Delia Parr has created a suspenseful and emotionally powerful story for the discerning reader."
—Romantic Times

"The town of Sunrise and its inhabitants virtually come alive in this unique story...A very enjoyable reading experience."
—Old Book Barn Gazette

"SUNRISE is a well thought-out and engrossing book that delivers."
—Rocky Mountain News

THE MINISTER'S WIFE

"With great power and true understanding of deep emotions, fears, longings, and love, Delia Parr delivers another unique story that etches itself into your heart."

—Romantic Times

"Parr's latest is brimming with forbidden temptation, old scandals, dark secrets, darker betrayals, and the power of faith."
—Publishers Weekly

Turn the page for more acclaim...

"THE MINISTER'S WIFE may be the 'breakout' novel that establishes Parr's reputation.... [It] reaches a new level of emotional suspense and dramatic complexity... Parr's writing is fresh and original."

—*Milwaukee Journal-Sentinel*

"[Parr's] characters are delightful... Parr's book is one in which the reader can search for hidden meanings of life in the various situations she presents, or reading the novel can be taken strictly as a recreational pastime. Either way, the reader wins."   —*Raton* (NM) *Range*

THE IVORY DUCHESS

"A heartwarming romance... an emotional love story of hidden pasts, assumed identities, and unexpected love."

—CompuServe Romance Reviews

"Delia Parr has done a wonderful job in balancing an emotional love story with humor... highly recommended."

—*Under the Covers Book Reviews*

"Ms. Parr is one bright star to watch!"—*Romance Forever*

BY FATE'S DESIGN

"Delia Parr vividly depicts everyday Shaker life, and BY FATE'S DESIGN showcases both triumph and anguish for the human heart and soul. Ms. Parr's star is definitely on the rise."   —*Romance Forever*

"Delia Parr has given us an intriguing historical, laced with delightful characters, passionate romance, and a heartwarming tale of love, growth, and trust—an incredibly beautiful love story."   —*Rendezvous*

The Promise of Flowers

DELIA PARR

St. Martin's Paperbacks

THE PROMISE OF FLOWERS

Copyright © 2000 by Mary Lechleidner.

All rights reserved. No part of this book may be used or reproduced in any manner whatsoever without written permission except in the case of brief quotations embodied in critical articles or reviews. For information address St. Martin's Press, 175 Fifth Avenue, New York, N.Y. 10010.

ISBN: 0-312-97505-8

Printed in the United States of America

St. Martin's Paperbacks edition / September 2000

St. Martin's Paperbacks are published by St. Martin's Press, 175 Fifth Avenue, New York, N.Y. 10010.

10 9 8 7 6 5 4 3 2 1

*Dedicated to
my agent, Linda Kruger,
whose professionalism and boundless enthusiasm
challenge and inspire me beyond all measure.
You are truly the "wind beneath my wings."*

Foreword

✦

Readers often ask where ideas for stories come from, and I don't usually have a specific answer. For *The Promise of Flowers,* I do.

The Powel House near Fourth and Spruce Streets is an historic home in Philadelphia, the city where I had decided to set this book. While researching, I found a detailed architectural study of the house, now restored and open to the public for tours. I also discovered there is a single sketch showing a large, three-story tower that has not survived, but once adjoined or stood very close to the main house. There is no other historical evidence to document the tower ever existed, the reason it was torn down, or even the purpose it served.

Thus, I borrowed the house, the tower, and the mystery to create the fictional Dunn mansion and let Violet Dunn tell me the story I share with you now.

I am extremely grateful to my most gracious tour guide at Powel House, but any misinterpretations belong to me.

For his help in researching the history of modern jigsaw puzzles, originally called dissected pictures, I am indebted to Bob Whitworth, whose Internet site (www.printsgeorge .com) and e-mails were tremendously helpful.

Delia Parr

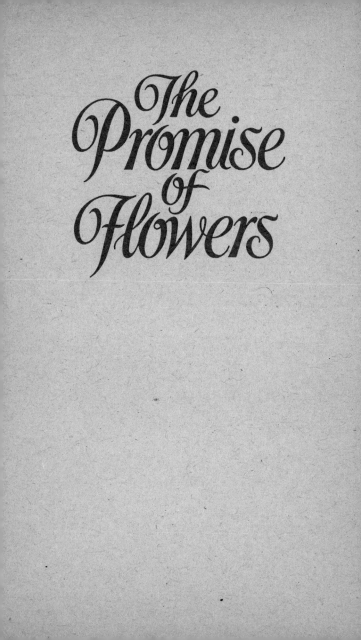

The Promise of Flowers

Prologue

OCTOBER 1833
PHILADELPHIA, PA

$\mathcal{V}$iolet prayed for the best, but expected to find the worst when she finally came face-to-face with her sister, Rosemary.

Just before sunset, she opened the door to the four-story tower adjoining her home where her sister had been confined in solitary isolation for the past week, punishment for slipping out again late at night. Guilt weighed heavy on Violet's heart, but the burden of constant vigilance, of keeping a close eye on Rosemary both day and night, was not always easy to carry, especially alone.

Determined to make amends now that she had finally gotten permission to bring Rosemary back to the house, she entered the second-floor sitting room. She bolted the door behind her, along with any gratitude she had for her father. Since Rosemary suffered from the same mental distraction that had claimed their mother, banishing her to the tower again was punishment that was as cruel as it was dangerous, but she had learned to expect nothing more from him.

Constance Montgomery had been one of Philadelphia's richest heiresses. As her husband, Charles Dunn had enjoyed the fruits of his wife's wealth. But as her widower, he was powerless to keep the Montgomery fortune from passing directly to Violet and Rosemary, their inheritance controlled by trustees carefully chosen by Asa Montgomery in his will.

Deeply disgruntled, her father had retaliated against the

two innocents who now stood between him and the fortune he had coveted. She suspected his unnatural disdain for his daughters was only part of his scheme to one day regain control of the fortune he had lost to them.

She glanced around the room before painful memories held her captive. Shadows from the curtainless, barred windows crisscrossed the sitting room, but Rosemary was not there. Taking a deep breath, Violet bypassed her worktable, went directly to the bookshelves along the far wall, and reached behind the bottom row of books to remove one of her childhood daybooks from its hiding place.

She was grateful she had been able to keep her father from discovering her secret treasure, and she pressed it to her chest. Between the dusty leather covers, yellowed pages held a precious few mementos of her mother. When she committed suicide, abruptly ending a lifelong battle with melancholia that labeled her as hopelessly mad, Violet had only been eight. Too little to understand her mother's illness or prevent her death. Old enough to remember her mother's final words: "Always protect and defend those you love."

Fighting tears, she vowed to remain true to her mother's counsel and carried her daybook with her as she made her way to the circular staircase that led to the third-floor sleeping chamber. She paused at the bottom step and listened hard, but no sound broke the eerie silence. She tried to quiet her fears, as well, but her heart still pounded with worry for what she would find upstairs.

Would Rosemary be withdrawn and unresponsive, locked in a state of complete despair that would signal another episode of melancholia? Or would she take one look at Violet and erupt into a whirlwind of frenzy, so highly agitated she would be difficult to control?

Facing either prospect was daunting, but not knowing how Rosemary would react was even worse. Unfortunately, Violet had no one to help her, and she started up the staircase. Resentment against her father grew with each narrow step she mounted, opening old wounds that tested her courage and determination.

She stopped and tightened her hold on her daybook. She closed her eyes and tried to put her own needs aside, to concentrate only on helping her sister. But the desperate desire to have someone at her side, offering support and encouragement, as well as strength, was nothing more than an impossible dream—one that threatened to weaken her resolve, reminding her, once again, of the price she had already paid to always remain strong.

Violet had learned, through painful experience, to hide her strength behind weakness to placate her father. Gifted with a strong, healthy mind, she had feigned episodes of melancholia and taken responsibility for Rosemary's mischief to protect her from him. She had succeeded more often than not, but she had failed completely when it came to protecting her from gossipmongers who called both of them mad.

As a consequence, Violet was completely alone. She had never had the chance to make any friends. A constant turnover in servants offered little opportunity for any to become her confidants. Her one ally, Elijah Dennus, had been a friend of her grandfather's, but Father had banned him from the house months ago.

With the yoke of responsibility always heavy on her shoulders, she had to be conscious of every word she dared to speak. She had to suppress whatever spontaneity might once have been part of her spirit. Uncommonly guarded with anyone she met, especially her father's friends and business associates, she simply could not chance risking her ultimate goal: independence and freedom—for herself and Rosemary.

Halfway up the steps, she faltered at the curve and leaned against the railing for support. She took several deep breaths as the events of this past week unfolded again, reminding her she must remain strong for much longer than she had hoped. Under the terms of her grandfather's will, she had had to wait until her twenty-first birthday to claim her inheritance and escape her father's domineering control. But she had marked that birthday only days ago by signing a document giving her father the right to control her inheritance, as well as her life, for another two years, until Rosemary herself would turn twenty-one and be able to claim her inheritance and her freedom, too.

In exchange, all she had was his word she would be allowed to remain by Rosemary's side whenever she was ill and his promise not to place her sister in an asylum should she suffer another episode of melancholia.

Armed with the mementos of her mother, she reembraced her role now as the only one who could help and protect Rosemary. From herself. From gossipmongers. And from their father—the one man who should have been a loving protector to them both.

She mounted the rest of the staircase with steps that were strong and sure. When she neared the top, she glanced up at the ceiling. Overhead, the treatment room was on the fourth floor. Harrowing memories of Rosemary being treated in the tranquilizer chair, with leather straps that held her limbs and body still and a boxlike cage that restrained her head movement and restricted vision, for hours, perhaps even days, made her tremble with outrage.

Dr. Poole used the chair to break her spirit and her will, to make her conform to Father's dictates, to make her meek and controllable. As far as Violet was concerned, treatment in the tranquilizer chair only triggered episodes of deep melancholia that would last for months.

But no treatment could change Rosemary's basic nature. Vibrant and precocious, she was completely unpredictable, a free spirit who needed excitement and adventure to survive as much as air to breathe. And one day, she would be free, Violet vowed.

When she reached the top of the steps, she glanced around the sleeping chamber. Her sister's bed was empty and the covers undisturbed while Rosemary sat huddled in the corner of the window seat. Her gown was badly wrinkled. Her hair was unkempt, a mass of blond tangles and knots that cascaded in disarray down the length of her curved back. With her legs bent and drawn up to her chin, her head rested atop her knees. She faced the window, apparently unaware of Violet's arrival.

Violet swallowed hard. She waited with bated breath until

Rosemary finally sensed her presence, stirred, and turned to face her. When she saw the telltale symptoms of the melancholia, her heart constricted with pain.

Rosemary's facial expression was bland, even detached. No hint of interest, only a brief flash of recognition flared in her dark blue eyes before it disappeared, leaving her gaze dull and unnaturally calm, like the waters of a lake no breeze of hope or joy dared to disturb. With her shoulders slumped and her hands lying listlessly at her sides, she offered the barest hint of a frown before she laid down her head and closed her eyes.

Unbidden, tears welled in Violet's eyes. She blinked them away and refused to give in to despair. Maybe if she acted quickly and used the daybook this time, she would be able to help Rosemary before she sank so deeply into melancholia she would have to be treated by the doctor.

She sat down next to her sister and prayed she would find the right words to help her. "Rosemary?" she murmured as she tugged on her sister's hand. "Father gave me permission to take you back to your room tonight. Will you come with me now?"

No response.

"I've been so worried about you," she crooned, caressing her sister's head.

A shudder. "You should have left when you had the chance."

Her heart trembled at the deep despair that laced her sister's words. "I could never leave you," she admonished. "You're my sister. I love you. And I'm going to stay right here with you until we can both leave together. But I can't help you, unless you let me."

A deep sigh. "Why should I try? Nothing has changed. It never will."

Violet was too stubborn to believe that was true, but she knew better than to argue with her sister when she was poised on the brink of total despair. She tucked her legs beneath her and opened the daybook. Memories of sunny spring days spent outside in the garden with her mother sprang to life the moment she opened the first two pages.

She took her sister's hand and placed it atop the yellow blossom that had been pressed between them. "Do you remember how Mama used to take us out in the garden? You picked this dandelion when you were only six. Mama told you it meant you were promised a lifetime of happiness."

She paused and watched her sister's face for some response. After many long heartbeats, her sister finally opened her eyes. When she reached out and traced the dried flower with her fingertips, one corner of her lips turned up to shape a lopsided smile.

Violet allowed herself a sigh of relief.

Half a smile was a beginning.

There was a long journey ahead before Rosemary would be well again, but it was a journey they would take side by side.

One smile at a time, until they were free to reclaim all of their hopes and dreams.

Together.

$\mathcal{T}$onight was a night to celebrate a new beginning, not dwell on memories that belonged to the past.

Sam Glennings closed and locked the front door to the town house he had only recently inherited from Aunt Lily. With a jaunty step, he headed down the street to meet his lawyer, Ben Hastings, to celebrate Sam's new business venture in Philadelphia.

As he passed rows of brick town houses and city mansions and his footsteps echoed on cobblestone walkways, images of Sunrise, a small country village in western Pennsylvania where he had been born and bred, flashed through his mind. Only squares away, heavily sailed vessels sat high in the Delaware River, instead of the Susquehanna, waiting to be loaded with exports his new firm would soon be able to supply.

With a fire bell clanging in the distance, he crossed the street and approached the tower adjoining a city mansion that occupied a full square of land. Soft light filtering between the bars on the third-floor windows illuminated the silhouettes of two figures huddled together. From all accounts he had been given, one Dunn sister was as insane as the other. They were definitely two women he would avoid like yellow fever.

He glanced away before his mind could conjure up images of two other women. His former wife, Polly, would be spending the rest of her life in an asylum behind locked doors and barred windows so she could not destroy anyone else ever again, while his beloved sister, Jane, was rebuilding her life even now . . .

He quickened his steps to put distance between himself and the tower, but he could not elude the bitter memories he thought he had left behind in Sunrise. A little over a year ago, their whole world had exploded into a nightmare his worst fears could not have imagined. Polly had not only betrayed her vows, she had murdered her lover, Jane's husband, Hiram Foster, and had done her best to see that Jane was wrongfully convicted of the crime. Despite city-lawyer Daniel Colton's best efforts, Polly nearly succeeded.

Until Daniel called her to the stand to bear witness to Jane's character. When the bailiffs finally led her away, she was a confessed murderess whose leap into irrevocable madness was as dramatic as the events she had just described, and Jane was set free. Within days, Daniel had wed Jane, left his lucrative practice in Philadelphia in Ben's hands, and taken his bride to France for a year to recover while Sam stayed in Sunrise, scarred and pitied, yet supported by a community still reeling with its own collective guilt.

Once Daniel and Jane returned to Sunrise, where Daniel settled in as a small-town lawyer, Sam knew he had to leave Sunrise, too, if he ever intended to find the same peace and contentment.

Aunt Lily's unexpected death had given him the wherewithal to forge a path to healing all his own. Now, after only two weeks in Philadelphia, he was well on his way. The town house was ideal, and he had quickly found a house-keeper willing to spend a few hours a day tidying up and

preparing a meal for him to eat whenever he arrived home
from work. After sharing his home in Sunrise with Aunt
Nester, bless her doting heart, he enjoyed his solitude.

He had his divorce decree, now a year old, stored in the
safe in the study. In his pocket, he had the keys to a small
office on High Street he had leased just this morning. He had
a list of suppliers from his former hauling business to get him
started. A newly hired associate, Tremore Flynn, had ambition that exceeded his valuable experience on the docks—
experience Sam needed to be successful.

And Sam aimed high. He would settle for nothing less than
being the biggest broker in Philadelphia and this pitted him
against a formidable competitor, the Montgomery Packet Line
operated by Charles Dunn.

With a pang of conscience, he glanced back over his shoulder at the tower. It was now enveloped in full darkness, so
he had no view of the poor tortured souls inside, and he dismissed any worry about their welfare. Through discreet inquiry, he had learned their inheritance from their grandfather,
Asa Montgomery, was well protected by trustees who would
hold a tight rein on Charles Dunn's control of the packet line.
That company was but one of the enterprises funding the
trusts established for the young women.

He turned away from the tower and resumed walking. He
had no time to waste. In two years he intended to topple
Dunn's control of the exports from the western hinterlands
and acquire a fortune for himself as well as Flynn, who would
be earning wages along with a percentage of the profits.

Then Sam would take his fortune and his success back to
Sunrise. As a gentleman farmer, he would work the land
claimed by his ancestors. Financially secure, he would not be
chained to drudgery or victimized by bad seasons and poor
crops as most farmers were.

When he finally returned home, well-earned respect would
put a stop to the pitying glances from neighbors and friends.
He would stand tall and proud as a man of character and
honor in his own right. For once and forever, he would over-
come the scandal and shame now attached to his name and
step out from beneath his sister's shadow.

Chapter One

❧

$\mathcal{V}$iolet's errand today could very well make the difference between success or failure in her bid to win freedom for herself and Rosemary.

She held her breath, tiptoed down the front staircase, and prayed she would escape the house without attracting her father's attention, if not his wrath.

She tightened her hold on her valise, packed with half a dozen new dissected picture puzzles. In her heart, she carried new hopes for the future, but well-founded fear held her joy in check. She could not afford to let down her guard now. Not when she and Rosemary were so close to ending their father's rigid control by claiming their inheritances and beginning lives far away from here where they could escape their reputations and dictate their own lives.

For over a year, Rosemary had been completely healthy in both body and mind, a miracle for which Violet continued to offer daily prayers of thanksgiving. No more bouts of melancholia. No more midnight wanderings through the streets of Philadelphia or adventures along the public docks. No more tantrums or mischief, either.

Perhaps the treatments Rosemary periodically had endured for years had finally effected a permanent cure as Dr. Poole suggested, although he stopped far short of declaring Rosemary permanently cured. More likely, she had simply matured and focused all of her energies, her hopes, and her dreams on her twenty-first birthday when she would be able to claim her inheritance.

With two months still remaining until that happened, Violet could not afford to be complacent or careless about anything, most especially where her father was concerned. Although he had mellowed considerably this past year, she did not accept his turnabout at full value. She and Rosemary had been on the receiving end of his malice and manipulation for far too many years not to expect he would attempt to stop Rosemary from claiming her inheritance in August. Violet also suspected he would try to force her to sign yet another document when the original she had signed two years ago expired in October so he could retain control of her fortune, as well.

She reached the bottom step and paused to shift her valise to her right hand. Swallowing hard, she moistened her lips and walked through the foyer toward the front door. She had tied the ribbon on her bonnet too tight, but did not stop to loosen it or check her appearance in the mirror.

She made her way through the foyer as quietly as she could. As she approached the front door, she let out a sigh of relief. When her father stepped into the foyer from the front parlor, she gasped out loud. Her heart lurched against the wall of her chest, but she did her best to keep guilt from staining her face a bright shade of red.

He took one look at her, spied the valise she carried, and scowled. "Is it necessary to deliver your puzzles in person? Why can't you just send them to the shop with Hudson?"

Her heart pounded in her chest, and she tightened her hold on the handle of the valise. "He—he took Rosemary to the dressmaker's, and I—I was looking forward to . . . to taking the walk," she offered.

His gaze hardened, but he stepped aside and opened the door for her. "I'll expect you home by one for dinner. In case you've forgotten, I have a guest coming to join us."

"I won't be late," she assured him, but resisted the urge to ask him yet again about the mystery guest he had invited. She gripped the handle on her precious cargo tightly as she walked to Dennus's Stationery Store on High Street.

Surprisingly, her father had not objected when Elijah Dennus offered her the opportunity to place her picture puzzles for sale on consignment in the store operated by his son. Fortunately, her father did not consider the little profit she made to be significant enough to warrant any more than polite interest, although he had no idea how many puzzles she had either made or sold.

In truth, her profits this past year had helped to fund a contingency plan should her father make any attempt to prevent Rosemary from claiming control of her inheritance. Violet tilted up her chin as she walked, more determined than ever to stop him. If these new puzzles sold quickly, Elijah would be able to deposit a tidy sum in the secret account at Philadelphia Savings Society he had opened for her when her works first sold.

Her steps quickened, and her heart swelled with a flower of gratitude. Thanks to her friend, she would have more than enough for both herself and Rosemary to escape if that became necessary. To augment her savings, she would continue to make her puzzles to support them. When their lawyers waged a legal battle on their behalf for control of their inheritances, she and Rosemary would both have to be strong in court to prove they were mentally stable and capable of handling their own affairs.

When she found herself on High Street, she replaced her troubled thoughts with visions of a hopeful future. Feeling fanciful, she let her imagination run free and conjured up the image of the clerk who worked in the shipping business next to the stationery store. On more than one occasion when she had delivered her puzzles, she thought she had caught him glancing at her through the display window, although honesty dictated she admit he probably was just inspecting the window display for new merchandise.

Emboldened by dreams she dared to hope might one day come true, she chose to believe, instead, he might be truly interested in her. The very notion made her giggle out loud like a schoolgirl suffering from her first infatuation instead of a young woman who should have known better.

"Well, it is my first," she murmured aloud, reluctant to admit that a man as strapping and handsome as the clerk would be unattached at all. He was at least several years older than she was and surely married, but not in her mind. And it was, after all, her own private fantasy.

Sobered by thoughts of how he might react once he knew who she was, she set her fantasy aside. As a wealthy heiress, she could hardly trust any man to be more interested in her than her wealth. As a reputedly *mad* heiress, she would likely attract men like her father.

The mere thought cast a dark shadow on her fantasy and the very special dream that she might one day find true love.

She did not glance to the side when she passed the office where the clerk worked. Instead, she kept her gaze averted and entered the stationery store. The unusually large crowd of patrons did not faze her or ignite any fears she might be recognized here, since few of the social elites in her father's circle of acquaintances frequented any stationery store other than Carroll's. She scanned the crowd, caught Elijah's harried gaze, and understood his nod as an unspoken plea to join him behind the counter where he was attempting to serve several customers at the same time.

"Simeon's upstairs sick today, along with his wife," he whispered as he tried to wrap up a copy of *Webster's American Dictionary*. Unfortunately, his arthritic hands refused to cooperate. "Be a darlin' girl and set your puzzles right into the display case. It's been near empty for the past week, and customers have been asking for more."

Without wasting a moment to remove her bonnet or cloak, she quickly set half her wares into the display case and left the rest inside the valise. The sight of the poor man still attempting to wrap the dictionary on his own touched her so deeply she did not hesitate for more than a heartbeat. She walked to the back room, stored her bonnet and cloak on a wooden peg, found a clerk's apron, and tied it into place before she rejoined him behind the counter.

"I'll take over here," she suggested as she slid the dictionary and crumpled paper away from him. "You sell. I'll wrap."

He grinned from ear to ear. "As long as you don't tell your father. He'd peel off my skin and have me boiled alive to serve for dinner if he found out you were working behind the counter as a clerk."

Giggling, she felt a blush steal its way up her neck. "Not today. We're having a guest."

"Then I'm safe. Now, Mrs. Pell," he prompted as he re-directed his attention back to his patrons, "what kind of sheet music did you say you were looking for?"

For the next several hours, Violet wrapped more packages than she would have ever imagined. With the shop still attracting a steady stream of patrons, the pace remained hectic and the drone of muted conversations filled the air. When the next patron waiting to be served stepped up to the counter to make a purchase, her heart literally skipped a beat as she gazed into the eyes of the very clerk who had inspired her schoolgirl fantasies.

He was even more handsome up close than he had seemed at a distance. And taller. He topped six feet, at least. With thick sandy hair, he had dark brown eyes that simmered with undisguised interest as he gazed at her. She dropped her gaze immediately and focused on the ink-stained cuffs of his shirt, but it was his presence—commanding and masculine, yet gentle—that sent her heart racing again.

This man surely belonged in a dream far too wicked for her to imagine. Pressed to occupy her mind with less outrageous thoughts, she stepped aside, bent down, and un-loaded the rest of her puzzles into the glass display case.

"Looks like you were right, Elijah. You do have a new selection for me to inspect today," the man suggested as her benefactor rejoined her behind the counter. "After the crowd of patrons streaming in and out of the store all morning, I was worried the puzzles might all be sold."

"As you can see, we're just setting the rest of the new ones into the case."

Finished with her task, Violet rose and backed away from the counter to allow Elijah to wait on his customer, her gaze glued to the floor.

"Come closer, Violet," he urged. "This, my friend, is the young lady who makes the picture puzzles. I'd like you to meet my son's neighbor, Sam Glennings. He's looking for a gift for his little niece. She's what? Two? Three?"

When Sam smiled, he nearly stole her breath away. "A little past a year, but rather precocious, so I'm told. I'm very pleased to meet you, Violet. I've admired your work for some time."

Like a sudden wildfire, a blush stole up her neck and spread to her cheeks. Heat engulfed her body from head to toe. She swallowed hard and lifted her gaze. "Thank you. You're very kind."

And far too experienced with women, she noted, as his sensuous gaze locked with hers.

"Have you a suggestion?"

Incredibly romantic, totally improper visions danced through the flowers in her heart and left them wilting. Her cheeks were so hot she expected the skin to peel right off her face and flutter to the floor.

"For my niece," he prompted with a twinkle in his eye that told her he had similar visions of his own.

"Your . . . your niece. Y-yes. Yes, of course," she stammered and pointed directly to the puzzle closest to her in the rear of the display case. "Appleton's Alphabet. It's rather a large puzzle," she blurted before she had the wherewithal to remember he was not a wealthy businessman, but a clerk who could scarcely afford such an expensive item. "It's cleverly detailed, as you can see by the label, and it's actually quite useful as an educational aide."

"What about this one?"

She had to take a step closer to the case to see that he pointed to a smaller puzzle in the front of the display. "That's also a good choice and equally practical for teaching numerals and sequence."

She tried to keep her voice steady, but failed, embarrassed

that she had not suggested the smaller, less expensive puzzle first.

He cocked a well-shaped brow, and the corner of his lips teased into a smile that would melt the blades on the saws she used to craft the wooden boxes. "You sound like a governess or a teacher."

"Violet's been both," Elijah offered before she could fashion an answer of her own. "She and her sister were very ill as children. Eventually, she became her sister's tutor. That's when I taught her how to make the puzzles. I thought they might pique her sister's interest in her studies and give Violet something to do to fill her empty hours."

Actually, Rosemary was far more interested in maps and geography than either orthography or figuring sums, but Violet was loath to reveal this to either man for fear of inviting further discussion of her private life.

"All the more reason to heed the young lady's suggestions," Sam suggested.

When he hesitated making his final decision on which puzzle to purchase, she worried the price for either was too high. "I have several smaller puzzles that are nearly finished. Perhaps they might be more appropriate for a child so young."

What was entirely inappropriate was the way he gazed at her and how her heart raced each time he smiled at her.

"Since I can't seem to make up my mind, I should probably take both of these new puzzles for Olivia," he drawled as he leaned his hip against the display case and leaned so close to her she could feel the heat of his body.

Frightened by the intensity of her reaction to him, she glanced away and looked up, only to see two new patrons entering the store. When they returned her gaze with shocked expressions, immediate panic raced the length of her spine.

In the next heartbeat, panic turned to total disaster when Mrs. Magee, the wife of her father's lawyer, pouted her lips. "Violet Dunn! Whatever are you doing here working as a . . . as a common clerk?" she admonished.

Her companion, Mrs. Poole, sniffed. "I can't imagine a man with your father's standing would ever allow you to—"

"My father knows exactly where I am," Violet responded, although she was certain he would be furious when he learned she had been serving customers instead of simply delivering her puzzles. She tilted up her chin, but held her breath as she looked back at Sam and studied his face for any sign he might have recognized her name.

She waited less than a heartbeat.

His smile froze in place, and his eyes clouded with confusion. "Dunn? You're Violet *Dunn*?"

With all the magic gone from their chance encounter and her fantasy destroyed by reality, she nodded. "Perhaps you know my father, Charles Dunn. He operates the Montgomery Packet Line here in the city."

Pity extinguished any and all semblance of interest in his eyes. "Indeed, I do," he murmured.

His immediate rejection cut straight to her heart, slashing her wilted fantasies about him into shreds of foolishness and shame she would not ever forget. "I'm afraid I must be going now. We're having a guest to dinner, and I'm afraid I'm late," she offered to Elijah. "Thank you, again, Mr. Glennings. I hope your niece enjoys your gifts."

Without giving either man a chance to respond, she retired to the back room, removed her apron, and donned her bonnet and cloak before she retrieved her now-empty valise. She managed to make an acceptable exit past the two shocked women and ran home as fast as her blurred vision allowed.

Gulping hard to keep tears at bay and to try to settle her rolling stomach, she bid her fantasy man a quick and final farewell and embraced the only dream she had any right to claim: freedom for herself and Rosemary. Far, far away, where no one knew their names or their pasts.

Nothing more.

But nothing less, either.

By the time she reached her front doorstep, she was out of breath, and her mind scrambled for a suitable explanation that would excuse her tardiness and placate her father as well as his guest.

She was scarcely inside the door when her father emerged

from the parlor. Standing rigid, with controlled anger sparking through his eyes like flames licking wet logs, he pursed his lips. Only the presence of the man who sat observing them from his seat in front of the parlor windows could possibly account for her father's ability to maintain his control.

"Congratulations, Violet. You've managed to keep both me and our guest waiting for nearly an hour," he gritted in a harsh whisper.

She quickly removed her bonnet and cloak and handed them both, along with the valise, to a maid quaking at the base of the staircase. "I apologize," she said meekly when she returned and faced her father.

"That's all? You apologize? With no explanation for your rudeness?" he whispered, again through clenched teeth.

"None that you would find acceptable," she confessed. Knowing full well he would hear about her efforts to help Elijah, she decided to take the initiative now and tell him when he would have good reason to temper his anger. "Elijah's son and his wife are ill today and I had to help in the shop. Mrs. Magee and Mrs. Poole send their regards."

His lips twisted into an angry frown before he grabbed her elbow hard to escort her into the parlor. "For your sake, you'd best think of a more suitable explanation before I introduce you to your future husband. You've already managed to slight him by being late."

Chapter Two

❧

$\mathcal{V}$iolet's legs nearly buckled, and she frantically searched her father's gaze for some sign she must have misheard him. To her horror, she found only a solid wall of black determination staring back at her. "F-future h-husband?"

"Fortunately," he snapped before he turned to lead her into the parlor, "he's already signed the marriage contract. You're to be married and off to your new home within the month."

Shocked senseless, Violet's mind locked and froze. She was unable to feel a single emotion beyond horror or to take a single step. Married? Within the month?

"Captain Jeremiah Miles, ma'am," offered the veritable giant of a man who emerged from his seat. His broad shoulders blocked the daylight streaming through the windows and cast his bearded face in shadows, but his deep voice resonated with firmness that equaled his massive frame.

The floorboards creaked as he walked closer to her, took her from her father, and guided her to her chair. "Perhaps you'd better sit down. You shouldn't be embarrassed. Or afraid. Most folks find my size rather intimidating. I'm quite accustomed to it, although I must say it proves worthwhile when commanding a crew."

She sank into the seat. Intimidating? She would have to stand on the chair just to look at him eye to eye!

"Perhaps a glass of brandy might help," he suggested.

"No. I'm fine. I'm ... I'm afraid there's been some mistake," she croaked. Her mind raced through a maze of thoughts, scrambling for the right words to make the man understand she was not opposed to him because of his unbelievable size, but an arranged marriage. She could not marry him. She did not even know him. And how could she leave Rosemary behind, now or ever?

Or was that exactly what her father wanted? With Violet gone, no one would be here to protect Rosemary as she turned twenty-one and was entitled to claim her inheritance.

She leaned to the side and looked directly at her father. "Rosemary. Where's Rosemary?"

He shook his head and smiled sadly. "She's with Dr. Poole. I'm afraid she's suffered a setback. Hopefully, time in the tranquilizer chair will calm her down."

Visions of Rosemary strapped into the treatment chair tugged at her very soul and unleashed memories that chilled her heart. Heart pounding, she bolted to her feet, rushed past the titan and her father, and charged up the staircase to the tower. She pushed the door as she twisted the glass knob, but the door had been bolted shut from the other side. She pounded on the door and cried her sister's name until she was hoarse. Tears of frustration covered her face when she finally collapsed against the door for strength to remain standing.

Silence, save for the sound of her own fractured breathing. Then ominous, controlled footsteps.

She turned, leaned back against the door, and raised her gaze to greet her father with cold dread wrapped around her heart. "What have you done?"

He cocked a brow, then shook his head. "Nothing more than any devoted father saddled with not one, but two mentally distracted daughters. I've had to search far and wide to find you a respectable husband. As for your sister—"

"What did you do to her?" she repeated, but in a sudden flash of insight, she knew exactly what he had done. "You told her, didn't you?" She charged forward. "You told her I was to be married. That I was leaving her. Didn't you?"

He grabbed her arms and shook her so hard her teeth chattered before he pushed her away from him. "Yes. I told her exactly that. And more."

Terrified by the hard glint in his eyes, she backed away from him and rubbed the numbness from her arms.

"Unfortunately, your sister's mind is far more fragile than even the doctors suspected. When she learned of your impending marriage, she became rather agitated, even hysterical. I fear she created quite a scene at Mrs. Dunsmore's—"

"You told her at the dressmaker's shop?"

"I had already instructed Mrs. Dunsmore to suggest a suitable gown for Rosemary to wear to your wedding. She argued so vehemently Hudson left to summon me to the shop to restrain the poor child. She has such a feeble grasp on her temper as well as reality."

Chest heaving, Violet balled her fists. "What reality is that? That you've arranged for my marriage without my knowledge or consent? Or that you deliberately chose a public place to tell Rosemary? Why? In all that's holy, why?"

He shrugged his shoulders. "It's very simple, my dear. Our agreement expires in October, and it appears you're well enough to take control of your own inheritance. Marrying you off before you suffered a relapse seemed imperative, and I'm quite satisfied with my arrangement with Captain Miles."

Violet locked her knees to keep them from shaking and forced the bile back down her throat. "Precisely what arrangement would that be? How much is a distracted heiress truly worth in the marriage market?"

"A ship. One commodity hard to come by when you've been cursed by bad luck. Three shipwrecks in as many years can quickly ruin a captain's reputation."

She swallowed hard. "What ship? You've no right—"

"You gave me the right to oversee your investments on your twenty-first birthday, remember? Unfortunately, the profits from the Montgomery Packet Line have dwindled to nearly nothing, thanks in no small measure to Glennings."

Her eyes widened, and her mind latched on to a most impossible notion as the face and form of Sam Glennings flashed before her mind's eye. "Glennings?"

"Sam Glennings. He's a ruthless broker dealing with western exports," he spat. "When honest competition failed, he used sabotage to acquire his fortune at the expense of yours. The miserable cur has no scruples."

She scarcely listened as her father rattled off a list of Sam's character flaws. Instead, she replayed her earlier encounter with Sam Glennings. He was not a clerk after all. He owned the firm next to the stationery store. Had he known who she was all along?

She would never know for sure, but of one thing she was quite certain: Sam Glennings was responsible for forcing her father into taking drastic action which in turn put Rosemary at risk and sentenced Violet to marriage to a total stranger!

"I've decided to sell the entire enterprise and use whatever profits remain to begin a new venture, after transferring title to the *Carousel* to Captain Miles, of course."

Hearing the name of her intended husband snapped her back to reality. "He's really marrying me for a ship?"

He snorted. "Hardly, my dear. You're an heiress, albeit a tainted one. I've no doubt he'll convince you to let him handle your remaining financial resources, particularly since he expects you to accompany him on his voyages. Given his size, you'd be a fool to resist."

"Or mad," she whispered. Shivering, she closed her eyes briefly to block out the images of her life with the sea captain that crashed together in her mind with images of Rosemary—alone and completely shattered.

"As for your sister, the poor troubled soul, she was quite inconsolable, especially after I told her you had been secretly betrothed for months and agreed to the marriage as a way to escape the bondage of caring for her." He shook his head. "I fear I shall have to see about having her committed to an asylum. It's all quite sad, yet unavoidable given her history of mental distraction. Unless, of course, she recovers in time to assign control of her inheritance to me in exchange for keeping her confined in the tower instead of an asylum."

She narrowed her gaze and squared her shoulders. Few flowers of hope remained in her heart, but determination was one flower not yet destroyed. "I'll stop you. Somehow, I'll stop you."

"Stop me? From taking what's rightfully mine? Had your mother lived—"

"My mother has nothing to do with this . . . this abomination!"

"She has everything to do with it. I married her when no one else would dare. Do you think it was easy living with someone who was truly mad? Or standing by as she passed her madness to my issue? And then her fortune bypassed me as well when she died so young."

Shaking, he wiped the spittle from his lips and glared at her. "If you dare to defy me now, I will find an asylum for you far away from here where administrators are most anxious to admit well-paying guests. Rosemary can live out the rest of her life at Pennsylvania Hospital where I can visit to make sure she never leaves."

Desperate to save her sister as well as herself, Violet squared her shoulders and held her head high. "Take the money. All of it. We'll sign whatever is necessary. Just let us go. Please."

He blanched. "What I want you can't give me. I won't bother to trouble your feeble brain with the details, but make no mistake. I will be respected and admired in this city and silence those who mock me as your grandfather's pawn long after his death. If you both sign your inheritance over to me, I'll be seen as a heartless knave who took advantage of you, but if I set one of your free . . ."

She trembled. "Then no one would doubt you would have done the same for the other," she murmured.

He nodded. "Or question my motives when I must commit her to an asylum. As you can see, there's nothing you can do to stop me. If you try, I'll have you declared incompetent and rise above the shame by relinquishing control of your inheritances and survive on my own investments."

Completely outraged, she squinted her eyes and tilted up her chin. "There are always choices, not all of which you can orchestrate or control."

The corners of his lips lifted with sardonic glee. "Such as taking funds from your secret little account so you can run away? Don't bother trying. I closed that account for you last week. If you still wish to try to defy me, remember one thing: With your death, the entire fortune passes to your sister and ultimately, to me, a prospect that should temper any notions you might have of replicating your mother's leap from the roof of the tower. Now if you'll take a moment to fix your appearance, I suggest we rejoin Captain Miles and have dinner. He's most anxious to get to know his future bride. If you act agreeably, I'll think about letting you visit your sister later."

Still reeling from shock and disappointment, Sam had no sooner returned to his next-door office and stored away his purchases than disillusion approached, this time in the form of Tremore Flynn.

Fortunately, their business association would terminate at the end of July with the sale of Glennings Enterprises, and Sam would go home flushed with success and the fortune he had worked so hard to acquire. If this morning was any indication, however, the contentment he intended to take back to Sunrise might evaporate before he even left the city.

Seated behind his desk, he braced for another one of the confrontations that had marked their association since shortly after it began, but escalated after he had announced in the spring he would be selling the firm.

Flynn was barely in the door before Sam took the initiative. "Problems?"

Beneath unruly red brows, hazy blue eyes sharpened with defensiveness. With his arms held straight against his wiry frame, Flynn remained standing. "Not unless you want to go over the inventory again or inspect the warehouses for yourself."

Sam cocked a brow. "Any reason I should?"

Flynn's eyes flashed with a hint of anger. "Of course not. I have everything under control at the warehouses and the docks. You just worry about keeping the books straight and broker with the suppliers till Edmund Squires takes over. There's no reason to question my abilities now, is there?"

"No," Sam admitted. Still on edge after finding out the pretty lady he had admired from a distance had turned out to be Violet Dunn, he had no reason to anticipate an argument with Flynn that apparently was not forthcoming. Combining their talents and experience had proved a profitable merger for both of them, although Sam should probably have paid closer attention to Flynn's efforts at the docks instead of merely relying on his word.

"I need the final figure for my percentage of the profits after you settle with Squires," Flynn prompted. "I assume you know better now what that sum will be."

"It should be close to the figure I gave you last week. I still wouldn't make any commitments to other investments until the final papers are signed later this month and I have the funds from the sale. In the meantime, any major changes in our inventory could affect the selling price—"

"And my share of the profits." Flynn's expression hardened. "There won't be any major changes. I'll make sure of that. I'm keeping my eye on a few potential problems, that's about it."

A warning bell sounded in Sam's mind. "Anything that needs immediate attention?"

Flynn waved his hand in the air. "Not really. Patton backed out of shipping the coal, but I got Swell to cut the same deal. Couple of warehouses might be needing a new roof, but not before you sell out."

"Let me know if that changes."

Shoulders squared with pride. "I always do. I might be anxious to put five hundred miles between me and the docks, but I'm not a fool. Not when it comes to business."

Relieved their conversation had not turned combative, Sam worked away the tension that had bunched his shoulder blades together. "I take it you're not going to marry Kathleen and take her with you."

A wide grin split Flynn's face in two and instantly lightened his mood. "I'm leaving alone as soon as I have my funds. Like I said, I'm not a fool. When a man starts over, he has to make a clean break with the past."

"You'll get no argument from me on that point."

Flynn chuckled. "I didn't think I would."

With that parting remark, he left Sam to ponder the notion he had indeed broken ties with his past when he came to Philadelphia.

Being away from Sunrise had helped Sam to put his disastrous marriage and the scandal into proper perspective. He felt whole again, even ready to experience love, now that he thought he knew what that meant.

He could not imagine a less acceptable female who had been the center of his fantasies than the woman he had finally met today. For months, he had watched her pass by when she delivered her puzzles to the stationery store. With soft brown eyes and dark hair, she was quietly efficient and so intriguing he had finally decided to pursue his interest in her today, only to learn she was Violet Dunn.

His competitor's daughter.

An heiress.

A *mad* heiress.

Had he been cursed by Fate? Why had he been drawn to a woman with a fragile mind, not once, but twice?

He tried blocking her image out of his mind, but the look of utter devastation that paled her face when he reacted so badly upon learning her identity had made an indelible impression.

Shame filled his spirit and yanked hard on his conscience. He knew firsthand what it felt like to be pitied or scorned, and he should have been able to spare her the same misery.

He could blame his poor behavior on the shock of learning her real identity, which rendered his interest in her as ill-fated, or on her apparently misguided hope her history of mental instability could ever be overlooked by any rational man.

He was hardly rational, however, at the moment, tormented by a question that had haunted him all afternoon: Why would an heiress reputed to be as wealthy as Violet Dunn be plying her wares like a common trader?

The obvious answer—need—slammed into his gut and stole his breath away. Either his discreet inquiry into the holdings of the Montgomery fortune had been wrong or was terribly dated now, two years later.

Guilt yanked his conscience even harder. Rumors he had dismissed about the packet line folding assumed new validity. If the line accounted for the bulk of the Montgomery fortune, Sam would have to admit Violet might be forced to augment her dwindling inheritance with her handiwork.

Pride kicked back at his conscience. Fierce but honest competition with Charles Dunn had occupied all of his energies for the past two years, and he had done nothing disreputable. He would have been incompetent, if not a fool, not to strike hard when a run of bad luck put Dunn at a disadvantage. Well-earned success in business for one firm often meant casualties for competitors, but he would spend many a sleepless night if he had forced two vulnerable women into financial ruin along with Dunn.

Unless he was leaping to conclusions.

He pushed his chair back from the desk and looked outside, only to find twilight instead of bright sunshine. He closed up the office and hurried down High Street to get some answers. He hoped he would find out Violet Dunn had simply turned to making puzzles as a form of therapy—one that kept her hands busy and her mind stable. If not, he had yet one more problem marring his final days in Philadelphia to resolve.

With a few meager bites of dinner sitting in her stomach like cannonballs, Violet watched her future husband consume enough food to supply the almshouse for two days. Surprisingly, his table manners were beyond complaint, although she wondered how any man could sit so ramrod stiff. Was the man made of iron?

Or only his heart?

Nothing else could explain how nonchalantly he treated this arranged marriage, unless he was as desperate to reclaim his reputation as her father appeared to be determined to regain his own.

Tears welled, but she forced them back. Instead of dining with either of them, she should be upstairs with Rosemary, now abandoned by Dr. Poole to suffer her confining treatment alone in deafening silence that would surely trigger a quick descent into melancholia. Unless Violet intervened quickly, Rosemary might become distraught enough to try to harm herself like their mother had done—a long-suppressed fear that chilled Violet's very soul.

With her hand shaking, she dabbed at beads of nervous perspiration that dotted her upper lip and drew in short gulps of air. Captain Miles reacted immediately.

"You've hardly touched your plate. Are you not feeling well?"

She deliberately kept her eyes averted from him as well as her father and stared at her lap. "Only a bit light-headed."

"Perhaps too much . . . excitement."

"Perhaps," she murmured. "I do apologize for being such poor company. If I could lie down for a bit . . ." She paused and counted each beat of her heart while waiting for permission to leave the table.

As if anxious to save face, her father quickly relented and escorted her to the staircase. "Visit your sister, if you must," he whispered.

She spun to face him and issue a denial.

He pressed a finger to her lips. "Don't bother. I know how your mind works better than you do yourself. But for Captain Miles, I would accompany you myself to watch your efforts to calm your sister into accepting what must be done. I wonder if she'll even want you near her."

She pulled away from his touch. "She's my sister. I've done nothing to harm her. Never!"

He smiled sadly. "Imagine, if you will, that the very person you love most in the world betrays you."

Her pulse began to pound. "I've never betrayed Rosemary."

"You're leaving her behind to marry and travel the world. I do hope you won't bother to write her or send trinkets as mementos of your voyages. She would find that most upsetting."

Her stomach heaved, but she managed to stand upright. Horror widened her eyes. Memories and images of Rosemary's obsession with the sea and dreams of travel rocked through her mind and churned in her very soul, crashing against her attempts to take the blame for their misadventures at the docks. She stared into her father's eyes and saw the truth glittering back at her. "You knew. All along, you knew," she whispered.

He nodded. "You'll live the life your sister has always wanted. You'll have the sea captain as the husband—"

"That should have been hers." She scarcely managed to give voice to her words and grabbed onto the banister for support. Far too late, insight triggered a new understanding. Of her father. Of her sister. Of the years of mental distraction, feigned or real, that her father had tolerated or meticulously orchestrated to destroy both of his daughters.

She closed her eyes and listened to the sound of his footsteps as he walked away and left her there. By having feigned melancholia in the past to protect Rosemary, she was now completely at the mercy of his diabolical plan—one in which Sam Glennings had played a significant role. For all she knew, he might have been in league with her father from the start.

Loyalty and devotion to her sister, however, far outweighed any concern for herself and tempered her fear of her father and her disgust for Sam Glennings. Gathering up what little strength she still possessed, she scampered up the stairs, determined to save Rosemary as well as herself. In time, she would make sure her father and Sam Glennings were well rewarded for what they had done.

Chapter Three

✤

Rosemary refused to say a word or even acknowledge Violet's presence.

Working as quickly as her trembling fingers allowed, Violet first freed the leather straps around Rosemary's ankles, then her wrists. She loosened the neck strap and lifted the caged box up and over her sister's head.

Once freed from the chair restraints, Rosemary slumped forward and buried her face in her hands. She made no sound, uttered no bitter words, even as Violet knelt and rubbed the chafed flesh encircling her younger sister's wrists.

"Don't accept what Father has told you," she pleaded. "It isn't true. Please believe me. I've never lied to you in the past, have I?"

No response other than a series of shudders that wracked her sister's solid frame and shook the length of the blond braid trailing down her curved back. Violet briefly closed her eyes and prayed the loving bond between them would be stronger than their father's wickedness or her sister's fragile mind.

She cradled Rosemary's head with gentle hands and slowly lifted it until she could see her sister's face, swollen with tears now dried on her flushed cheeks. Anguished blue eyes met her own, and Rosemary's bottom lip quivered.

With their gazes locked together, Violet held her breath

and watched Rosemary's very spirit wage an inner battle that would determine both of their futures.

Rosemary batted her lashes. "You're not leaving me, are you?"

Violet sighed with relief and rubbed her sister's temples with the pads of her thumbs. "No. Not if you're able to help me."

She twittered nervously. "Help you? I can scarcely sit without falling forward." She paused and glanced away. "Did Father tell you what happened at Mrs. Dunsmore's?"

"He was quite happy to provide all the lurid details, I'm afraid. From now on, I don't want you venturing out without me, day or night," she added for good measure.

Rosemary sighed, leaned against the back of the chair, and closed her eyes. "He's evil, Violet. I warned you not to trust him."

"Yet you did today at Mrs. Dunsmore's. You believed him when he told you—"

"About your betrothal to Captain Miles and how you're going to spend your married life at sea?" She sighed so deeply her chest caved in and looked as though her lungs had collapsed. "Captain Miles probably doesn't even exist," she murmured as she twisted her hands together.

"Actually," Violet conceded, "he's quite real. I met him only an hour ago. He's rather . . . unique-looking, but I expect you'll learn that for yourself soon enough once we convince Dr. Poole you're quite recovered."

Rosemary opened her eyes wide, and they clouded with confusion. "Then you are betrothed! I thought you said—"

"There's a marriage contract, but the other details aren't important right now. You are." Violet took a deep breath, held it, and let it out slowly. "We'll talk about this and make our plans in the morning after you've had a good night's sleep."

Rosemary grabbed her sister's hands and tugged them to her heart. "You'll stay with me tonight in the tower?"

"Don't I always?" she responded. She guessed that the door to the tower had probably been locked already to prevent either of them from returning to their bedchambers in the main house. "Come. Let's get you downstairs and into bed," she crooned.

She guided Rosemary down from the fourth floor of the tower to the sleeping chamber below and vowed with each step she would keep her promises to her sister.

*D*ressed in formal wear, Ben Hastings stood in the foyer of his home, shook Sam's hand, and frowned. "I gather you won't be going to the theater after all."

"Theater?" Sam glanced down at his rumpled trousers and the ink-stained cuffs on his shirt and winced.

"You've forgotten. Again. The Walnut Street theater? Front-row tickets?" he remarked when Sam lifted a brow.

"That's tonight? I thought—"

"Never mind. Obviously, you've got something far more important that's troubling your mind." He reached behind Sam, closed the front door, and led Sam into the office he kept at home.

After accepting and downing a glass of ice water, Sam sank down into an upholstered chair facing Ben, who had taken a seat behind his desk. "I apologize."

"Again." Ben chuckled, leaned back in his chair, and pushed away a lock of shaggy, prematurely gray hair while waiting for Sam to explain the purpose for his visit.

Sam raked his hand through his hair and cleared his throat. "Two years ago, before I started my business and hired Flynn, you conducted an inquiry for me into Charles Dunn and the Montgomery fortune, including the packet line."

Another nod.

"I'd like you to do it again. Quickly, but discreetly. Find out everything you can about Dunn, the packet line, and his daughters."

Without commenting, Ben opened a desk drawer, pulled out a fresh sheet of paper, and began writing. When he finished, he looked up at Sam. "Why the daughters? It can't be morbid curiosity. I know you too well to suspect that of you."

Sam swallowed the lump of guilt in his throat. "I don't

need personal information about them. I need to know how badly I've hurt the line's business and how that might impact their financial futures."

"I doubt the Montgomery fortune depends solely on the packet line. My guess is there would be some effect, but hardly enough to jeopardize the young women's well-being. Their grandfather had a multitude of investments, all of which he protected by appointing trustees for the girls' inheritances. That's been public knowledge for years."

Reluctant to reveal Violet Dunn had been reduced to peddling her wares, Sam kept his own counsel. "Exactly how much control does Dunn have over the girls' funds?"

The attorney shrugged his shoulders. "Since Montgomery made no secret of his dislike for his son-in-law, especially after his daughter's unfortunate death, I would think very little. Is there some particular reason you need this information?"

Sam's backbone stiffened, but he did not avert his gaze. "None I'm willing to discuss at this time. How long will it take?"

"Several weeks. Perhaps a month."

"That long? I need this information now," he blurted.

"Asa Montgomery's probated will is a matter of public record and readily available. Finding out the rest will take time if you expect my inquiry to be discreet. Otherwise, I could assign one of my associates or a clerk—"

"No. I want you to handle this personally. The fewer people involved, the better."

"Then I'll proceed first thing in the morning."

Disappointed, but not entirely stymied, Sam rose and extended his apologies for forgetting about their theater plans. He left with only one destination in mind, to get answers from the only man he knew who might settle Sam's conscience long enough for him to get a night's rest: Elijah Dennus.

$\mathcal{V}$iolet awoke with a start. Ribbons of moonlight sliced through the barred windows, casting eerie shadows on Rosemary's sleeping form. After hours filled with Rosemary's nightmares, which had been none too easy to calm, she rubbed her eyes to make sure, but a long glance at her sister's peaceful expression reassured her Rosemary was finally resting well.

Having fallen asleep kneeling beside her sister's bed with her head resting on the mattress at an awkward angle, Violet attempted to stretch her kinked muscles. Sharp pain stabbed the length of her neck and knifed across her forehead. Tingles raced up her legs from ankle to thigh.

Suppressing a groan, she carefully and very slowly stretched her limbs and turned her head from side to side before rising and making her way to the window facing east.

With a clear sky and a bright moon overhead, she had a magnificent view over treetops and roofs to the river itself. Like a flock of butterflies feasting on a floating flower garden, sailing ships lolled on the water, waiting for sunrise to bring workers scurrying about the public docks to fill the holds of ships with goods bound for the four corners of the earth.

Without regard for her one physical weakness, motion sickness, she squinted her eyes and tried to sight a sail emblazoned with the crimson cross that marked a ship belonging to the Montgomery Packet Line. Unsuccessful, she turned away from the window and leaned back against it as her stomach pitched and rolled as if she had actually stepped off land and onto a ship. She could scarcely look at the sea without immediately feeling nauseous, a fact her father, no doubt, had failed to tell her future husband.

Somewhere along the riverbanks was anchored the ship that would soon belong to Captain Miles. Given the man's incredible height, it was hard to imagine how he managed to fit below deck.

But at the moment, she had more pressing concerns, not the least of which centered on formulating an escape plan for herself and Rosemary. Blossoms of hope swelled in her weary heart and left no room for weeds of despair. Her father might have confiscated her secret savings account, but Elijah still owed her for the two puzzles Sam Glennings had purchased.

Although the sum would do little more than provide coach passage out of the city and sustain them for a few days, it was all she had.

She could have had much more.

Her father rarely took her grandmother's jewelry out of the safe and always confiscated the heirlooms immediately after they had been worn. She had not seen them for over a year. She would not be surprised if she never saw them again, but she could not afford to wait to see if she did.

She needed her coins, assuming Sam had not decided against his purchase after he learned who had crafted the puzzles.

Agitated, she paced back and forth across the width of the chamber—walking on tiptoe for fear she might wake her sister. Since her father did not allow Elijah to visit her at home, she would have to go to him to collect her coins. Although she did not relish venturing out at night to prevent her father from knowing what she was doing, she shoved common sense aside.

She was too desperate to know if she had any funds coming to her at all. If not, she would be in dire straits indeed and would scarcely sleep a wink until she knew for sure.

She checked her sister, found her still peacefully sleeping, and prayed her father was as confident of himself as he appeared to be and had not instructed the servants to lock the outside tower door on the ground level.

Without stopping to waste time worrying about the consequences should she be discovered missing, she rushed down the staircase and selected one of Rosemary's favorite puzzles. She slid back the lid, secured a puzzle piece, and returned to the third floor to press the piece into her sister's hand.

If Rosemary did wake up before Violet returned, she would find the puzzle piece. As had happened often in the past, the cryptic message would tell Rosemary where Violet had gone and reassure her of her prompt return.

She was practically out of breath by the time she reached the first floor. When she found the door to the outside unlocked, she drew in a deep gulp of air for courage and slipped out into the private garden hidden from passersby by a tall wooden fence. Being careful to stay in the shadows to avoid being seen by anyone in the house, she hurried to the service entrance near the stable in the rear and slipped out the gate.

Long familiar with the grid of intersecting city streets, she kept to narrow alleys and side streets to avoid passing rowdy taverns, theaters, or the larger hotels where people might see her and recognize her. Sultry air gave way to cooler breezes the closer she got to the river. Only a square away from the alley where Elijah Dennus lived, an approaching carriage sent her scurrying to hide behind a column at one end of the High Street Market to avoid being seen.

Overhead, above the curved façade, the watch tower awaited the arrival in the morning of a policeman who would monitor the throngs of buyers crowding the market along with an endless variety of pickpockets and thieves. Fresh produce, meats, and cheeses would not fill the empty stalls on either side of the square-long, open-ended structure behind her until dawn.

When the carriage began to slow to a stop directly in front of her, she backed inside the market before the wheels ground to a halt and the light from the carriage lanterns revealed her presence.

A creak of the carriage followed by footsteps and the murmur of excited but muted conversation announced the approach of the carriage's passengers on foot. She held perfectly still. Fear of being spotted and, worse, being recognized by someone who knew her or her father, sent her to her knees, and she crawled forward to hide beneath a stall.

Splintered wood overhead caught and ripped the sleeve of her gown and snagged her hair. Cobwebs brushed her face and caught on her lips. Sawdust coated her hands as well as her skirts, but when a furry creature scampered across her ankles, she clapped one hand over her mouth to stifle a scream and nearly toppled over.

Heart pounding, she managed to keep her balance and closed her eyes like a child blocking all view of the world, thinking it would make her invisible. Trembling, she listened as several people, at least one of them a woman, paused at the entryway to peer inside.

What kind of tourists would come to the market at ten o'clock at night? She could hardly imagine, since they all spoke a foreign tongue she did not recognize, but she prayed their interest would be short-lived as she feared her heart would soon burst.

Endless moments later, they turned away, but instead of returning to the carriage and leaving, they paused and continued their conversation only a few yards away, captivated, no doubt, by the ornate cupola above the watch tower. Groaning softly, she maneuvered herself around to face the archway, but they stood beyond her limited view for an eternity before climbing back into their carriage and leaving.

Relief swept through her entire body and calmed her thumping heart. She crawled to the center of the narrow aisle separating the stalls and got to her feet. Before she took time to pin up her hair again, she bent down, lifted her skirts, and tried to wipe the cobwebs from her face.

" 'Tis a fine ankle you have, lass, but I should like to sample more of ye."

She flinched, dropped her skirts, and tried to swirl away, but she was not quick enough. A firm grip on her ankle held her fast.

Absolute terror held her immobile for several thudding heartbeats. Horror filled her shadowed view of the man who lay beneath the stall directly opposite the one where she had been hiding. As he nudged himself toward her into a shaft of moonlight, beady eyes and a snide grin revealed the man's vile intentions.

"No-o-o!" She kicked at his face, again and again, until her toes were numb with pain.

Howling, he eventually relaxed his hold on her to grab at his face, and she tripped over her skirts in a desperate dash to escape. She hit the cobblestones hard enough to see stars, scrambled back to her feet, and raced across the street.

He came lunging after her. "Come back here! I'll make you pay for this, whoreson's bitch!"

Blinking back tears, she charged around the corner. His footsteps faltered, but the echo of his words chased her still. She ran to the end of the alley and pounded on Elijah Dennus's door. "Help me! Please! Let me in!" she cried, but her words sounded more like a frantic groan.

When the door swung open, she flew forward at the man who dared to block her way inside.

Chapter Four

❧

Sam grabbed hold of the rambling, hysterical woman. Guttural sounds scarcely resembling words that were coming from her throat sounded inhuman, and she fought to get inside with unbelievable strength given her size and stature. She clutched and clawed at his shirt so hard her nails scored his chest. Instinctively, he forced her back and held her at arm's length for his own protection.

Trembling and wide-eyed, with her terrified face framed by wild, unkempt hair and her dark brown gown crusted with filth, she looked like a witch who had crashed her broom into a ditch.

Or an escaped lunatic desperately fleeing the confines of an asylum.

Memories long-buried rushed to the forefront of his mind. He was transported back to another time. And another place. Polly sat on the witness stand in the Lancaster courtroom, trembling and gently weeping, a model of decent womanhood overwhelmed by tragedy. Within moments, she launched into an hysterical diatribe that distorted her beauty before she catapulted into perpetual mania, curled her fingers, and attempted to rake them down Daniel's face.

I should kill you, too!

Her screeched words echoed in his mind, keeping him

locked in the vortex of a nightmare that had exploded his world and haunted him yet again.

A smart shove rocked him back into the present and off to the side, and loosened his hold on the woman. He watched with amazement as Elijah stepped between them and wrapped his arms around her. "Hush now, Violet. Sh-h-h. It's all right, sweet girl. You're here with me now," he crooned.

"Violet Dunn?" Sam blurted her name out loud as his mind tried to juxtapose the image of the quiet, graceful woman he had observed and met only that afternoon with the tattered creature he beheld now.

One sleeve of her gown had been ripped, and her skirts were stained as though she had crawled on her hands and knees through the streets to get here. Blood splattered one of her slippers. Based on what he could observe with his own eyes, the rumors about the distracted heiress had not exaggerated or distorted the truth.

Violet Dunn was mad.

Pity consumed whatever disdain he might have felt while Elijah led the whimpering creature to a chair. Sam went to the small kitchen in the rear of the small house and pumped a glass of water for her. By the time he returned, Elijah had her seated and she appeared relatively calmer. He had pulled another wooden chair next to hers and had an arm wrapped around her shoulders.

Terror still paled her face, but her red-rimmed eyes focused warily on him as he approached her. She accepted his offering, sipped greedily, and handed the empty glass back to him. "Thank you. Both," she added, her voice trembling. "I don't think I've ever been so frightened in my life."

"What frightened you?" Elijah asked, his white brows wrinkled with concern.

Sam listened attentively as she explained what had happened to her at the market. His fingers tightened around the glass so hard he thought it might splinter. Considering how quickly he had judged her to be mad instead of terrified, as she had every right to be, it would serve him right if the glass did break and sliced open every finger on his hand.

Assuming her tale was true.

Assuming the man who had allegedly accosted her was not a figment of her imagination.

He set the glass on the windowsill and started toward the door, just in case she was telling the truth.

"Don't bother, Sam," Elijah argued. "The vermin is probably long gone. And nursing a broken nose or a split lip, judging by the blood on her slipper."

She pulled her foot back and hid her slipper beneath her skirts.

Sam glowered at the older man. "He deserves a lot more for attacking a defenseless woman."

"I'm more concerned about Violet at the moment," he countered before turning his attention to her. "Whatever sent you out to see me in the middle of the night that couldn't wait till morning?"

Her cheeks flamed, the bright red color accenting how pale her features had become. She lowered her gaze and toyed with her hands. "It's . . . it's rather personal. I mean no offense to Mr. Glennings . . ."

Elijah gave Sam a nod. "While I tend to Violet's concerns, perhaps you could go upstairs. Fetch some fresh towels. There's a basin on the washstand. Bring that as well. I'm sure Violet will feel a whole lot better once she freshens up."

Without argument, Sam climbed the narrow, winding stairs. Flickering light from the thick candle in a sconce at the top of the stairs guided his way, but it would take the light of a thousand candles to chase away the shadows of concern for Violet that had deepened far beyond what Elijah had managed to tell him before she arrived so unexpectedly. To give her a little additional time, he would strip off his shirt and tend to the welts on his chest before he went back downstairs.

Violet waited until Sam's footsteps sounded overhead before attempting to speak. She wrapped her hands around the very warm one Elijah offered to her and held on tight. Completely unnerved by her harrowing experience at the market, she had been ill-prepared to find herself face-to-face with Sam Glennings. To say the least.

With no more than a few precious minutes to explain herself before he returned, she quickly explained only brief details of her shocking betrothal and Rosemary's episode at the dressmaker's.

Elijah drew his brows together. The flesh on his bald head stretched thin, and his lips tightened into a taut frown. "Contemptible. That's what he is."

"Father found out about my savings account and closed it," she blurted. "He's confiscated my earnings from my puzzles, and I need them to take Rosemary away with me. Did Mr. Glennings buy my puzzles today?"

He looked at her and raised one brow quizzically. "He said he would before you left."

She dropped her gaze. "I thought he might have changed his mind," she whispered, convinced that after tonight's fiasco, he would be quite certain her reputation for being mad was well deserved.

"Sam's a good man, Violet. You can trust him. He's not one to break his word, once he gives it."

Caught by surprise, she glanced up and found him smiling at her with eyes where no doubt about his words could be found. She trusted Elijah. She was not so sure she could trust anyone else, especially Sam, but she did not have the energy to examine her thoughts about him now when her future was so uncertain. "Did you bring my coins home with you?"

He frowned an apology. "I left feelin' poorly by the end of the day so I stored the coins at the shop. I was hopin' to take them to the bank tomorrow. I can bring them home with me, instead, unless you want me to keep them at the shop. It would be easier and a whole lot safer for you to come there to collect them."

Disappointed, she nodded. "If I can get Father to let me out of the house, perhaps I can come to the shop, although he would likely try to take the coins away from me when I returned. I—I think it would be best if you brought them home. I'll think of a way to come here. In daylight," she added with a shudder.

He smiled and urged her closer. "You just rest a bit before you try heading home," he suggested.

Barely stifling a yawn, she laid her head against her friend's warm shoulder and closed her eyes. Given all that had happened in the course of a single day, her grasp on reality was tenuous, and she was repeatedly forced to question whether she would ever be able to accept anything she encountered as it appeared. For months, her father had been both kind and attentive, whittling at her suspicions about him until she had actually begun to trust him a little.

Yet all the while, he had been plotting against her, as well as Rosemary, scheming as he had in the past. Only this time he had woven a web of deception that might very well spell doom for any hopes she had of ever escaping his grasp.

To compound her distress, Sam Glennings added more confusion and uncertainty. No mere clerk as he had appeared, he was in reality a wealthy businessman, one who could be acting in concert with her father or against him, although Elijah apparently found him to be a man who could be trusted. She had yet to unravel the bonds of friendship that connected him to her only ally in the world, but she feared an ulterior motive on Sam's part as much as the remote possibility she might be wrong.

Irregardless of what kind of man Sam really was, she and Rosemary would be the parties who suffered most in this convoluted scenario. Adding Rosemary's fragile mental state to the mix of emotionally charged events of the day had taxed Violet to near her breaking point, but thoughts of her sister triggered immediate concern.

When she opened her eyes and sat up, she found Elijah had fallen asleep in his chair. Sam stood guard over both of them from his seat on the bottom stair.

He placed one finger over his lips, rose, and walked toward her. "I set everything out for you in the kitchen," he whispered. "There's warm water in the basin, towels, and a brush for your hair. While you freshen up, I'll write a quick note to tell him I've escorted you home."

She nodded, eased from her seat, and went directly to the kitchen. After her experience earlier, she was grateful not to have to return home unescorted. She relished going home alone with Sam Glennings as much as she might look forward to meeting her attacker again, but she could use this opportunity to learn more about him and plan a suitable payback for unfairly competing against the packet line and putting herself and Rosemary in these very dire circumstances.

$\mathcal{T}$he air was still and humid, the streets virtually deserted, and conversation stilted as Sam escorted Violet back to her home.

"You're not from Philadelphia originally, are you?" she prompted.

"Sunrise. It's a small town on the Susquehanna River. How did you know?"

"Tell me about it," she urged, ignoring his question.

She sounded sincerely interested as opposed to politely curious, but he needed no further invitation. For the next several squares, he gave her a quick sketch of the village itself and felt his heart lighten a bit as fond memories strengthened his longing to return home.

"Do you still have family there?" she asked, surprised he made no mention of a wife.

He nodded. "Several generations. Aunt Nester is the oldest, I suppose, and my sister is expecting my second niece or nephew come fall."

"Are you close to your sister?"

His jaw tightened. "She's all I had after our parents died. Jane raised me, supported me, and made sure I walked a righteous path, especially after she discovered the path I used to sneak back into the house in the middle of the night. I owe her far more than I'll ever be able to repay."

The memory of how close Jane had come to forfeiting her life because of the woman he had married and brought home to Sunrise still tugged at his spirit. He chose to concentrate on happier days ahead. "I should be home for good before long."

She hesitated and slowed a step or two. "You're leaving Philadelphia? What about your business here?"

"Family comes first in my life. I never intended to settle here permanently like Aunt Lily."

"Then you do have family here."

"No, she died before I arrived."

"Oh, I'm sorry."

He swallowed a lump in his throat. "Aunt Lily was a remarkable woman. She made no enemies and loved her family well and that is precisely what we had etched on her tombstone after we brought her home to Sunrise," he murmured. He slowed his steps as they approached the rear of her family home. His lightened mood sobered the moment he saw the outline of the ominous tower adjoining the mansion.

He had almost forgotten about her mental instability during the course of their walk and realized she had carefully but consistently steered the conversation in his direction. As a result, he had learned very little about her.

She unlatched the gate and stepped inside. "Thank you again, for your help and for escorting me home."

"In the future, you might want to confine your outings so you can be home before dark."

She hesitated before she closed the gate. "About tonight. You won't tell . . . Please don't mention anything to my father or . . . or to anyone."

His heart lurched in his chest, but her plea tugged at his pride, as well. "Your father is my competitor, Miss Dunn, not my friend or ally."

She nodded and quickly closed the gate. He waited until her footsteps faded before turning away. Her image flashed in and out of his mind's eye as he walked home, along with the echo of her voice. Despite all the gossip he had heard about her lifelong battle with mental distraction, he still found her disturbingly irresistible, and his physical attraction to her was far stronger than what he had felt for Polly, who could only be described as exquisite.

Violet, on the other hand, had an earthy, homespun quality about her that reminded him of country life and home—a paradox in itself since she had reputedly been born and raised in the city and had never gone farther than the family's country estate along the Schuykill River.

Her intense loyalty to her sister, which Elijah had glowingly described, made her all the more remarkable and reminded him of Jane.

He did not completely understand the reasons for the power of his emotional response to Violet, but he was darn certain he would be able to control his physical attraction to her. His infatuation with Polly had blinded him to flaws that had proven fatal to Jane's first husband and nearly to Jane herself. Fortunately for him, Violet's history of mental distraction gave him all the self-control he would need to keep his baser urges as well as his heart under safe wraps.

His conscience was quite another issue.

Although Elijah had been unable to provide any details about the state of the Montgomery Packet Line, he had shared one disturbing fact: Charles Dunn had taken control of Violet's fortune. No doubt he had plans to do the same to Rosemary's within months, leaving both young women completely at the mercy of a fortune-hunting father who did everything he could to perpetuate and exacerbate his daughters' reputations as mad.

If Sam had dented that fortune to the extent he feared, he unwittingly had forced Dunn's hand and should share part of the blame if anything happened to either of the young women.

He quickened his steps, but he could not walk away from his sense of guilt any more than he could escape the notion that he had not seen the last of Miss Violet Dunn.

Violet slipped into the tower and closed the door behind her as quietly as she could. Anxious to rejoin her sister, she wound herself up the darkened staircase and never stopped to catch her breath until she reached the third floor. When she found Rosemary still sleeping peacefully, she eased the puzzle piece from her hand, undressed, and climbed into her own bed wearing only her shift.

She was too tired to worry about her ruined gown and petticoats, or her bloodstained slippers; she would hide them in the morning. But she would have to think of a way to explain her scraped hands if her father chose to appear for a visit.

Even after she closed her eyes and felt her body go limp, her mind raced with questions about Sam Glennings that kept sleep at bay. He had been kind and attentive to her tonight, hardly the behavior of a man who had been described by her father as ruthless and without conscience. He was devoted to his family, that much was clear when he proudly described how his aunt had never made an enemy on this earth, and she could not think of why Elijah would be friends with Sam and urge her to trust him if he was everything her father claimed him to be.

Perplexed as to Sam's true nature, she focused her thoughts on his hometown, instead. From his description, Sunrise sounded like the very kind of place she might take Rosemary to hide. Seventy miles would be far enough from the city to escape their tainted reputations, yet close enough to allow her to be in contact with lawyers in the city she would hire on their behalf.

The one and only drawback was that Sam Glennings would be there, which made Sunrise the least likely place on earth she would ever go.

She would rather walk the proverbial plank, not a far-fetched possibility if she failed to escape, wound up married to Captain Miles, and ever attempted to defy him. If forced into marriage to that giant and a life of perpetual seasickness, she would not hesitate to fashion the plank herself. With that incredibly ridiculous scenario in mind, she made a mental note to be sure to include her saw with the rest of her tools and quickly fell asleep with a prayer on her lips and a plea in her heart that Sam would keep his word, as well as his own counsel, about what had happened to her tonight.

Chapter Five

◦❧

For Sam, the next two weeks were filled with frustrating days and troubling nights.

Within days of the heraldry and wild celebrations that had marked Independence Day, most city elites had abandoned Philadelphia for country estates to escape the suffocating heat and humidity that would probably last for the duration of summer.

Hordes of tourists invaded the slumbering city to crowd the streets, fill the hotels, and jam local shops, a scenario that reminded Sam of the trading season in Sunrise that transformed the sleepy village into a bustling stop for rafts and river arks floating farm exports and resources down the Susquehanna en route to Columbia.

His days, however, had been productive. He had signed the final agreement for the lease of the town house to a merchant, Theodore Bartlett. Once the actual sale and transfer of funds for his business had been set for July 27, he had arranged to ship most of his personal effects home that same day. The following morning he would be on his way home after turning over the keys to the town house to Bartlett.

His nights were plagued by haunted visions of the tower where he occasionally saw the silhouettes of Violet and her sister. He was not sure why he had reacted so strongly when Elijah told him about Violet's unexpected betrothal and forthcoming marriage, but her sister's near lapse into melancholia again did not surprise him.

Or deter him from making sure he was not responsible for having put Violet and her sister into financial ruin because he had not followed up his first inquiry into the Montgomery fortune with periodic updates.

The unexpected delivery of the package containing Ben's report only moments ago held the answers he needed. With his privacy guaranteed at his home, he removed his frock coat and cuffs before rolling up his shirtsleeves and consigning his cravat to the top of his desk.

Ignoring thoughts of the supper tray in the kitchen, he spread out the documents on his desk and perused each one very carefully. When he finished, he leaned back and stared at the ceiling to avoid any glimpse of the tower looming in the distance. What he had just read shook the very foundation of his soul and threatened to taint the fortune he had worked day and night to acquire.

The contempt he had struggled to control when he read the report escalated into stunning outrage—at both himself and Dunn.

According to the documents, Sam had achieved financial success by severely damaging the earnings of the packet line and making it nearly worthless as a source of income for Violet and her sister.

A serpent of disgust snaked through his veins, ready to strike a lethal dose of venom, which he felt he richly deserved. He had not done anything illegal or unethical, but he had been negligent if he judged himself objectively. For the first time, he realized his ambition and drive had blinded him to anything beyond being successful. He had been so consumed with making his own fortune, he had given no thought at all to how the investments funding the Montgomery fortune might have been changed.

Knowing he had never engaged in anything but honest, ethical business practices did little to assuage his sense of guilt.

The greater portion of his anger, however, he reserved for

Charles Dunn, along with the lawyers who had aided and abetted a scheme as diabolical as it was cunning. Ben Hastings had managed to trace through a series of intricate legal filings, some as recent as only days ago. In effect, Dunn had stolen the bulk of the trust fund, leaving but a pittance to support both Violet and Rosemary. Dunn's chicanery, as well as any perception of business as an honorable profession, soured the taste in Sam's mouth. His desire to return home and spend the rest of his life farming the land deepened into implacable resolve.

But not until Dunn had been stopped.

Otherwise, the fortune Sam had honestly earned would be tainted by the knowledge he had acquired it at the expense of two very vulnerable women.

He set the report aside and closed his eyes to block out any distractions so he could concentrate on one issue at a time. Most importantly, he was fairly certain Violet and Rosemary had no inkling of what was yet to happen. His conscience gave him no choice but to alert them to their father's chicanery, but he could not help the Dunn sisters or extricate himself from this quagmire of deceit and betrayal alone.

Ben might be able to offer some guidance, but Daniel was far more experienced in dealing with swindlers disguised as social elites or reputable merchants.

With Jane heavy with child, Sam was loath to ask his brother-in-law to come to Philadelphia. He was also reluctant to remind Daniel of his past. Once a renegade lawyer who skirted the boundary separating ethical behavior from illegal, Daniel had changed and grown as a direct result of defending Jane.

Asking Daniel to help unravel and reveal Dunn's legal machinations, which were designed to claim all of the Montgomery fortune left after the folding of the packet line, would be selfish and unfair to everyone involved, with the possible exception of Violet and her sister.

Stymied for the moment, he concentrated instead on the copy of the marriage contract Ben had somehow obtained and focused on the man who was about to marry Violet. He labeled the jealousy that surged in his heart as ludicrous, a consequence of guilt, but nothing more.

He knew nothing about Captain Jeremiah Miles except what was noted in a separate report. Reputedly from Delaware by birth, he made his living plying trade with the Orient, an obvious connection to Dunn since the Montgomery Packet Line had had its origins in trading with the East.

What kind of man would willingly chain himself to a wife with a family history of madness that spanned two generations in exchange for a ship? Was he cut from the same cloth as Dunn, in league with him, or just desperate?

As impossible as it might seem, Violet could very well be in danger now from two men: her father and her betrothed.

With all his experience at the docks, Flynn should know something about Miles, and Sam made a mental note to see him on the matter in the morning.

Caught in a maze with one question after another creating new stumbling blocks to finding a solution to his dilemma, he did not realize dusk had given way to full nightfall until a sharp rapping at the front door jolted him out of his reverie. After fumbling about in the dark to reassemble the report, he made his way to the door and greeted Ben, who stepped inside and walked right past him.

"Have you no candles? This place is as black as a tomb. I thought you might not be home."

"Then why did you nearly pound down my door?"

Ben sighed as Sam proceeded to light one of two pairs of candles resting in wall sconces in the foyer. "Unlike my friend, who appears to be plagued by a number of foibles, including uncommon forgetfulness at times, I am the epitome of perseverance, a quality for which you should be grateful."

"Not to mention efficient," Sam commented as he finished his task. He bit back the urge to make any reference to Ben's worst foible: his temper. While Sam's penchant for forgetting social engagements was embarrassing as well as annoying, Ben's volatile temper had cost him dearly. Provoked into attacking a prosecuting attorney on a case shortly after taking over Daniel's practice, Ben had nearly destroyed his own career and ended up with a broken betrothal, as well. Since Sam had known him, Ben had won the struggle to keep his temper in check, in part by hiring two additional lawyers and adding clerks who lightened his caseload, but mostly by persevering and winning back his reputation one case at a time. Nearly implacable, he did not let anything goad him beyond mild but rare expressions of anger, which may have accounted for his rather congenial mood tonight.

"I thought you said you needed a good month to assemble the report on Dunn," he suggested.

Ben grinned. "That's simply good lawyering. Never make a promise to your client you can't keep and always over-estimate how long it will take to keep it. Had I told you I could conduct your inquiry in two weeks, you would have been pacing the floor and visiting my office these past few days demanding the report. And I might have been tempted to blast you with a good dose of the temper I've kept too well under control to lose now. As it stands, you got your information ahead of schedule, which should please you immeasurably."

Sam cocked a brow. "Pleased is not quite my mood."

"I suspected it wouldn't be, which is why I persevered," he remarked and flexed the fingers on his right hand. "You no doubt spent the past few hours completely preoccupied with unnecessary guilt, and I assume that explains why you're not properly dressed for Mrs. Belle's."

Sam gritted his teeth. Forced once again to admit he had forgotten their plans for the evening, he had little desire to attend a dinner party with hundreds of others. "I'm sorry. You'll have to go alone this time."

Ben squared his shoulders. "I'll wait while you change."

Sam crossed his arms over his chest. "Since you wrote the report, then you obviously know the truth. If I hadn't been so almighty fixed on being successful, I might have given thought to following up on my initial inquiry into the Montgomery fortune. So forgive me if I'm not in a festive mood."

"You haven't done anything illegal or immoral," he countered.

"Maybe not," Sam argued, "but Dunn has. And I intend to stop him. With or without your help. Now unless you can give me one good reason why I should attend Mrs. Belle's instead of making plans to see Dunn's scheme shot straight to Hades, I suggest you attend without me."

Ben grinned. "Violet Dunn will be there with her intended, Captain Miles. Now get dressed. We'll talk about what we're going to do to help her on the way."

$\mathcal{W}$idow Olympia Belle's monthly dinner parties, where as many as three hundred common mechanics mingled with philanthropic civic and business leaders, had been a Philadelphia tradition for nearly a decade. Violet was quite certain her appearance there tonight would provide fodder for gossip for the rest of the season and eclipse the names of notorious guests for which Mrs. Belle had become infamous herself.

As if her presence alone would not be enough, she would be escorted there by Captain Miles, a man who might very well be mistaken for one of the Greek-styled pillars at the entrance to the palatial Belle mansion if he stood still. Beyond that, she had few expectations about the man. She had only seen him once since the day they met, but he had had little to say when he had escorted her to the dressmaker's for a fitting for her wedding gown.

Other than that single outing, her father had refused to allow her to leave the house during the day. After her last experience, she dared not venture out at night. Stymied in her efforts to collect her coins from Elijah, she hoped her acquiescence to his plans for her marriage would somehow work to her advantage. The moment her father lowered his guard and gave her some freedom, she would collect her coins and take Rosemary away.

Her worry that Sam Glennings might tell her father what had happened had not materialized into a problem. More worrisome, however, had been her father's suggestion that Rosemary accompany him to the event tonight. He had even insisted they wear their grandmother's jewels and had also returned a brooch each had received from their grandfather the day of their births.

While Violet had a multitude of misgivings about tonight's affair, Rosemary saw the outing as a grand adventure. Rosemary and adventure always spelled disaster. The sinking feeling in the pit of Violet's stomach told her that was precisely what their father had in mind, particularly since Rosemary had fooled even Dr. Poole and seemed completely restored.

"At the moment," she murmured.

Ensconced once again in the suite of rooms they shared on the third floor of the mansion, she dismissed their maid, Bridget, joined her sister in front of the full-length mirror, and checked both their reflections.

No two sisters could possibly look so distinctly different. Fashionably gowned in ivory silk and wearing a necklace of astonishing rubies, Rosemary had her blond hair piled high in tight curls and appeared even taller, although she did top Violet by several inches.

In contrast, Violet wore an Empire-style gown of deep burgundy and had her dark brown hair knotted at the nape and capped with lace, a study in simplicity undermined by the heavy rope of pearls that banded her throat.

Rosemary's cheeks, flushed with excitement, only accented Violet's pale complexion, but it was the twinkle of devilment in Rosemary's blue eyes that prompted Violet to voice her concerns. "You must stay with us at all times."

Rosemary grinned and swirled about the room. "Shall we all dance together, too?"

"Stop it, Rosemary. Right now."

With an exaggerated pout on her face, Rosemary curtsied. "Yes, my queen. Have you any other commands for your humble servant?"

Violet threw up her hands. "This isn't going to work. Why on earth did Father insist—"

"I'll behave. I promise."

Suspicious, Violet frowned. "Why should I believe you?"

Blue eyes darkened with disdain. "Because the titanic Captain Miles will be there to make sure I do. Opportunistic,

fortune-hunting monster! I'd rather be strapped in the tranquilizer chair for a week than spend any time with him, but
I'm coming along to protect you for once."

Violet shuddered, but held her own counsel. While
tempted to remind Rosemary that tolerating the man's presence for an evening hardly compared to spending a lifetime
with him, she knew better than to argue with her sister. If
even mildly agitated, she was likely to accost the man and
give him a dressing-down before they were formally introduced. Violet did not want to antagonize a man large enough
to need only one hand to strangle the life out of either woman.

When the clock in the hall struck nine, she winced. "He's
waiting downstairs. I hope he's not out of sorts because we're
late."

"Wait until you don't show up for the wedding," Rosemary
teased and scooted from the room in a flurry of skirts and
energy before Violet could respond. She managed to catch up
to Rosemary at the half-landing, yanked on her elbow, and
forced her to descend the rest of the way at a more genteel
pace.

Telling Rosemary about their father's plans for her and
consoling her with details about how Violet intended to outwit him appeared to have been a mistake she would undo if
she could.

Before she lowered her gaze, she caught sight of Captain
Miles. Dressed in full formal uniform, he was standing at
attention at the base of the staircase looking as daunting and
impressive as the main mast of a ship. Dwarfed, her father
stood far behind him at the front door.

Violet held on to her sister and paused when they reached
the bottom step to gain the advantage of a few inches. She
might have been eye to eye with her father, but she found
herself staring straight into the center of the captain's chest.
She tilted her head back to see his face and prayed she would
not be greeted by eyes flashing with indignation.

Violet caught her breath and held it. Captain Miles was
not even looking at her! His gaze was riveted on her sister,
and the expression on his face made it appear he had been

cast under a spell—one that, astoundingly, had snared her sister, as well.

Violet's heart began to race, and she drew in a sharp gulp of air charged with enough electricity to light the sky over the entire continent. For several long heartbeats, she glanced back and forth from her sister to the captain and felt the blood rush from her face.

Awed by the intense physical and emotional attraction that sparked between Rosemary and Captain Miles, Violet grabbed the banister for support and closed her eyes.

Disaster had struck, and they had not even left the house.

$\mathcal{B}$athed in the light of a thousand candles in an opulent ballroom that rivaled Versailles for extravagance, Violet welcomed the final notes of a waltz. Her fears about being the focus of attention had been thankfully ill-founded. There were so many people packed into the event, she was but one of hundreds of anonymous faces.

She practically hobbled from the dance floor with a taut smile plastered on her face. If her father was as inept at business as he was at mastering the art of dancing, there would be precious little inheritance left for anyone to worry about.

She swiveled her neck and scanned the crowd. She had little chance of spotting Rosemary, but was not overly concerned. Her father had arranged for several trusted associates to fill her dance card so that would certainly keep Captain Miles away from her. She should have been able to see Captain Miles since he stood shoulders above every other man in the room. With no sign of him, she was curious to know where he had spent the past hour, but exhausted enough not to care or argue with her father. She followed her father's lead as he led her by the elbow through the throng gathered to watch the dancers as the orchestra began yet another melody.

Her feet were bruised and sore. The choker of pearls around her neck stuck to her skin and felt like a noose. Her mouth felt as if it were stuffed with cotton. The only reason she did not dissolve into tears was the fact that the evening was nearly over. As soon as they found Rosemary and Captain Miles, they were all going home.

She slipped the ribbon that held her dance card from her wrist. When a passing servant paused to offer refreshments, she exchanged her dance card for a glass of lemonade. Before she managed a single sip, her father grabbed her arm and the lemonade sloshed over the rim and saturated her glove.

"We don't have time for you to indulge yourself. It's time to find your sister as well as Captain Miles and go home," he snapped.

She scarcely had time to replace the glass on the tray before he ushered her away. They searched the ballroom for more than half an hour, but found no sign of Rosemary. Captain Miles was also absent. While Violet went to check the dressing rooms set aside for the ladies' use, her father went downstairs to see if she had gone to the first-floor buffet. They agreed to meet at the front entrance in twenty minutes.

She paused long enough upstairs to remove her glove and rinse the sticky residue from her hand. One of the maids in attendance handed her a towel.

"Miss Dunn?"

"Yes?"

"I have something here for you," she whispered. "I promised your sister I'd give this to you." She pressed a folded dance card into Violet's hand.

Violet quickly scanned a note scribbled between the names of dance partners, tore it into small bits, and promptly discarded it all before she put her glove back on and hurried toward the stairs. More furious with Rosemary than she had been for a long time, she hurried her steps and wondered how she would ever explain this to her father.

Obviously, she could not, but she had no idea what she was going to do or say when she met him downstairs. She hurried back down the stairs, only to find Sam Glennings waiting for her.

"May I have a moment?"

She paused, took full note of how handsome he looked in

formal attire, and felt her heart leap. "I'm sorry. My father is waiting for me downstairs. We're . . . we're leaving now."

Disappointment flashed briefly in his eyes. "I've waited all night for the opportunity to speak to you. I promise not to keep you long."

"Perhaps another time," she murmured, certain she had nothing to discuss with him.

When she turned to walk away, he suddenly appeared in front of her again. "Perhaps later tonight. I'll wait for you at the rear gate. It's important," he added as if he could read the denial on her lips before she set it free.

"I can't promise I'll be able to meet you tonight," she insisted. She had a far more pressing problem to solve at the moment, one that most definitely did not involve Sam Glennings. "If you'll excuse me, I don't like to keep my father waiting."

He smiled a warning. "I'll be there at midnight. Tonight and every night until we have a moment to discuss a matter of great importance to you and your sister."

With her traitorous heart flip-flopping in her chest, she ignored the opportunity to remain and convince him he would be wasting his time; instead, she walked around him and made her way down another flight of stairs to reach the front entrance.

She had no intention of slipping out of the house to meet him tonight or any other. She knew enough of her father's plans for her and her sister. She did not need to know more, and anything Sam Glennings might tell her would not change her mind about leaving before her father destroyed both of his daughters.

The moment she saw her father pacing the width of the marble steps, all thoughts of Sam were dispatched to the back of her mind.

Mottled with rage, her father's face was florid. He greeted her with a snarl. "Get into the carriage. Now. Your sister took ill and went home over an hour ago."

"Ill?" She swallowed a lump of anxiety. "What happened?

Why weren't we summoned to help her? How did she manage—"

"Apparently she managed quite well," he snarled as he assisted her into the carriage. "She left with Captain Miles."

"How fortunate he was there to help her," she mumbled and prayed with all her heart Rosemary would be home by the time they arrived. If not, she would personally help her father lock Rosemary in the tower once she arrived home!

As for Captain Miles, she would need a little time to think of a way to repay him for his role in tonight's disaster, but she most definitely would.

Chapter Six

❧

I know my responsibilities only too well." Captain Miles paused, but his words, as well as his stance, brooked no further argument.

Violet quaked as she watched the standoff between her father and her betrothed. When he finally glanced at her, his expression did not soften. "Please accept my apologies for not escorting you home. Forced to choose between leading your sister through a throng to find you and your father or finding immediate relief for your sister, who was feeling faint and exhausted from the night's outing, I trust you will not doubt my intentions."

"Your apologies are accepted, of course," she murmured. While his words were eloquent and perfectly phrased, his gaze remained hard. Search as she might, she found no trace of the simmering desire and smoldering sensuality she had seen when he first met Rosemary.

He obviously had no expectations their union as husband and wife would be anything more than a business arrangement. If all her efforts to escape her father as well as her impeding marriage failed, at least she would have no illusions to be destroyed, as she'd had when she first met Sam Glennings.

And she would never again experience the pain of seeing

interest in a man's eyes fade to pity and disappointment when he looked at her.

Her father puffed out his chest. "It's late. We'll discuss this in the morning, Captain," he said. He dismissed Violet with a sharp wave of his hand. "See to your sister. I'll expect a full accounting when you both join me for breakfast at eight."

She caught the captain's gaze, nodded, and forced herself to take slow, measured steps up the staircase. When she passed the half-landing and was out of view, she hitched up her skirts and raced the rest of the way to the third floor.

Rosemary was already in her nightdress and sat curled up on the window seat that faced the river with her legs tucked beneath her and her forehead leaning against the pane. When the younger woman turned to face Violet, her eyes dazzled with wonder that sent chills to Violet's heart. "I've seen his ship! It's glorious. Did you know he's been to China four times? And India, too? He—"

"Don't do this to yourself, Rosemary. Please. Do you know what would happen if Father found out you left Mrs. Belle's to spend time alone with Captain Miles? You should thank every star in the heavens you were here when we got home. Whatever possessed you to deliberately lie about feeling ill and then disappear for over an hour? If Father asks Bridget what time you arrived home—"

"Oh, she won't tell. She's been keeping company with Sean in the stable after he delivers ice. As long as I don't tell, she won't."

Violet tapped her foot. "The housekeeper—"

"She spent the night with her daughter, remember?" Grinning, she got up, met Violet, who crossed the room to meet her, and tugged on her hands. "Please don't be angry with me. It was only for an hour. He was the perfect gentleman, and he's sweet, considerate . . ."

When her voice trailed off and her eyes glazed over, Violet gently shook her sister by her arms. "Stop it. This isn't some romantic fairy tale. This is real and terribly dangerous. Have you forgotten who he is?"

"D-dangerous?" her sister sputtered and yanked free, her eyes flashing with blue fire. "He didn't even try to take any liberties. He's not what you think."

"If I don't find a way out of here for both of us, he's going to be my husband in a fortnight! He's toying with you."

A pout. A shake of blond curls. "He's not. He wouldn't mislead me into thinking—"

"He's an 'opportunistic, fortune-hunting monster.' You called him so yourself. He bargained away his freedom and intends to marry a woman no one else would have in exchange for a ship! And if he had taken liberties with you, who would have believed you weren't imagining it all? You're the perfect toy for him. Can't you see that?"

Chest heaving, Violet drew in shallow gulps of air. The prospect of spending her life with a man who had the un-mitigated gall to take advantage of her very own sister sent cold shivers down her spine. In her mind his character was tarnished beyond redemption, and that only reaffirmed her determination to leave before the wedding could take place.

Rosemary collapsed facedown on her bed and wept into her pillow. Violet sat down on the edge of the bed and patted her back. "Hush now. He's just an infatuation. One day you'll meet a good man. Once who will love you and honor you above all others," she murmured.

Giving voice to a dream she had tucked away in her heart for herself did little to calm Rosemary. Crooning softly, Violet talked on and on about finding a new home and new beginnings in a place where the past would matter less than future dreams . . . until Rosemary had cried herself to sleep.

𝔉ollowing their disastrous evening at Mrs. Belle's, sheets of rain blanketed the city for three straight days and nights. The air had turned raw. The wind blew so relentlessly it woke Violet from her sleep. Again. Shivering, she rose and added another shovel of coal to the warming stove. She crawled back under her covers, folded her arms, and hugged them to her chest.

Held captive by the weather, she had made no progress in executing her plan to escape. But she had not wasted the past three days trying to figure out whether her father had become careless or merely too preoccupied with business to notice he had not put their grandmother's jewelry back into the safe.

Selling the jewelry would provide a small fortune for Rosemary and herself, but she did not know how to manage selling them without being caught. Reputable jewelers would recognize either her or the necklaces. In either event, they would unquestionably notify her father.

The necklaces might as well be made out of paste for all they were worth to her now, and all she could do would be to make certain to take them with her when she left.

Yet another gust of wind rattled the windowpanes and interrupted her thoughts. She held her breath for fear the glass might shatter. When it did not, she exhaled softly and found it hard to imagine anyone venturing out tonight.

She knew one man who would.

A guilty conscience tugged her back out of bed and over to the window where she pulled back the drapes and peered outside.

He was there.

Again.

She might not be able to see him, but she felt his presence to the marrow of her bones.

The idea the man waiting on the other side of the gate, night after night in such inclement weather, might be someone other than Sam Glennings was so far from being rational she dismissed the possibility at once.

If the weather had not turned so foul and prevented her from slipping away unnoticed to collect her earnings from Elijah, she would have sorely resented Sam's sentry duty at the rear gate. The horrid weather was also the only thing that kept her inside and gave Sam a reprieve from being told in no uncertain terms she had no interest in anything he had to say.

She worried her bottom lip, let out a sigh of complete consternation, and surrendered to guilt. "You'll probably catch lung fever and die, if brain fever doesn't strike you down first," she grumbled as she rummaged through the trunk at the foot of her bed. She grabbed hold of her pale gray winter cloak, pulled it free, slipped it around her shoulders, and tied it tight at her waist. After fastening her hair with a ribbon, she hesitated, then decided to leave her hood down until she was outside.

She left her bedchamber and stopped at the door to Rosemary's room to peek inside. The form beneath the covers lay still. Poor Rosemary. She had slept through most of the storm out of sheer boredom, although Violet was watching her closely to prevent another plunge into melancholia.

Satisfied Rosemary was asleep, Violet crept down the stairs, tiptoed past her father's bedchamber, and paused at the half-landing to cock an ear.

Eerie silence, broken only by the ticking of the clock below.

Instead of going downstairs to the main floor, she crossed through the rooms in the back buildings to keep her walk outside in the dismal weather as short as possible. Once through the old nursery and playroom, then the sewing room, she reached the back room used as a schoolroom and descended the servants' stairs to the kitchen.

Without a candle to guide her, she made slow progress. Her heartbeat raced far faster than her feet could safely travel. To keep from turning back, she had to keep reminding herself she had no choice but to convince this man he was being a ridiculous, obstinate fool who was risking his health to talk to a woman who did not want to hear a word he had to say.

The kitchen door creaked open, and her heart sank the moment she realized the rain had not slackened one iota. Gritting her teeth together, she tugged her hood into place and tied it tight just below her chin. With a deep breath for courage, she stepped out into the storm. After she slipped twice on the brick walkway separating the private gardens from the house, she slowed her pace. Like a turtle wearing blinders, she had no peripheral vision, but easily kept the stable in sight straight ahead.

By the time she finally got to the stable itself and then found the service gate, her slippers were soaked clear through and her cloak was on the verge of saturation. Her toes ached with cold. Her teeth chattered together so hard she thought they might chip. The ironic thought that she might be the one to contract lung fever instead of the obstinate fool on the other side of the gate did not sweeten her temper or rein in a quickly escalating litany of complaints she was ready to hurl at Sam Glennings.

She unlatched the gate, swung it toward her, and struggled to keep it from blowing out of her hand and banging against the fence. As if given new opportunity, the wind howled through the opening in the fence and gusted beneath the hem of her cloak. Rain pelted her face and stung her eyes.

Instinctively, she turned against the wind, slammed her eyes shut, and pushed down the hem of her cloak. The gate swung out of her grasp and hit the fence with a loud crash. Before she could cry out to get Sam's help, strong hands clapped over her mouth and across her chest and wrenched her back against the wall of a man's chest. Fear thundered through her body and scrambled her brain, but sheer terror turned her to stone when she felt the blade of a knife pressed to her throat.

"Don't struggle agin me this time, lass. I've only come to sample my due."

Sam woke with a start and bolted upright. Disoriented by the sound of a whinnying horse as much as his surroundings, he glanced around the stable while his brain slowly unscrambled and he discovered where he was and his purpose for being here.

He leaned back into the bed of hay he had fashioned for himself. "Big mistake," he grumbled. He got to his feet and brushed the hay from his clothing. When the marble-coated horse in the stall on the opposite end of the stable whinnied, Sam cast the animal a glower. "So you warned me not to get too comfortable, and I didn't listen. It's all her fault, anyway," he muttered.

Foolish woman. Didn't she have sense enough to know he would not have asked her to meet him in the middle of the night unless it was important?

He regretted the phrasing of his thought as soon as it echoed past his conscience. Maybe she did not have enough sense. He had to keep reminding himself that Violet Dunn was scarcely a normal, able-bodied, stable woman.

Despite their congenial conversation when he escorted her home from Elijah's home after her lucid explanation of what had happened to her at the market, her hysterical arrival and leap into his arms had painted an image of her on the canvas of his mind he could not easily forget.

Or dismiss.

The fact that he had seen no sign of her alleged molester when walking her home or found any evidence of struggle at the market when he stopped en route to his own home less than half an hour later made it all the more likely she had imagined the whole affair.

He could not fathom the depth of terror that plagued her mind. All the more reason, he mused, to warn her she was betrothed to a man either cursed by bad luck or completely incompetent at the helm of a ship, according to Flynn, and alert her to her father's scheme as soon as possible.

Only his driving need to protect a woman as vulnerable as she was kept him returning, night after miserable night, in the hope she would meet with him. He was not, however, a complete fool. After one night of standing outside in the rain, he had spent successive nights here in the stable where he could be protected from the elements, yet still hear her when she approached the gate.

Tonight was the first time he had fallen asleep. Worried he might have missed her, he pulled out his pocketwatch. He did not bother to retrieve and light the lantern hanging by the stable door. Instead, he opened the crude matchbox beneath the lantern, found and struck a match that he held to see the time. "Blast! It's nearly one!"

He snapped the case on the watch closed and put it back into his pocket. After blowing out the match, he held it between his fingers until it cooled before tossing it to the ground. With howling wind and drenching rain outside, he would probably not have heard her approach had he been awake, anyway.

As her protector, he was no better than her own father! He hissed and let loose a string of expletives.

The clanging sound of wood smacking against wood silenced him and immobilized him long enough for him to also hear a muffled cry that nearly stopped his heart in mid-beat.

He tripped over a bucket in his charge to the door and clawed his way back to his feet. When he pulled the stable door open, he saw two figures. A struggle. A woman's muted scream. A man's grunts.

"Violet!"

Without regard for the outercoat he had stored on a peg to dry, he bolted ahead of the sound of his own scream, grabbed hold of the hair on the man's head with one hand, and yanked hard. He clapped his other hand on the man's shoulder, but the fabric of his coat was slick and he could not maintain his grip.

Angry expletives. A wild cry. The man twirled about. He counterattacked with strength beyond his size, slipped, and toppled both of them to the ground. Snarling viciously, he lunged for Sam's face.

Sam managed to ward off the blow by blocking his face with his forearm. Metal sliced through fabric and flesh before it hit bone. Pain seared a wide swath and unleashed rage that gave him the strength to hurl the man aside. Panting heavily, Sam managed to get to his knees. A gust of wind caught and held his breath. A rain-drenched lock of hair blinded him momentarily, long enough to give the assailant time to flee.

Ignoring the maniacal need to follow and catch the vermin, Sam turned all of his attention to the small figure huddled against the fence. He dragged in raw air that stung his throat. Nursing his arm, he stumbled toward her. "Violet? Are you all right?"

"Sam!" She lunged at him and grabbed hold so hard and so fast he had to fight to keep them upright. He wrapped his good arm around her quaking shoulders and hugged her to his chest.

Any doubts he had had about her earlier tale of a molester dissipated into anguish as he realized he had given the man a second chance to accost her. It would indeed be a far colder day in July before he would ever let that happen again.

Waning in strength, he helped her to the stable, but they were not alone. The ghost of his guilt went with them.

Chapter Seven

Violet wrapped her arms around Sam's neck and buried her face against the column of his throat. She collapsed against him, burrowing closer, pressing harder, as if she might be able to crawl beneath his very skin to find refuge from the terror that filled her soul.

Wrapped in the safe haven of his embrace, she felt her heart thumping against the wall of her chest and echoing in a wildly erratic, pounding rhythm against every pore of her skin. She clenched her jaw and clamped her lips together to keep from giving voice to the horror that still shook through her body.

With a low hum that rested in the base of her throat, she blacked out the clang of her attacker's vile and disgusting words, which still resonated in her ears.

With lightning speed, snippets of her harrowing attack blinked back, again and again, to reinvade her senses. The feel of the sharp blade of the knife. The smell of stale sweat and liquored breath. The touch of frenzied hands mashing her breasts. The sound of heavy, labored breathing. The realization of his nightmarish intentions to violate her body as well as her soul.

All kept her nearly paralyzed, unable to think or respond to anything beyond the need to hide and escape the terror, even unable to acknowledge she had been rescued.

"You're safe now," Sam gritted as he dragged her with him toward the stable.

His words sounded distant, like the echo of a voice cried from a mountaintop and carried to her ears on the wind through the valley of her fear. His hold on her was firm, but his breathing was uneven. And his steps faltered as he fought against the wind and rain to get them to shelter.

Once he managed to get them inside and closed the door to shutter out the storm, he collapsed back against the door itself and carried her with him. She could feel his heart pounding as his chest rose and fell with frightening speed. She burrowed closer, inhaling his scent and welcoming the safe power of his embrace.

Molded against him, heart to heart and hip to hip, she let bold and bitter tears begin to wash away her fear. Sobs tore from her throat and finally set terror free. Tremors raked through her body to chase away the remnants of her attacker's touch.

And the hands of time slowed to create a special moment for healing.

Soft, crooning words of comfort. Caressing hands. Gentle strength. Sam offered them all to her. Sobs eased to gentle weeping. A soft breeze of peace and security invaded the very essence of her spirit.

She felt safe. Protected. Even treasured.

And still vulnerable, not to attack but to dreams best saved for the future and, most definitely, another man.

She wiped the tears from her face, but when she eased from his embrace, a wave of dizziness left her legs weak and shaky. Before her knees buckled, he caught her up in his arms and carried her to a bed of hay. He sat her down and urged her to lie down.

Shivering, she curled into a ball and heard him step away into the darkness. She fought against the nausea that heaved in her stomach, closed her eyes, and huddled in the hay.

Alone. Again. Always so alone.

With his forearm on fire, and tucked next to his waist, Sam

searched blindly but frantically for the lantern he had seen earlier.

"Blast!" He yanked his hand back from the planked wall next to the door frame just as the tips of his fingers brushed against the lantern's globe. The splinter in his throbbing thumb felt as big as a toothpick.

After several tries, he managed to pull the splinter free and lifted the lantern off the hook. Although his one-handed attempts were awkward, he eventually had the lantern lit, and a bright glow he hoped would be hidden to anyone outside the stable filled the room.

He was not shocked by the blood that splattered his trousers. The gash in his forearm was deep. Even now, blood oozed from a wound that would need a row of stitches to stem the flow of blood.

He was more concerned Violet had been struck by the assailant with the knife, as well, but unless he stopped the bleeding quickly, he would have little strength left to help her.

When he held the lantern up to illuminate her makeshift bed of hay only a few feet away, what he saw made his heart skip a beat and then pound alarm through his veins. Already saturated with rain, folds of her soft gray cloak were stained with blood.

Was it his, or had she been too traumatized to realize she had been cut by a knife?

He dropped to his knees and set the lantern to the side. "Violet? You'll have to help me. Undo your cloak. Let me see if you've been injured."

She scrambled to her knees and presented him with her back. "I'm—I'm fine. Just a little shaken. There might be a few bruises, but nothing more."

"You're still in shock," he argued. "The man had a knife! He could have hurt you—"

She bowed her head. "He didn't." Barely a whisper, her voice broke. "Just give me a few more moments before I . . . before I go back to the house."

"Not until I'm certain the scoundrel didn't—"

"No. I'm ... I'm not dressed ... properly," she stammered.

He caught his breath and exhaled it in a rush. "You're worried about the style of your *gown*?"

When she nodded, Sam's mind focused on memories of Polly. She was narcissistic, and her obsession with her appearance and her extreme vanity were only small components of her mania. If Violet could be concerned about her appearance in the aftermath of such a frightening experience, instead of whether or not she had suffered a serious wound, she was obviously not hurt badly enough to require his immediate attention or his concern.

"So be it," he snapped. "I'll settle for a piece of your petticoat."

She turned her head to the side to glance back at him, but the refusal sparkling in her eyes died before it reached her lips. "You're hurt!"

He shrugged his shoulders. "It's nothing a few stitches won't cure, but I need something to bind around the gash to hold it closed. I'll replace your petticoat, of course," he remarked to forestall any reticence she had about ruining one of her petticoats. "Your cloak, as well," he added.

He caught the look of hurt in her eyes before she turned around and got to her feet. She bent down and tore off the hem, but tossed it aside. "It's caked with mud," she explained and ripped off another strip that she used to wrap his arm. "The fabric isn't very strong, but it should hold well enough." Avoiding his gaze, she chewed on her lower lip. "A sling would help."

Before he could argue, she turned around again and tore a wider swath from her petticoat that she folded into a triangle. He held out his bandaged arm so she could drape the fabric against the plane of his chest.

While holding one end behind his neck, she pulled on the opposite corner until his arm was cushioned in a sling at a comfortable angle near his waist.

When she knotted the ends together, her fingers brushed

against his neck, and his flesh tingled with sensations that warmed his blood to a dangerous level.

When she finished and stepped back, he glanced down at her handiwork and frowned. He would have a hard time explaining to the doctor how and why he had a sling decorated with wildflowers! Polly never wore petticoats made of such soft material, and none had embroidery as delicate. She reserved such finery for her nightdresses. He swallowed the idea that Violet was wearing her nightdress, instead of an old gown, as too incredible to be true. "Thank you," he murmured.

"You're welcome. And there's no need to replace my nightdress. Helping you now in any way I can is the least I can do after you risked your life to save me."

He nearly choked on his amazement and a good measure of guilt. "You're only wearing a . . . a nightdress?"

A soft pink blush painted her cheeks. "I told you I wasn't dressed properly."

"B-but a nightdress? Whatever were you thinking when you decided to go outside on a night like this, at an ungodly hour, without being properly dressed?"

She blanched, but her eyes flashed brightly. "Perhaps I was thinking of the obstinate man who had spent the past three nights standing outside in the rain waiting for a woman who thought she made it perfectly clear she had no interest in anything he had to say!"

Stung by her response, his temper roared and silenced the guilt; she would never had been attacked had she not gone outside to meet him. "Your actions speak louder than your argument," he countered. "You obviously wanted to hear what I had to say, or you wouldn't have come to the gate. What astounds me is your complete disregard for propriety and your own safety. If you hadn't opened the gate before you knew—"

"And just precisely how did you get inside? I didn't let you in. Did you forget the hour and arrive late enough to find the gate open?"

"I never forget an engagement or a promise," he quipped.

He wondered if she knew any more of his foibles, but refused to acknowledge even one of them to her. "And I wasn't late. I was early, in fact, but I had little inclination to get soaked clear through again. I simply climbed the fence—"

"No one can climb a solid, six-foot fence, especially one slick with rain."

He cocked a brow. "I can. With a little ingenuity. I was raised in the country and climbed trees practically before I could walk, so my sister tells me." He paused, realized she had once again cleverly maneuvered the conversation back to him.

"This is all completely off the main point of this conversation." He would have continued, but suddenly found himself unable to fashion a single thought beyond how lovely she looked, even after such an ordeal. Her hair lay plastered against her scalp, glistening in the lantern's glow, and accented fine high cheekbones and gently arched brows. Impossibly long lashes framed large brown eyes flecked with green and gold, as though an artist had painted them to be so unique they would capture and hold a man's interest for a lifetime. Her lips were a bit thin. Her chin came to an unfashionable point, except when she smiled.

Not beautiful, merely fascinating.

She donned her hood and tied it into place. "You were saying?"

He raked his hand through his hair. "I just don't understand why you'd venture out in your nightdress. It's that simple. Can you tell me why without evading the question? Just this once?"

She flinched.

Had he spoken too harshly, or had she read his mind and discovered how intriguing he found her to be?

"Indeed I could, but I won't," she countered. "Blame whatever reason suits you. Perhaps I was worried you might take ill if you stood out in the rain another night. Perhaps I wasn't planning to meet with you at all and just wandered out into the storm, oblivious to propriety as well as the weather. Or the unlikely possibility someone would be waiting to molest me."

She paused and dropped her gaze. When she finally looked back up at him, her eyes were swimming with tears. "Or perhaps I am simply mad."

Her words added layer upon layer of more guilt, but it was the echo of her sad, lonely footsteps as she walked slowly out of the stable that pierced his heart.

Snuggled deep under her covers, Violet lay awake and stared into the darkness. Her body was stiff and sore and her heart was aching from bruises she should have expected.

Although this night's terror would one day be nothing more than an unpleasant memory, she would be forever scarred by her reputation as distracted. Melancholy. Lunatic. Or touched in the brain. Put more plainly: mad.

While it had suited her needs to carry a label most people feared to protect her sister, she always believed she would one day be free to simply be herself. Now she was not sure if she would ever be able to do that.

Despite years of feigning mental frailty, she still recognized the line separating sane from insane behavior and never once crossed over it. Although she often questioned her judgment of people and found it hard to distinguish truth from lie, she did not question her sanity.

Any confusion she now felt was merely the consequence of her constant vigilance over Rosemary, the shock of her betrothal, and the prospect of leaving her sister behind with her father if Violet failed to undo his plans for her.

She tasted salty tears and kept sobs silent by pressing the back of her hand to her lips. With her eyes closed, she relived those precious few moments in Sam's arms when he held her close and offered her his strength and his comfort.

For one long heartbeat after another, she recast the scene. Instead of being a man who jeopardized her fortune and forced her father's hand, Sam was a man with a tender heart who found her irresistible. Far from being a woman tainted by the scandal of madness, she was his beloved.

With her heart filled with her impossible vision, she let her dream lead her to sleep. The question of why he had insisted on speaking to her remained to greet her in the morning.

Chapter Eight

❧

Dawn announced relief with clear skies and brilliant sunshine. Long before the servants' feet had hit the floor to start another day, Violet had stored her torn nightdress and bloodsplattered cloak in a trunk in the attic alongside the other apparel she had ruined within the space of two weeks.

She had tucked the question of why Sam thought it urgent to speak with her inside the trunk, as well, although she did pray his wound would not fester and healed quickly.

By moving carefully, she did not jar her wrenched shoulder, and she had concealed a deep purple bruise on her throat by wearing a high-necked blouse held in place by the brooch her grandfather had presented to her on the day she was born.

She paused in front of the cheval mirror to give her appearance one final check before joining Rosemary and their father for breakfast. Her dark hair was neatly knotted at the nape of her neck without a single strand out of place. The white lawn blouse actually made her complexion look less pale, but it was the brooch that drew her attention and invited memories to resurface.

She stepped closer and fingered the delicate spray of violets expertly carved from amethyst so they almost looked real. Small diamonds in the center of each blossom sparkled softly, and a single gold stem held leaves of jade. Her sister had a similar brooch, one with a single rose sculpted from ruby.

She had no real memories of her grandfather, only stories that had been told and retold so often by her mother during her childhood they seemed real. Tales of sailing ships and pirates, foreign lands and adventure. All shaped the image of the sea captain who had retired to Philadelphia.

Against all odds, whether in war or competition, he had founded the Montgomery Packet Line and parlayed his savings into a fortune—only to meet the one foe he could not defeat for his only child: madness.

With only ten days remaining until her marriage, Violet had little time to squander on painful memories. She lifted her lids, looked herself square in the eye, and straightened her spine. She would not honor her mother's memory by being weak or becoming mired in self-doubt. She would not risk another midnight escapade to secure her funds from Elijah, but get them she would.

Today.

Before the day reached eventide.

She would have to enlist Rosemary to the cause. Given the amount of rest she had had these past few days and her penchant for mischief, Violet was confident she would get no argument from her sister. In fact, the greater concern was keeping Rosemary reined in during the course of some sort of outing today. That serious thought followed her as she left her room and descended the stairs.

$\mathcal{D}$r. Morgan elbowed Ben Hastings out of the way. "Give the man some breathing space, and give me room to tie off one last stitch!"

"You shouldn't really close that gash until you give him a good dose of common sense."

With his jaw set to bite back the pain, Sam glowered and hissed through clenched teeth. "Do you mind keeping your own counsel? Let the man finish! Even I have sense enough not to crowd a doctor during a procedure."

Ben caught the glower and tossed it back. "Someone has to watch over you. You can't remember to keep engagements you yourself suggest any more than you give second thought to wandering the streets and alleys in the middle of the night."

"Ouch!"

"Done," the doctor pronounced as he wrapped a fresh bandage around his handiwork. He patted Sam on the back. "Put your shirt on while I get something suitable for a sling. I should have something in the trunk I keep in the carriage."

"And a muzzle for my friend," Sam snapped as the doctor made an exit. His arm stung like fire ants had permanently nested beneath the row of black stitches that spanned at least six inches.

While Sam eased into his bloodstained shirt, Ben crossed his arms and cocked his head. "So when do I hear what really happened?"

Sam shrugged his shoulder and awkwardly tucked the end of his shirt into his trousers. "You already did."

"Hardly."

After inhaling a long, deep breath, Sam let it out slowly. "I told you twice, and I'll repeat myself one last time. I couldn't sleep. I got up early and took a walk—"

"In the rain."

Sam frowned. "No, the rain had stopped by then, but the streets were slippery. That's why I fell and cut my arm on a broken bottle."

"The one lying in the street?"

Completely out of patience, he hissed. "No. The one I had in my hand." He raked his hand through his hair. "Of course the one in the street! Have you ever known me to get addled and carry spirits with me as I caroused the city?"

Ben narrowed his gaze. "You never touch the stuff."

"Exactly."

"Not good enough, friend. Dr. Morgan might not challenge your tale, but I will. If what you say is true, just tell me why that gash appears to be a defensive wound. Who attacked you?"

Sam swallowed hard. He had intended to get medical help by himself. Weak from loss of blood, he had run out of strength and barely made it to Ben's. Before knocking at the door, he had had the wits to remove the sling and bandage and stuff the remnants of Violet's nightdress into the pocket of his coat. To protect Violet, he had concocted a perfectly logical story—one Ben challenged again.

"I told you. No one—" His denial caught in his throat, reminding him of the times he had tried to lie to his sister while growing up. It had not been easy being raised by the woman with the reputation as the most honest woman east of the Mississippi; she had set an example for him that had not been easy to emulate.

When Ben held out a piece of the embroidered cloth, Sam was speechless. "And where does the woman who fashioned this for you fit into your tale?"

Their gazes locked together. Like horned bulls tangled together in a desperate bid for dominance, neither man blinked or took as much as a single breath.

Until Sam grabbed the delicate material and shoved it into his pocket. "I never thought you'd take advantage of a friend, especially when he's injured. I can't believe you went through my pockets!"

Ben gripped Sam's upper arm. "I'm your friend, but I'm also a lawyer. I suspect you might need both right now. If you're mired in some sort of trouble, let me help."

"I can handle this alone."

"Can you?" he murmured and dropped his hold.

A lump lodged in Sam's throat, and he fingered the cloth in his pocket as he calculated an answer for his friend. He had rescued Violet tonight, but in the aftermath, he had not had the opportunity to discuss the real reason that had brought him to her home. After tonight's fiasco, he did not think it wise to tempt Fate and insist on another clandestine midnight meeting.

Given his adversarial relationship with Charles Dunn, he could scarcely call on her at home. Propriety, if not the size of her betrothed, dictated it unwise to extend an invitation to her for a social outing.

Ben was right. Sam faced no viable options, save one, which forced him to swallow his pride and ask his friend for help. He easily dismissed any fear Ben's temper would flare out of control and trusted him above anyone else here in Philadelphia to be able to convince Violet both she and her sister were in danger and needed his help.

When he heard the front door open and close as the doctor made his way back to his patient, Sam nodded. "You're right. I'll need your help. Later. After I've had a chance to freshen up."

$\mathcal{V}$iolet would have chosen any of a dozen outings other than Fair Mount Water Works on the banks of the Schuykill River.

Unusually crowded with tourists and local residents during the summer season, the public gardens and walking paths did offer a semblance of anonymity, and Violet had agreed to Rosemary's suggestion.

With her father's warning about being vigilant and keeping Rosemary from wandering off still ringing in her ears, Violet linked arms with her sister and held a parasol over their heads to protect them from the sun as they joined the parade of visitors. A refreshment saloon, newly opened in the remodeled engine house, offered shade as well as an opportunity to rest while savoring a meal.

It was the architectural wonder of the water works itself, which provided an endless supply of quality drinking water to the entire city, as well as the magnificent view of the river, cool breezes, and fresh air that drew hordes of tourists.

Impressive Greek-styled buildings housed the wheels that raised water to the reservoir on the crest of the mount. Marble statues were centered in sparkling fountains while lush green foliage along the maze of paths and bridle trails added a country feel to the atmosphere.

Violet knew almost immediately she had made a mistake by agreeing to come here. She was already exhausted from her harrowing night, but the heat quickly evaporated what little energy she had left.

Rosemary, however, was nothing short of packaged energy and quickly grew bored with Violet's slow pace. "We'll never get to walk all the paths today," she whined. "Why are you so tired?"

"I'm not," Violet protested. "I'm just feeling the heat more than usual."

Rosemary tugged her to a shaded bench that was free and sat near a fountain. "Rest here," she insisted.

Violet lowered her parasol, sat down, and patted the empty place beside her. Provided with a perfect opportunity to enlist Rosemary's help in the next few hours, she smiled. "Sit with me. There's something I want to ask you."

Rosemary grinned. "Not yet. First I'll get us some lemonade." She dangled her reticule in front of Violet's face and giggled. "See? I even managed to get Father to give us a few coins for refreshments," she teased and practically skipped her way off before Violet could mount an argument.

By the time she bolted back to her feet, Rosemary had already disappeared into the throng. Violet had the sinking feeling she had somehow waltzed right into one of Rosemary's schemes and sat back down on the bench.

If she was right, Rosemary had a good head start on the adventure she had concocted for herself. If Violet was wrong, she might very well be gone on a fruitless search when Rosemary returned.

"She has ten minutes," she muttered and checked the watch that hung from a silver chain around her neck. "It's eleven-fifteen. Ten minutes. No more," she repeated. "She can't possibly get into trouble by then."

Ten long minutes later, Rosemary had not returned. Violet hesitated, waiting ten more just to allow for the size of the day's crowd and the long lines at the vendor stands. Annoyance kept Violet's foot tapping for another ten minutes.

By noon, she was worried.

By twelve-thirty, she grew alarmed and abandoned the bench.

"Foolish. That's what she is, utterly foolish," she muttered. Half an hour later, after none of the vendors could recollect seeing Rosemary, Violet started down one walking path. Then another.

No sign of Rosemary.

"Irresponsible twit," she grumbled and climbed the stone steps that led up to the walkway- surrounding the reservoir. She made faster progress without the parasol being up, and the heat of the full sun drained her energy twice as quickly. On the verge of utter exhaustion, she stumbled her way around the reservoir.

No Rosemary.

"This isn't a good time to play hide-and-seek." Her whimpered words echoed back to another time when Rosemary had been much younger and thought it rather delightful to hide from her older sister, often for hours, before reappearing when Violet was on the verge of tears.

"You're not a child anymore." Her words gave life to fear Rosemary might be in real danger because she was not a child, but a young woman who might attract the attention of a man with less than honorable intentions.

What better place could there be to meet and perhaps spirit off a young woman as naïve as Rosemary? Her sister might even be foolish enough to invite a perfect stranger to explore one of the two isolated glens she had discovered on previous visits.

Or Captain Miles?

Following a spark of inspiration that filled her heart with both dread and hope and fueled her with renewed energy, she rushed back down the steps. Her heart pounded faster when she reached the first glen and found it empty. When she was but a few yards from the second, her heart stopped and almost did not start again.

She leaned against the trunk of a tree for support. Her mouth dropped open. Her eyes widened with disbelief, but shock sucked the breath from her lungs and gave her no power to move or cry out. Horrified, she stared straight ahead to where Rosemary stood, wrapped in the embrace of a man who could be mistaken for no other.

Bile soured the taste in her mouth. Disgust unleashed nausea that made her sway on her feet. Outrage filled the air in her lungs and cast aside any thoughts but taking her sister straight home and keeping her there under lock and key, if necessary, to protect her.

Violet watched in stupefied fascination as Captain Miles turned away and left Rosemary standing there with her mouth red and swollen from stolen kisses before Violet could utter a single sound.

$\mathcal{A}$ stone had more expression than Rosemary's face.

After hours of pleading, Violet could not get her sister to even acknowledge her existence. She paced back and forth in Rosemary's bedchamber and nearly tripped over the supper tray Rosemary had simply set aside on the floor.

Being careful how she phrased her words was important. What *he* had done was beyond contempt, but what Rosemary had done was sheer lunacy.

Violet dared not use that word or any other that kept springing to mind.

Pleading overexertion to get permission from their father to take supper in their chambers had been easy, especially since he had been summoned to the country estate to handle some sort of emergency. Making Rosemary see she was being badly used and misled by a conniving, manipulating cad was nigh impossible when the girl refused to listen to a single word Violet had to say.

To make matters worse, she had still not figured out how the two of them had scheduled their assignation. Plans for Violet and Rosemary to visit the water works had been made only that morning at breakfast, and Rosemary had never been out of sight after that.

Recalling how Rosemary had sweetly but stubbornly refused to consider any other destination for their outing, citing perfectly reasonable objections to the other sites, Violet suddenly rocked to a halt. She remembered how still Rosemary had been when she checked her bed before slipping out to confront Sam.

Thinking of the long afternoon naps Rosemary had taken the past few days, Violet rummaged through the trunk at the end of Rosemary's bed as well as her wardrobe.

Stymied, but not daunted, she found what she was looking for stuffed beneath Rosemary's bed.

She tossed four pillows to the middle of the room and held out the water-soaked cloak in front of Rosemary's face. "You've been sneaking out at night to meet him, haven't you?"

Blue eyes flashed briefly, then shuttered.

Violet sighed, tossed the mantle to the floor, and knelt down in front of her sister. "Rosemary, please. Talk to me. If you won't, can't you at least pay attention to me?"

Not even a blink.

She wrapped her hands over one of her sister's and hugged it hard. "I love you, and I won't let him destroy you like this. He's a monster, a heartless fiend who cares nothing—"

"He loves me."

The whispered words were so softly spoken, Violet barely heard them.

Tears trickled down Rosemary's face, and her bottom lip quivered. "He's not a monster. He loves me and doesn't care about my illnesses or my money."

Violet's heart trembled with guilt. If she had not been so preoccupied with Sam and his stubborn insistence to see her, she would have known Rosemary was back to her nighttime escapades. "He's stolen your innocent heart, for which I'll never forgive him, but there's no place for you in his future. Only me."

She bowed her head, blinked back tears, and then gazed lovingly at her sister. "Captain Miles has signed a binding legal contract to marry me. If he dares to break it, which I assure you is definitely not part of his plan, he'll have no future for himself. Have you forgotten about the ship he received? That's all he wants. Not me, and I'm afraid, not you, either. Whatever his motives or his feelings, they aren't pure or good, and I will promise you this: If I fail to find a way for us to escape, I will never let him forget what he's done to you. Never."

With every beat of her heart, she swore it would be so.

A knock at the door interrupted her, and Violet sighed. "Come in, Bridget," she called as she got to her feet.

The door opened, and the maid barely stepped inside the room. "You've a caller, Miss Violet."

"A caller?"

On the verge of tears, she twisted her apron with her hand. "Mr. Ben Hastings. Says he's a lawyer, ma'am. He's waiting in your father's study. Said to give you this to make sure you made a few moments for him. Looks like he's set to spend the night if you don't." She handed a neatly folded paper to Violet, who stepped aside to open it out of the younger woman's view.

"Shall I tell him to wait?"

Violet took one look inside, saw the small shred of fabric, and nodded slowly. Distraught because Sam had sent his lawyer to see her, she was unable to voice a single word. She simply refolded the paper and slid it into the pocket of her gown before heading downstairs, certain Sam Glennings had finally proven himself to be a man she could neither like nor trust.

With every step that took her closer to Ben Hastings, she grew more confident she finally understood the enigma that was Sam Glennings. He was not a ruthless entrepreneur as her father had claimed. He was not the gentle, kind man she had thought him to be any more than he was a man Elijah thought she could trust, either.

If her suspicions were right, Sam was the most vile serpent ever to slither across the earth.

Chapter Nine

❧

*P*recisely what is your purpose here, Mr. Hastings? Extortion or blackmail? In either case, doesn't that violate some sort of ethics? Or have you none, like Mr. Glennings?"

Of all the possible reasons why Sam had hired a lawyer to represent him, Violet could think of none that were honorable. She was rather surprised he had not sent his lawyer directly to her father, but she was hardly in the mood to be grateful.

She kept her gaze steady on the lawyer and refused to be swayed by his gentle demeanor or the look of surprise and disappointment that lined his face. She had no thoughts to waste on Sam, either. Obviously, he was quite recovered if he had been well enough to engage a lawyer this quickly.

With a wide mahogany desk separating her from her unexpected caller, she held her head high and scarcely blinked. Despite the confidence she heard in her own words, she was unable to keep her heart from racing or her hands from worrying the folds of her skirts.

She also refused to let in the memories of when she had sat behind this desk nearly two years ago, intimidated by her father's lawyers when she signed control of her inheritance over to her father.

He coughed, but quickly recovered. "I assure you Mr. Glennings has no such intentions, and I wouldn't represent him if he did. When I said the purpose of my visit was financial in nature—"

"I have no funds of my own, but if Mr. Glennings wants to be reimbursed for his medical expenses, or to have his clothing replaced, perhaps something can be arranged," she conceded, although she had yet to retrieve her coins from Elijah. "Beyond that, I have nothing to say to you or to Mr. Glennings."

Warm gray eyes held no threat, only concern that chastised her more effectively than anything he might say. "Quite to the contrary, I believe it's in your best interests to talk to me. Obviously my visit has upset you. Perhaps Sam would have been better advised to wait until you had fully recovered from your ordeal and you were thinking more clearly before sending me to see you. Under the circumstances, however, we had little time to delay," he said.

He was good, maybe better at soothing a mistrustful client than any lawyer she had encountered over the course of the years that a series of trustees had administered her inheritance before her father took control. Against her will, her guard relaxed. Her heart dropped back to a decent rhythm. She laid her folded hands on her lap and quieted her suspicions, but only for the time it would take to listen to what this man had to say before she sent him on his way.

"We haven't much time. My father might return at any moment," she prompted.

A guilty smile. A . . . a wink?

"We have at least another hour, although I doubt we need that much time. The problem at the country estate isn't truly serious."

She cocked a brow. "How convenient."

He actually blushed, cleared his throat, and awkwardly placed the wide envelope he had been holding on top of the desk. "Sam wanted you to have this as quickly as possible. If you read through it now, I'll be able to answer any questions you might have. Sam would have come himself, but after last night . . ."

"Is he all right? Has he seen a doctor?" she blurted.

Despite her reservations about Sam's intentions, she had real concerns about the wound he had suffered while defending her.

"He's stubborn and forgetful at times, but he's not made of steel. The stitches will come out in a week or so. Other than that, he's only worried about you, particularly since he expects to be leaving on the twenty-eighth."

July 28.

Her wedding day.

She dropped her gaze and stared at the envelope. "Then he's sold his business, just as he said he intended to do."

"Yes. He's rather anxious to go back to Sunrise, but he couldn't leave without knowing . . . Please. Read the documents."

He opened the envelope and took the time to arrange them on the desk in what she supposed was a specific order. "I'll give you a moment alone," he murmured before he took a place in the shadows by the front window, where she assumed he would be watching for her father to arrive home.

She moved the candelabra closer to the documents. The first was a copy of the marriage contract signed by the two fiends in her life: the man who had literally sold her and the one who had bought her. As she expected, the terms of the agreement were exactly as her father had explained them to her.

Except for what she found in one paragraph. She paused and read it again:

> *Title to the said ship shall be transferred to Captain Miles on or before 14 July 1835 to facilitate repairs and alterations. Upon breach of this contract, title shall immediately revert back to said original owner.*

Two weeks before the wedding? Today was the eighteenth, which meant Captain Miles had already taken title. Why would her father take that risk? What kept Captain Miles from sailing off without fulfilling his end of the contract?

She perused the rest of the contract, but found nothing

related except a curious clause giving him free title if Violet were to be pronounced incapable of giving her consent to her vows. "Incapable, not unwilling," she whispered.

He's had three shipwrecks in as many years.

Her father's words were like cold fingers of fear clutching at her throat. Her father did not expect Captain Miles to leave without going through with the wedding. If he did, the ship would simply meet a fate similar to the others, but this time, Captain Miles would not survive.

No wonder the man had set his designs on Rosemary. He was exacting revenge of the worst sort, and Rosemary had fallen right into his trap. What better way to insure his bride-to-be was incapable than to seduce her sister and make very sure she found out? Under those circumstances, a normal woman would become hysterical. A woman like Violet, who was reputed to be distracted, might very well lose whatever slender hold she had on reality and go completely mad.

Captain Miles could then sail away with his ship as legally plundered booty.

Sam obviously thought she had the right to know why Captain Miles had agreed to marry her. Unaware her father had already told her, he must have the same concerns about her betrothed as she did, although he could have no inkling exactly what he planned to do to have her declared incapable. Neither did her father, which gave her a small, but definite advantage against both of them.

By sheer force of will, she set the contract aside along with her curiosity as to how Hastings had managed to secure such confidential papers. She would deal with Captain Miles one way or another, but not until she knew the full extent of her financial status.

The remaining documents included the one she had signed two years ago that gave her father control of her inheritance, but not Rosemary's. She immediately set it aside, but found the other three documents difficult to understand since she had little head for business or account books. By focusing on underlined segments of each document, however, she was able to piece together enough information to know she had misjudged her father.

He was far more devious than she had imagined and so were his lawyers. According to the documents, the trust fund set up for Violet and Rosemary was now virtually worthless, leaving them both financially dependent on their father, who had become a wealthy man at their expense.

With her heart pounding, she fought against fear and disbelief to remain calm and objective. She may have misread or misinterpreted the documents. Still, it would be impossible not to understand the statement detailing heavy losses sustained by the Montgomery Packet Line or to overlook one name in the list of investors in the other ventures that filled her with disgust: Dr. Orpheus Poole.

Surprisingly, she was indeed grateful to have a lawyer at hand—one who could either explain away her fears or confirm them. When she motioned for him to rejoin her at the desk, he did. "I won't waste your time or mine by asking how you obtained these documents. I'm more worried about what they mean."

Rather than trip through a series of unfamiliar business names and lists of stockholders, she cut to the core of her concerns. "Am I correct to conclude my father, Charles Dunn, is the primary stockholder in several new corporations, including the one that will actually own the former Montgomery line?"

Ben reached out and placed his hand over hers. "I'm afraid so. He's been shifting funds from your trust to a number of his enterprises for the past two years. His actions are legal and probably acceptable from a business perspective. But highly unethical. Since he ultimately ends up owning a controlling interest in all the new firms, he can easily manipulate the earnings due to the trust fund and keep most for himself."

He paused, and his expression softened. "The Montgomery Packet Line accounted for the bulk of your grandfather's fortune, and the heavy losses reported for the past year and a half had a severe impact. As of today, there's only a token amount left in your share of your grandfather's estate. I'm sorry."

She swallowed back tears. "What about Rosemary's share?"

"A little better, but not much. Funds must have been diverted from her trust by Lloyd Burgher, the trustee appointed by the courts a year ago after George Adams died. He's an associate with Peter Magee, your father's lawyer."

With no inheritance, Rosemary and Violet had no hope of ever escaping their father's control and leading independent lives. She stiffened. So did her resolve. She would not allow her father to fleece the trust fund and steal the inheritance that rightfully belonged to his daughters, even if it meant unleashing a public scandal by hiring her own lawyers and taking him to court.

"Are these documents enough to bring before a judge?"

"I'm afraid they're not sufficient proof for a court of law without a full accounting of each enterprise involved. More importantly, you'd also need the books and records for the packet line. I think there's every reason to suspect those losses might have been exaggerated to cover funds he transferred to his new enterprises."

"Sam." She dropped her gaze and whispered his name as shame filled her spirit. She had badly misjudged him. Again. It was no wonder he had sent his lawyer to see her, since Sam's business had ended the packet line as a profitable enterprise. Her father, however, might very well have painted Sam's competition as ruthless and unscrupulous as a way to hide the fraud he had perpetuated. If so, Sam did not need to feel guilty about the financial predicament she now found herself in. But she could not dismiss her own guilt quite so easily.

If she had not tried to protect Rosemary by claiming distraction, she would not have been equally vulnerable to scandal and her father's manipulation. If she had not assigned control of her inheritance to her father, she could have found a way to protect Rosemary. If she had not put all her meager earnings into a single account . . . if only . . . if only she had been stronger.

But she had been weak and afraid; her will was strong but her spirit was intimidated by the fear that her melancholia had never been feigned at all and complete madness would one day claim her, just as it had her mother.

There was little she could do now to change the past. Even the present seemed a muddled mess too complicated to easily clear up right now, but her future would be no better unless she took a stand.

She was not sure how she might resolve her own situation, but the least she could do for Sam was to give him a free conscience to carry with him to the future he would have at home in Sunrise.

A clear conscience. Is that what Sam truly wanted?

Would he have bothered to help two young woman now in financial jeopardy if they weren't both tainted by reputations as distracted? Since she would not have been attacked if she had not gone outside to see him last night, is that why he was trying to warn her?

Or could he be the same man who had comforted her? With his heart pounding against hers in that one splendid moment, he had held her as though she were as precious to him as a beloved, joined as equals in mind as well as spirit. Which man was he? Could he be both?

Too confused to trust her own judgment, too vulnerable to the yearnings of her heart, she simply could not risk involving him in her affairs any longer. "Please tell Mr. Glennings I appreciate his concern and absolve him of any responsibility. He's free to enjoy his profits without worrying about me or my sister. In the future, I'd appreciate it if he'd leave this issue in my hands. He's done quite enough."

Indeed, he must have paid a high fee to acquire the documents, especially so quickly. Already beholden to Sam for rescuing her last night, she could not add to her debt to him. Without funds to repay him, she had no other choice but to unpin her brooch and place it into the lawyer's hand. "Please return whatever fee Mr. Glennings has paid. This should cover everything. If not—"

"I can't accept this," he argued as he attempted to place it back into her hand.

When she pulled her hand away, the brooch slid across the desk. He caught the brooch before it could fall to the floor.

When he looked back at her, she smiled and wrapped her arms at her waist. "Please keep it. If I'm to use the documents against my father, then I should pay for them. Otherwise, you can take them back to Mr. Glennings."

"I only began my inquiry several weeks ago. Given more time, I believe I'll be able to locate the packet line's duplicate set of books, which will show the funds diverted from there disguised as losses."

She gathered up the documents and held them against her chest to keep him from reclaiming them. "Good night, Mr. Hastings. I'll put my faith in what I have here. And in the courts. What my father has done is fraud, and the courts will—"

"The courts will want proof."

"And Mr. Glennings wants a free conscience," she argued. "Tell him he has it with my blessings and my gratitude."

The sound of carriage wheels approaching, then stopping directly out front, ended any thought of continuing their standoff. Before she realized what he was doing, he had grabbed away her documents, shoved a single new document into her hand, and tucked the original set inside his frock coat.

As agitated footsteps clomped toward the front door, he smiled and pointed to the document she held. "It's an agreement to name me as administrator of your inheritance once you're married and living at sea. Quickly. Crumple it up and just follow my lead. If you need to contact me, my home office is best. Sam can direct you."

With her heart pounding in her chest, she sank back down into her chair and created a ball out of the paper in her hand. In the meantime, Hastings assumed a stiff, formal position in his seat and put an arrogant expression on his face.

When her father charged through the front door, crossed

the foyer, and headed directly for the study, she did not have to feign tears or force her body to tremble.

Hastings cleared his throat. "I'd still like to speak to you again in a few days to answer any questions you might have, assuming—"

"What are you doing here in my home?" her father demanded as he stormed into the study.

Hastings rose, extended his hand, and introduced himself.

Her father knocked it away, and his glare would have turned the Arctic Sea into a tropical swamp. "Do you think I'm stupid?" her father fumed. "I know who you are, and I know you represent Glennings, the arrogant bastard. He sent you here, didn't he? Well, here's a message for your client," he warned as he poked his finger into Hastings's chest. "Tell Glennings I'll deal with him personally, and this time, he won't get away with his chicanery. Now get out," he ordered. He grabbed hold of the collar on the lawyer's frock coat and dragged him out of the study into the foyer.

Violet watched and listened with horror. Fearful the confrontation would escalate into physical violence when the lawyer yanked free and charged back at her father, she tossed the ball of paper to the desk and cowered in her seat. She dared not follow the two men out of the room. But although they were quite angry, they spoke in harsh whispers she had to strain to hear.

Rage flashed through Hastings's entire body, incinerated all vestiges of his gentle demeanor, and transformed him into a man as frightening as her father. "Your daughter," he spat, "is old enough to make her own decisions, and I have every right to represent her interests. Sam Glennings is but one of my clients, and your threat against him is as unconscionable as what you've done to your daughters' inheritance."

His gaze narrowed into slits of pure fury, and his hands balled into fists. "Glennings has no inkling of what you've done, but I do," he hissed. "If you want to keep the funds you've stolen from your daughters, you'd best rethink your stand and encourage Violet to allow me to represent her."

Her father squared his shoulders and took several steps

toward Hastings, but braced to a halt when the younger man extended his arm and held up his palm. "You can't intimidate me because I have the proof. Undeniable proof!"

"You have nothing," her father spat. His body shuddered and his breath came in rasping spurts like a bull that had raced full steam ahead only to face a stone wall.

. Hastings cocked a brow and lifted his chin in defiance. "Tell your lawyer, Magee, to stop by my office the day after tomorrow. I'll let him see what I have. Let him be the judge," he challenged. "You don't have a prayer of getting away with anything unless I allow you," he warned as he backed toward the door. "And unless you do exactly as I say when I return next week to finalize arrangements for representing your daughter, I'll personally give the proof to Glennings. He won't hesitate to use it, which makes me your only hope."

Before her father could answer, Hastings charged out of the house and slammed the door behind him. Violet cringed, terrified her father would assume she had heard every threatening word. If he even suspected as much, he would lock her in the tower. Or worse.

She did not have to feign tears. Crying out of fear for herself as well as Rosemary, she covered her face with her hands and listened as he approached her with angry steps. "That arrogant fool," he shouted as he entered the study. "What lies did you hear? What lies did he tell you?" he demanded as he charged toward her and snatched the ball of paper from atop the desk.

She dropped her hands from her face, and they visibly trembled when she tried to wipe the tears from her face. "I—I tried to tell him I didn't want t-to t-talk to him," she stammered. "He wouldn't leave until I agreed to see him. He scared poor Bridget half into a swoon."

Her father ignored her, smoothed out the paper, and held it closer to the light to read it. "He really does think he can bully his way right into administering your inheritance after your marriage!"

She flinched and let more tears cascade down her cheeks as she tugged on his sleeve. "You won't let him come back, will you, Father? Will you make him stay away? He frightens me."

He searched her face for several very long heartbeats. When his gaze finally softened, he reached out to pat her cheek. "Of course I won't. I'll protect you. Haven't I always?"

She forced herself to tolerate his touch, and the lump of relief that was lodged in her throat kept silent a bitter, but ill-advised response. For now, she was safe, and she could only pray Ben Hastings would be able to protect himself should he carry through with his threat against her father.

$\mathcal{F}$rom his vantage point behind a tree halfway down the square from the Dunn mansion, Sam flinched when he heard the front door slam. Already unnerved by Dunn's unexpected arrival home, he listened with growing concern as Ben stormed down the street. When he charged straight past Sam without stopping, he followed in hot pursuit. "Hold up, Ben."

His friend only increased his pace.

"Ben! Slow down!"

The lawyer called back over his shoulder. "Not now, Sam. I'll meet you at your house. Later."

Sam's heart lurched against his chest. He ran ahead at full speed and yanked on Ben's shoulder, and spun him around.

Although it was too dark to see the expression on Ben's face, the rigid set of his shoulders, the stiff upward tilt of his chin, and the hands curled into fists made Ben the silhouette of a man still in the throes of a fearsome rage—one he had yet to fully expunge.

"Yes, I lost my temper!" Ben spat. "Yes, I threatened that sorry excuse for a man. Yes, I let you down. Now leave me alone," he hissed. "There's nothing you can say or do to make me feel any worse than I already do."

Shocked and deeply disappointed, Sam scarcely recognized the man standing before him. "Can you at least tell me if you had a chance to convince Violet to let us help her?"

Ben exhaled slowly. "She wants to proceed on her own.

Lord knows she's not likely to want my help after the scene I just created, but Dunn's not likely to blame her for anything. At least I did that part right."

He reached into his pocket and retrieved something he placed into Sam's hand. "It's her brooch," he explained. "She wanted me to take it in lieu of the fee you're paying me." He snorted. "I don't deserve a single coin. Not after what I did, but Dunn's such an audacious bastard. I kept telling myself to remain calm, but when he dared to threaten you and then dragged me out into the foyer like a crate of yesterday's garbage, I snapped. I lost control. And I threatened to expose his entire sham."

When he paused, his shoulders slumped. "I'm sorry, Sam. I really am sorry I let you down. At least I recovered enough to take all the blame. He won't come after you or Violet. It's me he wants now."

Concern for Ben helped Sam to set his disappointment aside. "Let's go back to my house," he suggested. "Aunt Lily never got rid of Philippe's stash of brandy. We'll talk this through and work out something after you've had a chance to tell me everything that happened in there."

Ben nodded and walked alongside Sam as they headed toward the town house together.

Several hours and a decanter of brandy later, Ben finished his tale with a crooked smile. Sam sagged back in his chair from exhaustion, not overindulgence. "You did all you could do tonight. Under the circumstances, I don't think you should be too hard on yourself. Dunn——"

"If you even try to thank me, I might have to hit you," Ben teased, although he was in no state to harm as much as an ant.

Sam frowned. "I'm worried about Violet, but I'm even more concerned about her father. What are you going to do when Magee shows up at your office? If you show him the documents we have now, he'll know you were bluffing."

"I'll think of something," Ben countered with a snort. "I'd

better. My whole career is at stake because of my blasted temper."

Sam swallowed hard, but let his friend talk through his despair.

"You know something, Sam? I love the law. I love using it to protect innocents from people exactly like Dunn. I always knew that would involve risk now and again, but I never thought I would jeopardize my own career. I'm sure I'll survive anything Charles Dunn tries to do. The question is whether or not I can survive my own stupidity."

He paused for moment, then continued. "In the meantime, maybe Ludlam will have some luck finding the second set of books for the packet line—if you still want me to continue the investigation without Violet's approval."

Robert Ludlam was the investigator who had provided last-minute ammunition to use against Polly and save Jane from certain conviction. Sam nodded. "Ludlam might be the only one who can find proof Dunn deliberately distorted the losses the packet line had sustained. If he fails, I'll be no worse off than I am right now."

Sam rubbed at his eyes, which burned from weariness. He could not fault Ben for exploding when Dunn attempted to physically toss him from the mansion. In point of fact, Sam should never have asked Ben to go. He should have gone himself.

He should have been the one to explain in complete detail what her father had done.

He should have shouldered the responsibility, however unintentional, for helping her father find such success.

He should have held her and comforted her as he did last night, and by the feel of her body pressed against his, he would have known she believed him and trusted him.

She had no one else in the world who thought she was precious enough to protect.

He took the brooch out of his pocket to cradle it in the palm of his hand. "Pay Ludlam double his fee and have him work around the clock, if necessary. I want those books. And

I want you to be careful. Dunn is not a man who will take your threats lightly."

Although his concern for Ben was very real, his mind was focused more on Violet, and he was already busy trying to come up with a way to return her brooch to her before he left for Sunrise. Although it made no sense to him, his heart beat a little bit faster with the curious, yet preposterous idea that he would not be leaving Violet behind.

Chapter Ten

❧

The next morning, a new dawn shined hope on Violet's shaky world with the gift of a new day. The sudden, unexpected death of Elijah Dennus tied a shadowed ribbon of sorrow around the afternoon.

Whatever animosity her father felt toward the last of Asa Montgomery's friends gave way to propriety, which dictated paying final respects to Elijah Dennus. The occasion, she noted sadly, also gave Charles Dunn the opportunity to put his devotion to his two daughters on display and give the public a view of the mammoth who would soon be his son-in-law.

Violet could not find fault with Captain Miles's behavior today. He had been reserved, but attentive to her alone. But Rosemary claimed her genuine concern. The tearstained face and pale complexion usually hidden from the rest of the world had little to do with bidding a final farewell to an old man whose passing meant little more to her than accepting the unavoidable cycle of life.

Captain Miles, if not her own reckless naïveté, was solely responsible.

As Violet feared, her sister blamed her for interfering and misjudging his intentions. Rosemary engaged her in convoluted, overwrought discussions that still made her head spin with confusion. On the heels of narrowly escaping her father's wrath, she had spent the entire night using the new information she had learned about Captain Miles from the documents she had seen, along with the loophole in the marriage contract, to try to convince her sister not to see him alone again.

She thought she had been successful, but the moment he arrived to accompany them to pay their final respects, she knew by the look on Rosemary's face she had failed.

She entered the home of Elijah Dennus behind Rosemary and their father, and escorted by her titanic betrothed. The long, heavy veil she wore protected her from the stares of curious mourners lined halfway down the alley. None in the crowd had voiced complaint when Charles Dunn escorted his family ahead of them. Although shaken and distraught, she refused Captain Miles's arm and walked in under her own power.

Simeon Dennus, his wife, and their five children received mourners in the small front room where Violet had visited Elijah only a short time ago. Her future husband had to crank his neck to keep his head from skimming the beams on the low ceiling; nevertheless, he dominated the crowded room and captured everyone's attention.

But her heart and her gaze centered only on the candlelit room beyond the parlor where Elijah Dennus lay dressed and ready for burial in a few hours.

While her father expressed condolences on behalf of his family, she slipped away and stood alone next to her beloved friend and ally. Beneath closed lids, blue eyes twinkled no more. Hands bent with age and disease were stilled, yet freed now from pain. A heart once beating lay quiet, but the love he had so freely given to her was a gift death would never claim.

With her back to the rest of the mourners, she bowed her head in prayer. Still raw with shock at his sudden demise, she flinched when another mourner stepped alongside her and brushed her shoulder with his. She raised her head and turned to see that Simeon had joined her. "I'm truly sorry about your father," she murmured. "He was very dear to me."

He kept his gaze focused on his father's face while he quickly but surreptitiously pressed a tiny, heavy canvas drawstring bag into the palm of her hand.

She knew without asking that the coins were the earnings she desperately needed, but she had been too consumed with grief to give them more than a fleeting thought. She swallowed hard and tucked the bag inside her glove where she could keep the coins silent by curling her fingers around them.

He leaned toward her slightly and whispered, "After my father took ill, he insisted I give this to you privately if anything happened to him. He also wanted me to give you a message, although I can't fathom exactly what it means. Hopefully, you will."

Her vision blurred and her heart began to race, but she managed a nod.

" 'Trust him. Tell her to trust . . .' That's all he managed to say before he slipped away. I'm sorry," he whispered and left her standing alone once again.

Tears escaped and her throat clogged with a choked sob. Even when facing his last moments, Elijah had been thinking of her welfare instead of his own. The hand of death had done more than eclipse his message. It had claimed a devoted friend she would miss forevermore. She lifted her veil and pressed a kiss to each cheek, the stiffened wrinkles now cold to her touch.

"Live well in Paradise," she whispered. Once she had her veil back in place and her emotions under better control, she tried to finish her friend's message. Trust . . . whom? Which man did he want her to trust?

Did he mean her father? Impossible. Her betrothed? She shuddered at the thought, although as a retired seaman, Elijah Dennus might have known of Captain Miles, even though he had not said so when she mentioned her betrothal. Ben Hastings? She did not know for sure that Elijah even knew him, but Ben was Sam Glennings's lawyer, not hers.

Sam. Did he want her to turn to him and trust him now that Elijah was gone? He had told her he was a man worthy of trust the night she had first been accosted, and it made sense he would remind her again since she seemed less than enthusiastic about the idea at the time.

Like fine grains of sand caught in a gust of wind, her questions swirled through her mind and stung hard against sadness and worries about Rosemary as well as the future. Her fist tightened around the bag of coins, the only real thing she dared to trust now that she was left without her one true friend and ally.

When hushed murmurs behind her grew to loud whispers, she turned around slowly. Shock widened her eyes so her lashes brushed against her brows. With her mouth agape, she watched from behind her veil as Sam entered the room, and she waited for a virtual explosion to rock the house right off its foundation.

Sam stood only a few feet behind her father, and she studied him quickly. Other than being slightly pale, he bore no visible evidence of injury. He wore no sling, but she noticed he held his left arm pressed against his body more stiffly than his right.

With her heart doing flip-flops, she bit her lower lip while waiting for the confrontation her father might provoke. She exhaled slowly when he merely nodded to acknowledge his well-known competitor; she thanked the solemnity of the affair for prevailing over her father's temper.

When Sam looked at her from across the room, a completely unexpected explosion of emotion created a tunnel between them that blocked out both time and place. Held immobile, as if enveloped by a dream, she felt his very soul reach out and touch her own to share the pain of betrayal and devastating loneliness he too hid from the world. An understanding heart beat in perfect synchrony with her own and tugged on her heartstrings.

Awash with lethargic sensations that filled her with a sense of peace like she had never known, she moistened her lips just as, without warning, the hulking shape of her intended husband stepped in front of Sam and ended the dreamlike experience.

As Captain Miles walked toward her, her heart whispered

what death had stopped Elijah Dennus from saying: She could trust Sam.

With her troubles. With her life. With her heart, but only if she had faith enough to trust herself.

Her mouth went dry with the fear that shook her very soul—if she was wrong about Sam.

Captain Miles lumbered toward her and extended his arm. "Your father would like to leave."

Without argument, she let him escort her past Sam, who had his back to her now as he spoke quietly with Simeon and Stella Dennus. Her head lowered, Violet concentrated on watching where she walked to avoid leaning on the captain's arm and settled quickly enough into the carriage that would take them all home.

When her father announced an outing to the country estate where they would all spend the night, the carriage became a trap that had ensnared her as unsuspecting prey. She sagged back against the cushions and sighed softly. Not all traps were lethal. Rather than waste her energies on a fruitless plea to attend the burial services, she should be grateful her father had allowed her to say farewell to Elijah at all.

Being secluded at the country estate, where Rosemary and Violet were rarely welcome, might very well offer an unexpected opportunity to present an ultimatum to Captain Miles—one he would have no choice but to accept.

She only prayed Rosemary might one day forgive her.

$\mathcal{T}$he wooden coffin had been lowered into the grave and covered with dirt. Prayers had been offered, and mourners had long ago departed to go home and resume the business of living.

No marker yet identified the man who had spent eighty-seven years on earth. Only freshly turned earth and a sadly wilted spray of flowers placed there by his grandchildren.

After the burial services, Sam walked down High Street toward his office, but it was the little shop next door that tugged him to the display window his friend had only yesterday rearranged. When Sam tried looking through the glass, he saw his own reflection. He stepped closer to block it out to be able to see the new merchandise nesting alongside one of Violet's dissected picture puzzles, but his thoughts were occupied with memories.

His friendship with Elijah had developed gradually, deepening only this past spring. Time enough to feel sorrow. Time enough to feel shortchanged.

Although death was the natural consequence of birth, living a life of decency and honor was not a matter of chance, but of hard work. Elijah Dennus had made it look easy. So had Sam's father.

Paul Glennings had been gone for so long, Sam could not remember more than impressions, memories made vague by the passing of time. Shining through came a feeling of unconditional love that time would never diminish.

Sam had been blessed in his life more than troubled. The anchor holding him fast to a life of honor and good character had been set by two very different men who had been separated by both time and place, yet held firm by the example his sister had provided.

Lacking their counsel now, he leaned his shoulder against the window where a hasty sign announced CLOSED DUE TO DEATH IN FAMILY. REOPEN TOMORROW.

Death had cheated many when it claimed Elijah Dennus. A son had lost a father. Children had been cheated from the wisdom they would have gleaned from their grandfather. Shoppers had lost an ear always ready to listen. Sam had lost a new friend.

Although death had eclipsed Sam's plans to enlist Elijah's help in arranging a rendezvous with Violet, it had also brought the two young people face-to-face. Standing a room apart from Violet, together, yet unable to speak, he had not been able to see her face or control the longing to hold her again that clouded his common sense and rattled his self-control.

While they were in the room together, it seemed as though he felt the fluttering touch of her spirit caress his own. He dismissed the idea now as nothing more than surprise at seeing her at the wake and the tension of coming face-to-face with Charles Dunn, an unsettling experience at best, considering what had happened during Ben's visit.

He fingered the brooch he kept in his pocket. If he returned it to her by post or messenger, her father might intercept it. He would not ask Ben to deliver it for him, but could hardly imagine delivering it in person himself.

Or could he?

A grim smile that started in his heart lifted the corners of his lips. He pulled back from the window and put the brooch back into his pocket. With his throbbing arm held tight against his side, he headed toward his own destiny, for good or for ill, after a brief visit to Simeon Dennus.

Chapter Eleven

※

Charles Dunn brought supper to an abrupt end. "Captain Miles, I expect you'd like to spend time with Violet. Perhaps a stroll outside before it gets dark. Gentlemen, I suggest the rest of us adjourn to my study for brandy and cigars."

Violet unexpectedly had the opportunity she needed to confront her betrothed, and she was surprised to find such a precious gem nestling in the charred ashes of a day still smoldering with tension. While Captain Miles helped her from her seat, her father escorted his assemblage of carefully chosen guests from the room. She watched through downcast eyes as they obeyed their host's command and filed out after him. Peter Magee, her father's lawyer. John Caldwell and Markham Shaeffer, long-standing business associates. Thomas Rollings, merchant. Finally, Dr. Poole, who had earlier given Rosemary a sedative against Violet's protests.

All men whose names she had seen as stockholders in the myriad enterprises formed to defraud her and her sister of their inheritance.

All of them assembled, she presumed, to witness her mental stability as well as Rosemary's apparent relapse into melancholia.

They must all be quite pleased, along with her father. Would they all toast to their financial success tonight? Were they all fully aware of the price she and her sister would pay?

Driven by greed, were they also her father's pawns, to be discarded when they were no longer useful?

She was too filled with disgust for each and all of them to ponder either their motivations or their fates. She was only concerned, at the moment, with Captain Miles, who appeared to be completely bemused during supper. She was convinced his smile would quickly disappear once he learned she had discovered his vile plan to outwit her father.

When her giant betrothed escorted her outside, she drew in long breaths of fresh air filled with the scent of wild honeysuckle and mint. She rested her hand on the trunk of his arm, but refused to be intimidated by his size or his strength. When she measured him by his character, he was no larger than a sugar ant. The image brought a smile to her lips she could not contain.

"You don't do that often enough. You should, you know. A smile is nourishment for the soul," he remarked as they traveled the walking path that led to a secluded sitting area on the banks of a stream that filtered into Wissahickon Creek.

She nearly gagged. Listening to such sentiment from a man she knew to be an opportunist was like hearing a fish peddler sing opera. Her lips instinctively dropped into a frown, an unspoken message she would not smile again for him if it meant starving her soul to death.

A sigh rumbled from his lips. The muscles in his arm grew taut, but he did not voice a reprimand. "This is a difficult question, but I need an answer. Are you committed to this marriage your father arranged?"

She stiffened. "Have I a choice?" she murmured, shocked by his bluntness as well as his question.

"What if you did?" he ventured.

"Then I would have to be honest and say I would prefer to marry someone who finds choosing a wife a matter of the heart instead of his purse or his reputation."

Her answer hung in the air, unchallenged. Much to her dismay, he made no further attempt to pursue the matter or to otherwise engage her in any conversation at all. When they reached their destination, he helped her to a seat on a wrought-iron bench. Though sturdy, it would hardly accommodate his size or his weight, and he stepped a few feet away to stand at the edge of the small stream with his back to her.

A strong current rushed spring-cold water that cooled the air here, although the canopy of leaves and branches overhead kept most of the strong summer sun at bay. Moss crept across the earth beneath her feet, hiding from slices of sun that ripened wild strawberries closer to the path during the day and cast argentine ribbons of twilight now.

With her opportunity now at hand, she swallowed hard. Although undaunted, she was nevertheless uneasy. The well-rehearsed words she had stored in her mind to brook the subject heaviest on her heart kept rearranging themselves so that an awkward silence grew thicker by the heartbeat.

"How is your sister? Dr. Poole seemed quite worried when I saw him talking to your father. Is that why you were so silent during supper? Are you worried about her?"

Although he still had his back to her, his words held just the proper tone of sincere interest in her, rather than Rosemary. Violet needed every ounce of self-control she possessed not to shove him right into the stream. She might be a third of his size, but adding her contempt to the element of surprise would be enough to do it. Her conscience refused to allow more than the thought.

She gritted her teeth and balled her hands into fists. "Rosemary is resting comfortably. I'm sure she'll be feeling much better after a good night's sleep."

Did his shoulders actually straighten a bit?

She blinked her eyes several times, certain she must have been mistaken.

With twilight growing dimmer with each passing moment, she had no time to waste and plunged ahead. "I know of your vile intentions, toward Rosemary as well as myself. Either you stop now, this instant, or I'm going to tell my father what you've already done and still plan to do. I'm certain he'll be more than willing to make you stop. If you don't, the *Carousel* will undoubtedly end up at the bottom of the sea, your flesh will be eaten before it rots, and your bones will be scattered on the ocean floor as toys for sea creatures."

Her heart hammering against her chest and her mind envisioning her own quick demise if he did not believe her, she gulped down the lump of fear lodged in her throat.

He turned around slowly and riveted her to her seat with a gaze blazing with barely controlled anger. Only two quick strides brought him back, and he towered in front of her before she had the chance to draw more than a single breath. With surprising ease, he lifted her from the bench and set her back down, feet first, on the seat, but he did not release her. They were now nearly face-to-face, and the end of his closely cropped beard was so near she could almost feel it bristling against her face. His hold on her arms was only firm enough to keep her steady, but the flash of determination in the depths of his midnight eyes held her immobile.

"Rosemary told me you were very devoted to her and extremely protective. She didn't tell me you were also very foolish."

His breath was warm, but his words nearly scorched her cheek. His gaze melted her courage in the space of a single heartbeat, but her strong will somehow kept her spine from collapsing. "I am far less foolish than you might suppose."

Why had her words sounded like a whimper instead of a challenge? She tightened her jaw and held her gaze steady.

He stared right back at her. "There isn't a man alive who has challenged my character," he warned. "Your gender might protect you now, although your . . . your feeble female mind is no excuse for inventing false accusations—"

"Feeble mind?" She gasped and smacked at his arm. "I'm no more distracted than you are! I saw how you looked at Rosemary the night you met her. I saw you holding her in your embrace at Fair Mount with my own eyes. And I know she's been slipping out at night to meet you!"

He puffed out his chest and narrowed his gaze, but she did not give him time to argue.

"What kind of cad are you to be betrothed to one woman while trying to seduce her sister?" she charged. "A conniving, wicked man, that's what you are, but I know exactly what you're about. I found the loophole in the marriage contract you're trying to slip through, and I make this promise to you: Regardless of what happens between now and the day we pledge our vows, if we must, nothing will make my mind snap and allow you to use the loophole in the contract. *Nothing!*"

With her chest heaving and her lungs on fire, she was forced to draw in air or fall right into a swoon. The only visible signs her words had any impact at all was a small tic in his cheek and a subtle squaring of his jaw. His lips drew taut, but his hands were gentle as he set her back to the ground.

His face solemn, he looked down at her with eyes frighteningly calm. "I believe you. In fact," he admitted, "I intend to hold you to your promise."

"You're . . . you're *mad*," she whimpered. Did he think he could try to seduce Rosemary and then marry Violet without regard for either of them? Terrified and confused, she tried to back away from him, but the back of her legs hit the bench. She barely managed more than a squeak when he took her arm to escort her through the quickly descending darkness back to the house. En route, her mind conjured up all sorts of despicable scenarios in her mind, but none of them could explain what his words could possibly mean.

Or extinguish her resolve to protect Rosemary—at any cost.

Once they were inside the house, he guided her directly to the foot of the wide staircase that led to the second floor, where wings stretching east and west separated family sleeping chambers from guest accommodations. He lifted her hand and pressed a kiss to her palm that sent chills down her spine. "You have nothing to fear from me," he whispered. "Only your promise. Do not let fear or doubt keep you from fulfilling it. Good night."

He bowed, took the stairs two at a time with uncommon ease, and quickly disappeared down the guest hall.

Trembling, she needed the support of the banister to hold her steady long after his words and footsteps had disappeared.

When she finally recovered her wits, she mounted the staircase, still pondering her bizarre experience with him.

"Violet!"

Only halfway to the top landing, she heard her father's
voice call out her name. She turned around and saw him
standing at the bottom of the steps. His stormy expression
was one clap shy of being thunderous.

"Come down here."

Alarmed, she scampered back down the steps, but before
she could ask him why he was so angry with her, he held out
his hand. When she saw her violet brooch cradled in the center of his palm, her heart literally fell to her feet, and she
tightened her jaw to keep a cry from escaping her lips.

"Mrs. Ware summoned me from my meeting to inform me
Glennings has arrived to return your brooch. He's waiting in
the parlor. I'd like an explanation before I see him," he demanded.

Tears well beyond her control blurred her vision. Confusion set several free. She swiped them away, but her throat
was so tight with fear she could not utter a sound, let alone
words of explanation she dared not voice.

He snickered. "Sometimes I forget how truly weak and
pathetic you are," he grumbled. "Come along, then," he insisted as he grabbed her elbow and nearly dragged her along
with him. "I don't have time to waste while you find your
tongue. I'd rather confront Glennings, anyway."

She had no will of her own to resist. She did not even
have the mental energy to sift through the mist clouding her
mind to claim a single thought before another entered her
mind. And then another. After a day that began in such deep
sorrow and a confrontation with Captain Miles that ended
only moments ago, she was too deeply mired in emotional
quicksand that threatened to leave her a mindless, spiritless
shell to think beyond taking one step at a time toward the
certain disaster waiting for her in the parlor.

Apparently Sam had decided to confront her father now
with the evidence his lawyer had only last night threatened
to use against her father. Given the number of his close

friends and allies who were still at the country estate, Sam was walking into pure trouble.

Once her father found out she had given the brooch to Ben Hastings as payment for his fee and realized she had seen the documents he had offered to show her father's lawyer, there would be no hope of any reprieve for her or for Rosemary.

As she approached the archway to the parlor, she moistened her lips and tried to stand up straighter. If she was going to her final destiny, she would do so with only one goal in mind: to maintain her dignity.

Chapter Twelve

❧

Sam's idea to return Violet's brooch to her in person here at the country estate, in front of her father, was just bold enough to mitigate, if not redeem, last night's debacle at Dunn's city mansion.

Since Dunn's lawyer, Magee, might appear tomorrow in Ben's office to challenge Ben's claims of proof against his client, Sam had little choice but to learn all he could tonight. He waited anxiously in the parlor, hoping he could resolve the issues that had been pressing on his mind as well as his heart for the past twenty-four hours.

He wanted to trust Ben's judgment, but after what had happened, he needed to learn firsthand whether or not Dunn had seen through the charade and discovered the true intentions behind Ben's visit. He also needed to assess Dunn's current mood, if only to reassure himself Ben had not put himself in imminent danger by threatening someone as powerful and deviant as Charles Dunn.

Given any hint Dunn had retaliated against Violet or had plans to stop Ben, Sam was fully prepared to do anything, short of murder, to stop him here and now, even if he did have only one good arm.

The sound of approaching footsteps set his heartbeat back from a racing gallop to a dull, heaving pounding. He held his place and stood in the center of the room facing the open door that led to the foyer. When Dunn escorted Violet into the parlor, Sam took one look at her and kicked himself mentally for having one idea short of making him a complete fool.

He caught his breath and exhaled slowly to keep from crying out her name and reassuring her he meant her no harm. If he believed in spirits, he would have sworn she was a ghost searching for her own soul. He had seen women with twice as much color in their cheeks as she had fall into a dead swoon. The fear in her eyes dazzled brighter than any of the dozens of candles in the room and lit a flame of regret in the deep recesses of his spirit.

Jerky steps carried her to a chair near the open window. She dropped, rather than sank gracefully, to her seat and made no attempt to arrange the dark skirts that enveloped her as if she sat upon a wispy black cloud.

With a limp hand lying in her lap cradling the brooch, she drew in short breaths of air he measured by the rapid rise and fall of her chest. A light breeze caressed the short tendrils of hair framing her face and seemingly revived her enough to give her the strength to tilt up the tip of her chin.

Charles Dunn stood next to her chair, rested his hand on the back, and faced Sam without any apparent regard for his daughter's distressed state. He eyed Sam with disdain. Dark brows were knitted together above deep-set eyes shadowed by suspicion, but his entire demeanor exuded sheer arrogance.

"Glennings," he spat by way of acknowledgment without extending his hand. "Quite frankly, I've got little time to waste and even less patience. Since my daughter seems to be momentarily *distracted*, I expect a full explanation from you. Exactly how did you come to possess my daughter's brooch?"

Sam held his head high and kept his gaze locked with his opponent's. "Simeon Dennus found it today lying on the floor near his father's body shortly after you left with your family. Since he was already overwhelmed by Elijah's death, I offered to return the brooch for him."

Dunn cocked his head. "So you came all the way here to deliver the brooch as a mission of . . . mercy?" He snickered. "That hardly suits your cold, thieving nature."

"I thought Miss Dunn might be distraught at losing her jewelry," he responded. Out of concern and respect for Violet, he declined the bait Dunn tossed at him and refused to escalate their meeting into a fierce and bitter personal confrontation.

Dunn rewarded his self-control with a sneer. "Then you expect me to believe you're tenderhearted as well as benevolent. Try again," Dunn challenged with a shake of his head. "Never mind. It would be obvious to anyone who knows you as well as I do you don't have a single bone of goodness in your entire body. What is it you really want, Glennings? A reward? If so, I'm surprised you didn't send Hastings to collect it for you."

Sam ignored the slur against his character and counterattacked without pausing to take a breath. "Like you, I tend to my own errands, no matter how small or distasteful," Sam gritted. "I don't send someone else to do my work for me," he challenged.

Making an oblique reference to a visit Dunn's lawyer had paid to Sam over a year ago to warn him against further sabotaging the packet line might very well serve to minimize Ben's threat and force Dunn to accept a stalemate until next week when Ben was supposed to return to see Violet. By then, maybe Ludlam would have the proof both Ben and Sam needed to stop Dunn.

The air itself became thick with tension. Dunn's gaze became even more penetrating, but Sam refused to even blink and returned a gaze that was rock-confident and steady. His heart pounded so hard now he thought it might explode, and when Dunn finally blinked first, Sam sensed he had won and caught a sigh of relief before it escaped.

"Make no mistake. Madness is the only thing we have in common," Dunn retorted with just enough of a hint of defensiveness in his voice to satisfy Sam's initial impression of victory. "Since you're here, you might as well take a good look at my daughter. She bears no resemblance to your wife, Polly. According to the pamphlets I read, she was blond and quite beautiful while Violet is no more than mildly attractive."

Sam's soul actually flinched, but he tightened every muscle in his body to make sure his shock at Dunn's audacity did not betray him. He did not dare glance away to look at Violet and give Dunn even a slight advantage, but he was quite certain any relief she might have felt after learning Sam had not come to betray her was now replaced by shame.

He did not want to upset her any more than he had already done and chose to ignore Dunn's taunt. Since Violet bore no visible effects from last night, and only his own misguided appearance here tonight, seemed to distress her. Dunn did not pursue a discussion about Ben, so Sam had no reason to remain any longer. "I came to return the brooch. Now that I've done that, I'll be on my way."

He took a step forward, but Dunn held up his hand. "Stay where you are. I'm not finished and neither are you."

Sam paused and stifled the urge to knock Dunn to his knees. "Yes I am."

"No you're not," Dunn countered. "Since you're returning to the city, you can deliver a note to Simeon from my daughter. If benevolence truly is your only motivation, I assume you'll have no problem waiting while Violet writes her note."

Before Sam could answer, Dunn rang for the maid and instructed her to bring everything necessary for Violet to the parlor. As soon as the maid left, Dunn addressed his daughter for the first time, and his demeanor instantly softened. "How could you be so careless with your brooch that you didn't even realize you'd lost it?"

Color suffused her cheeks. "I'm sorry. I—I suppose I was fiddling with it at some point, but I didn't realize the brooch was missing until we arrived here. With your guests arriving for supper and Rosemary taken ill, I was afraid to tell you what I'd done."

He clucked and shook his head. "Afraid? Of me? You'll have Mr. Glennings thinking I'm an ogre."

She closed her eyes briefly before she spoke again. "I was afraid I'd disappoint you. Again."

"You've never been a disappointment, Violet. Not to me, and I pray, not to Captain Miles, although you can't expect him to be as understanding as I've been with you."

Dunn reached down, patted her shoulder, and smiled. "Since you're so remorseful, I'll let you keep the brooch. I doubt Captain Miles will tolerate such carelessness, so I won't tell him about this. You should do the same."

The arrival of the maid interrupted them, and she followed her employer's instructions without comment. She placed a tray with a writing pen, ink, and note paper onto a table next to Violet and left.

"Write your note," Dunn suggested. "When you thank Simeon, don't forget to apologize for burdening him on such a difficult day."

He waited until she had actually begun to write before turning his attention back to Sam. "While Violet pens her note, perhaps you can tell us both more about your former wife. You locked her away in a lunatic asylum before you divorced her as I recall. The details should prove fascinating, given Violet's experience with the same type of illness."

Now that Dunn appeared ready to reveal the past, Sam had no hope Violet would let him help her. Even if he proceeded without her approval, she would never trust him once she learned he had once been married to a woman tainted by madness and had set her aside. Without Violet's trust, there would be little he could do to stop her father, but he had learned one very important lesson: He should never underestimate the demon who had taken human form as Charles Dunn.

Sam's breath came out in a hiss. The horrified look on Violet's face nearly stopped his heart, but it was the expression in her eyes that would haunt him to his last breath. His plan to help her had just exploded into miserable failure—one he would long live to regret.

Madness. Divorce. Lunatic. Asylum. Her father's words clanged together in her mind like cymbals, deafening all the other words that linked them together.

Her fingers tightened around the pen in her hand, but she could not write another word until Sam offered some explanation for her father's outrageous and rude accusations.

When he looked at her, fury and pain churned in his eyes before he turned a steely gaze to her father. "My former wife murdered her lover and let my sister stand trial for the crime. She was indeed declared a lunatic, but I divorced her after she confessed to poisoning my brother-in-law. And *after* the state ordered her confined to an asylum for the rest of her natural life, not before. Since you obviously read the vicious pamphlets printed during my sister's trial, you have all the lurid details. You won't get any more from me."

Her heart trembled in her chest, but her soul shuddered after hearing Sam's response. She still had no idea why he had chosen to return her brooch tonight, but she was quite sure he had not expected to be confronted with a past that would make him the last person on earth she could ever trust if she believed her father instead of him.

A shudder wracked through her body, and she clenched her teeth. She did not doubt Sam's explanation. No man would reveal such an awful tale unless it was true. Besides, Sam's account could be easily disputed if it was a lie, something her father must have realized since he did not challenge Sam again. His only real purpose must have been to embarrass Sam, but he had only succeeded in revealing himself to be an arrogant, self-righteous monster.

Peter Magee's arrival interrupted her thoughts as well as the confrontation between her father and Sam. "Charles? I'm sorry to intrude . . ." He stopped abruptly when he saw Sam and stared at her father. "What's he doing here?" he snapped.

Her father shrugged. "He'll be leaving shortly. What is it?"

Magee moistened his lips. "Something's come up at the meeting that needs your immediate attention, but I can try to stall the issue for a bit longer—"

"That won't be necessary. As it stands, I'm quite certain Mr. Glennings is most anxious to return to the city." He nodded to Violet. "Finish your note as quickly as you can. I'll speak to you further in the morning. I'll send Mrs. Ware back to collect the tray," he said before leaving with his lawyer.

She set the pen down, lowered her gaze, and drew in short gulps of air. Her heart began to race when Sam approached her, but all she could think of was the expression in his eyes the first time he met her. No wonder his interest in her died the moment he heard her name. He had been cruelly betrayed by a woman whose mind had been destroyed by madness. She thought him remarkable to offer to help her, given her reputation, and did not judge him harshly for not telling her about his past.

"I'm sorry," he murmured. "I never meant to upset you by coming here. After last night, I needed to make sure you were all right and to tell you how bad Ben feels about what happened."

When she looked up, remorseful brown eyes met her own, but she found no pity, only deep regret in the planes of his face. "Father provoked Ben. It wasn't his fault. It was my father's," she insisted. "I'm sorry for what he did to you tonight. He had no right—"

"To abash me?" He shook his head. "I'm not proud of my past, but I don't let it shame me. Not anymore."

Already impressed by his self-control in the face of unspeakable provocation, she admired his ability to rebound so successfully. But that did not excuse her father's behavior. "Father distorts the truth whenever it suits him, regardless of who might be hurt."

Sam squared his shoulders. "I'd never do that. Not to you or to anyone else. I'd still like to help you. If you'll let me."

Touched deeply by his words, she blinked back tears. As much as she needed his help, she could not allow him to get further involved. "You don't know my father like I do. If he finds out—"

"Then we'll both be in trouble."

"There isn't much time—"

"There's at least a week," he insisted.

The maid's approaching footsteps forestalled any further discussion. Before she knew what he was doing, he had grabbed her half-written note. "You don't have to bother finishing it. Simeon isn't expecting the note, but he knows I've come here and will corroborate my tall tale tonight, if necessary. I'll contact you once I have the information you need," he whispered before walking toward the door.

She turned in her seat to keep him in view. "How?"

He grinned. "I'll manage. Just trust me," he murmured before disappearing into the foyer.

Trust me.

His words echoed in her heart long after he left the house and the maid had cleared away the tray, and she remembered the message from Elijah as well as her own experience at his wake earlier today.

Sam was the most unique and intriguing man she had ever met, if only because he did not let her father intimidate him or let his past control him, qualities she should have developed in herself long ago.

In fact, Sam was the one person in her life she could judge as remaining true to her initial perception of him—if she did not allow fear or doubt to muddle her opinion.

Her father vacillated between ogre and protector with such ease she could not trust a thing he did or said. Her betrothed was either an opportunist, a scoundrel, or possibly, a madman, depending on how she interpreted their perplexing conversation earlier tonight. Even Rosemary seemed changed. Where once she welcomed Violet's protection and advice, she now resisted, as resentful of Violet as she had been of their father in the past.

Only Sam held out any hope that she could set herself and Rosemary free. Only Sam asked nothing in return, except a clear conscience. Only Sam could understand how deeply she had been hurt in the past by the taint of madness.

He was a man of courage and deep conscience.

He was the very type of man she could learn to love.

And he was the one man who would never be able to love her in return.

With a heavy heart, she left the parlor to take to her bed, where she might find some respite from a day she would long remember as one of the worst days of her life. Muffled voices still coming from her father's study were out of hearing by the time she reached the landing on the second floor. Before she could retire, however, she thought it best to see for herself that Rosemary was all right.

She tiptoed into Rosemary's room. After stumbling around in the dark, she finally found a candle. When it was lit, she said a fervent prayer the sedative Dr. Poole had given to Rosemary would not put her into a slumber that might last for days.

With one look at Rosemary's bed, she knew her prayer, unfortunately, had been answered. The sedative, apparently, had not worked at all. The bed was empty, and there was no sight of Rosemary anywhere in the room.

She blew out the candle and set it back into place. Panic made her heart pound. Anger made her tremble, but also sent her flying out of the room, down the hall, and straight to Captain Miles's chamber door. She rapped softly when she really wanted to pound the door down. If he dared . . .

The door swung open, although she had scarcely touched it. She stepped inside and looked around. A single candle on the opposite side of the room from the massive bed straight ahead did little to shed light on the bed itself. Summer netting draped around the bed further obscured her view, but there was no mistaking his presence or the voice that nearly para-lyzed her with fear.

"Shut the door. Quietly," he commanded. "Unless you want the entire household to know your sister has fallen asleep in my bed."

Chapter Thirteen

꘎

A scream ricocheted from Violet's throat to her mind and back again, but no sound escaped her lips. Her heart raced so fast every pore of her skin throbbed with the frantic rhythm. Pitched from shock and outrage to desperate action in the blink of an eye, she charged to the bed. When she yanked back the netting at the foot and stared inside, her narrowed gaze widened into stunned disbelief.

Bathed in twilight shadows, Captain Miles sat abed fully dressed with his back against the headboard and his legs stretched straight beyond the end of the bed. His bulk nearly consumed a bed built to accommodate two, but he never looked up at her and kept his gaze riveted on Rosemary.

Curled atop his lap, she lay fast asleep with her head resting on his chest and her arm lying along his waist. One of his hands stroked the waves of her unbound hair; the other cradled her form.

The aura of sweet intimacy and gentle protection was so strong and overpowering Violet could scarcely draw a breath, but she was appalled by the total impropriety of what she beheld. "Are you completely out of your mind?" she gasped. Although her question came out in a forced whisper, in her mind it was a screech that echoed in the room.

He never looked up and tightened his hold on Rosemary. "I'm no more distracted by madness than you are. Or your sister." He pressed his cheek to the top of her sister's head before he softened his voice. "Do you know what happens to a wild bird forced into a cage? It fights for freedom and bangs at the bars till its wings are broken. When they heal, it tries again. And again, until it's too weak to fight anymore."

The sigh that escaped his lips seemed to come from deep within his heart. "Rosemary isn't as strong as you are. Not yet. But she can be. With me . . ." When his voice broke, he looked up at Violet with eyes swimming with deep devotion. "Rosemary has told me what you've done to help her and protect her, but I'm willing to do that now. If you'll let me."

Her heart skipped a beat, as though acknowledging and celebrating the love and commitment resonating in his plea. The truth of his words and his feelings for Rosemary shattered all of her illusions about his intentions and left her trembling. "You love her," she whispered, both awed and frightened to the depths of her soul.

He pressed a kiss to the top of Rosemary's head. "Beyond all you can imagine. I've searched the world for a woman like Rosemary. Now that I've found her, I won't ever let her go—or ever let anyone hurt her again."

"But what about my father? And the marriage contract? Or your ship? You can't just turn your back and walk away, especially not with Rosemary."

He glanced up, caught her gaze, and held it. "I'm not walking away. I'm going to sail from here right under your father's nose. There won't be a thing he can do to stop me because we'll be an ocean away before he discovers we're gone. We want you to come with us, too."

She truly believed he meant every word he said, but she knew her father better than he did. "You can sail to China, but he'll still find you. He has ships and crews willing to do his bidding on every ocean. Do you think he simply plucked you out of the scores of sea captains when he wanted to marry me off? He orchestrated the shipwrecks that ruined you to use you for his own purposes!" she blurted. She had no proof to support her charges; she was relying solely on her own intuition.

"Do you think I'm fool enough not to know that?" His gaze narrowed and hardened. "I am many things, madam, but I am no man's fool. I recognized sabotage more than once, but I didn't know who or why until your father summoned me here."

She sighed and sank down on the corner of the mattress with her fingers still wrapped around her brooch. "If you knew what he'd done, why couldn't you go to the authorities instead of agreeing to marry me?"

"I *suspected*," he argued. "The proof is leagues beneath the sea. My *life* is the sea, and he destroyed my reputation so no one would engage me to set a sail, let alone captain a ship. I would have married the devil himself to get my own ship!"

"Or a madwoman?" she taunted.

Guilt shadowed his gaze. "The moment I saw you I knew I had made a mistake by signing the contract. I had no right to drag you or any woman into my troubles. The contract was just paper and words, but you were very real."

He rubbed his beard and briefly closed his eyes. "At that point, it was too late to change my mind. Even if I could somehow get the contract voided, I was afraid your father would take out his wrath on you. I had no choice but to go with the rigging I'd set myself and sail out the storm. Then I met Rosemary. . . ."

At the sound of her name, Rosemary stirred awake. Her face lit the moment she gazed up at his face, and she snuggled closer to him.

He wrapped his massive arm around her in a quick hug. "We have company."

Rosemary peeked her head around. "Violet!" she gasped. She scrambled off his lap and climbed out of bed.

He pulled her back, set her alongside him, and put his arm around her shoulder. "Violet and I had a chance to talk while you were resting."

Rosemary's face clouded with doubt. "Violet?"

With tears blurring her vision, Violet held out her arms. Rosemary scampered into her embrace and clung to her. "He loves you. I can see that as clearly as I can see you love him, too."

As impossible as it might have seemed only hours ago, Violet knew love had bound her sister to a man who, by his size alone, could protect her from anything her father could design. Captain Miles offered her the kind of life at sea that had filled her dreams since childhood. He could give her a future that could banish forever the nightmares of the past—a future Violet could not give to her.

But would he watch over Rosemary and keep her from all harm, including harm she might do to herself?

The burden he would carry as her protector would be heavy, as Violet knew only too well, but she also knew it was a burden love would help him to carry, just as love for her sister had given her the strength to prevail all these years.

She hugged her sister's body. The little sister she had protected all these years had blossomed into womanhood. Was it time to let her go and entrust her to the care of another? If she didn't, if she tried to keep Rosemary with her and failed to outwit their father, Rosemary would live the rest of her life in an institution. If Violet succeeded and won freedom for them both, Rosemary might one day recover from losing a man she loved, but she would never forgive Violet.

Either way, Violet would spend the rest of her life knowing she had sacrificed all these years, only to fail her sister in the end.

"I just don't know how to help or what to do," she admitted. "There's nothing we can do to void the contract. You can't simply sail away, either. Sooner or later, Father will find you."

Unspoken words choked her throat. If Rosemary did somehow run off with Captain Miles, Violet would be left behind to fight for their inheritance alone, a task that would be impossible from the asylum where her father would no doubt place her.

Rosemary squeezed her hand. "My captain will protect me. I can't leave you behind. Father will destroy you. Come with us. Please."

"I can't leave and neither can you. Not yet."

Captain Miles rose and stood next to them. "Listen to your sister, Rosemary. She's right. We can't stay, and we can't run. Not unless we find a way to stop your father once and for all."

"There is a chance," Violet offered. She released Rosemary and looked up at Captain Miles. "There's someone who's promised to help me. To protect him, I won't tell you who he is or what he's trying to do, at least for now. If he's successful, Father won't be able to enforce the marriage contract. He'll have to relinquish control of our inheritance, as well."

He nodded. "Then I'll wait, but only till the twenty-sixth. If you haven't had success by then, I'm taking Rosemary away with me."

She nodded her agreement and helped Rosemary from the bed. "Can you trust me for a few more days? It means you'll have to stop seeing Captain Miles. In fact, it would be better if you could stay in bed. Feign another episode. I won't leave your side unless I must. Father will be so pleased to see you ill again, he won't suspect a thing. You'll be doing exactly what he prayed you'd do . . ."

She paused, mulled over whether or not to reveal their father's plans for Rosemary to Captain Miles, and decided the truth might sway him to cooperate. "He's told me he plans to set Rosemary aside in an asylum before her birthday. That's why he wanted our marriage to take place so soon. With me gone, he'd have no one to stop him."

Captain Miles put his hand on Rosemary's shoulder as she began to tremble. "On my life, I won't let him do that to you."

Violet looked up at him. "I'll need your help, as well."

His gaze hardened. "I'll do anything you ask."

"Then you should call on me every night. Arrange an outing or two. We could attend a play or take a carriage ride to Fair Mount so I can meet with my . . . my friend to find out what he's learned. We haven't much time, but it's our only hope."

"We'll do that," he vowed.

Rosemary did not protest.

"Good." Violet dropped her gaze, saw the words in the loophole in the contract in her mind's eye, and blinked them away. She had no intention of losing control of her wits or her mind and finally understood Captain Miles's cryptic statement earlier that night.

No fear.

No doubt.

She fingered the brooch still clutched in her hand. A spark of an idea gave her hope there was something she could do for Rosemary and Captain Miles if Sam failed to find the proof she needed in time. With a heavy heart, she accepted what she must do to protect her sister one last time.

She only prayed Sam would be true to his word and agree to help her accomplish what she had to do now, and hoped Rosemary would understand when Violet chose to remain behind.

Chapter Fourteen

❧

Sam was in no mood to be civil or understanding.

Four long days and four tortured nights after seeing Violet, he had had little sleep. His arm itched so badly it felt like a second generation of fire ants were nibbling at the row of stitches in his arm, but Dr. Morgan had sent a message to him at dawn to cancel his scheduled appointment to have the stitches removed, citing an emergency.

Sam had had no word from Ben Hastings, other than a brief note telling him Magee had never appeared at his office and Ludlam was still working on finding the second set of books for the packet line. He had not thought of a way to contact Violet, either.

When Flynn arrived at his office and dropped a virtual bomb in his lap, Sam exploded. "What the blazes is next?" he grumbled and tossed the paper he had been holding onto his desk.

Unflinching, his associate lounged against the doorjamb. "Considering there's only a week before Squires takes over, don't do anything. Let him deal with it. The shipment isn't due to be loaded for a couple of weeks yet. By then, you'll be back home and I'll be long gone, too."

"You know I haven't done business that way for the past two years. I won't start now," Sam argued. "If we've got a warehouse full of spoiled wheat flour, then we take the loss, adjust the inventory before we settle with Squires, and lower the selling price accordingly. And see that the roof is repaired on the warehouse before it rains again and I lose even more."

Flynn pushed himself to stand up straight. "*We* lose," he countered. "I have a stake in all this, too, and I'm counting on my share to set myself up on a good hunk of land out west. Why not let insurance cover the loss? You've never collected before—"

"Fire insurance won't cover water damage or fix a leaky roof that should have been repaired so this wouldn't have happened. You were supposed to let me know if anything needed immediate attention, remember?"

Flynn squared his shoulders and charged the desk. "I contacted Cummings myself and told him to submit a bid to you. Which he did. If you had approved the bid, the roof would have been fixed," he spat. He rummaged through the papers on Sam's desk. When he found what he had been looking for, he tossed it at Sam. "There. It's dated two weeks ago. I did my job. Guess you've been too busy to do your own."

Sam grabbed the paper, saw that Flynn was right, and swallowed his pride. "You're right. I'm sorry. I have been a little . . . preoccupied lately. It's a loss we'll just have to live with."

Working his jaw, Flynn shook his head. "Not necessarily. Damaged or not, all goods burn the same way. Nobody would know the difference from the ashes, now would they?"

"I'd know," Sam gritted, finding Flynn's suggestion of arson to be contemptible. He clenched his fists and swallowed the bile souring the back of his throat. He did not take time to ponder whether Flynn's apparent lack of ethics was something he had missed during the course of their association or was predicated on a desperate attempt to avoid a loss in profits he would feel much more than Sam.

In either case, he would not tolerate anyone in his employ who was less than completely honorable. Unfortunately, he depended on Flynn entirely to arrange for the actual storing and shipping of goods Sam had brokered. He had no one else he could substitute for Flynn, especially on such short notice, yet he had little alternative but to act surely and swiftly. "You're finished, Flynn. Effective immediately."

Flynn's mouth dropped open, and his eyes flapped wide with disbelief. "You're firing me? For suggesting something that's done more often than you'd like to pretend?"

"I'll have your wages and your share of the profits based on the original numbers ready for you to pick up at the bank in two hours. Get yourself out of Philadelphia. Tonight. I'm shutting down the business until Squires takes over."

Fury blazed from Flynn's eyes. "You self-righteous bastard! If it weren't for me, you wouldn't have half the fortune you're carrying home." The expression on his face hardened. "I'll be at the bank in two hours. Be sure the draft is for the full amount. There's a ship sailing at midnight. I'll be on it," he spat before he stomped out of the office, slamming the door behind him.

Still seething, Sam had barely taken his seat before the door swung open and a young street urchin rushed straight toward him.

"You Mr. Glennings?"

He nodded.

"Got this for ya." He handed Sam a folded paper and turned to leave like a whirlwind of energy that had suddenly changed directions.

Sam managed to get to the door and place his palm at the top to keep the boy from opening it. "Hold it, son," he urged when the boy kept pulling on the knob. "You're due a coin."

The boy looked up, glowered, and held out a coin. "Been paid. 'Less you wanna add more, I'm leavin'."

Sam cocked his head. "That depends. Wait and give me a chance to see if I want to respond to the note you've brought me."

The boy scowled and held on to the doorknob. "Time off the streets is money earned by somebody else."

Chuckling, Sam led him to the chair in front of his desk and urged him to sit down. "So you're a fledgling entrepreneur. I don't suppose you had enough to buy my firm? The price was fair."

Dull green eyes flashed with ambition Sam knew only too well. "Not yet, sir, but I will by the time I'm as old as you are. Cost you a coin for my time to wait and another to deliver your reply."

"Agreed," Sam murmured as he took his seat. He unfolded the paper and found a puzzle piece inside depicting the main fountain at the Fair Mount Water Works. When he turned it over, he found a short message:

7 o'clock. Tonight.
V.

Completely perplexed, he put the puzzle piece into his pocket. Why had Violet taken such a risk by contacting him? Had something unexpected happened? Or was someone using her initial to lure him to a meeting? Completely perplexed, he put the puzzle piece into his pocket. "Who gave you this message? Was it a lady?"

The boy rolled his eyes. "That was no lady! That was a big black bear of a man."

"Captain Miles?"

Bony shoulders shrugged. "Didn't give me no name. Just told me to bring this to you quick."

Worry escalated past fear and set his heart racing. He pressed several coins into the boy's hand and sent him on his way.

Had Violet enlisted Captain Miles to act as an intermediary? How? Sam was not familiar with her handwriting and did not know if she had even penned the message. If she had, there was no way of knowing if she had willingly written the message or not.

The possibility that either Dunn or Miles had discovered Violet's cooperation with Sam's inquiry chilled his blood. Fear for her well-being spurred him to keep the rendezvous and tempered the idea he might be walking into a trap.

He had no time to waste, especially since he had to complete the arrangements for Flynn and meet him at the bank before he could go anywhere else. He closed up the office, turned to lock the door, and found Dr. Morgan standing in front of him when he turned around.

His face was lined with exhaustion, and his eyes were filled with concern. "I've just come from tending to Ben. He's been hurt pretty badly, but he insisted I fetch you. I'll explain everything on the way."

*K*ill *him. Kill him. Kill him.*

The echo of the words Dunn had used to order the attack on Ben that had nearly been successful consumed every other thought in Sam's mind. Shocked and enraged by the viciousness of the attack on his friend, he stood at the bottom of Ben's bed.

He turned to Dr. Morgan, but had to take several deep breaths before he could find his voice. "You're sure he told you Dunn was there and personally told the thugs he hired to kill Ben and make it look like a common mugging?"

The doctor nodded. "Ben was in a great deal of pain, but he was coherent. Dunn issued the order, but he didn't stay to watch."

Ben swallowed hard and turned back to stare at his friend. Only the longish, gray-streaked hair, still matted with dried blood, convinced Sam the broken man lying in the bed was Ben Hastings. Below a wide swath of bandages encircling his head, angry bruises distorted his face and a garish row of stitches sliced through one brow. A blanket covered his long, lanky frame and detailed the stiff outline of a splint on his left arm. Hidden from view, wrappings held several cracked ribs in place.

Sam needed more than bandages or splints to check the lava of anger that spurred him to avenge what Dunn had ordered done to Ben. They had both badly underestimated how far their opponent was willing to go to preserve his own interests; neither of them suspected he would go so far as to have Ben murdered.

A raging concern was whether or not Dunn's failed attempt to murder Ben was a singular act or part of a conspiracy to silence everyone who could possibly be involved. Had Dunn discovered Ben was acting at Sam's request when he investigated the packet line? Was Miles involved? What about Violet?

That tonight's rendezvous, allegedly with Violet, was a ruse, a trap meant to ensnare Sam, seemed more than a possibility now, and he worried that Violet might be in danger, too.

When he envisioned what Dunn might do to her, his heart began to pound. Dunn would not have her beaten or killed. Given her medical history, he had more subtle forms of punishment: confinement to the tower or an asylum and treatments that could permanently cost her her sanity.

Guilt for involving Ben fueled the hotbed of emotions churning in Sam's gut, but heart-wrenching concern for his friend cooled his temper. He clenched his fists and tightened his jaw. "Will he recover?"

A hesitant nod. "He should, provided there aren't any complications. The injury to his head concerns me the most. Only time will tell if his vision improves or deteriorates, but it's entirely possible the damage to his eyesight is permanent. Whether or not he'll be able to see well enough to practice law is highly doubtful."

Images of Ben, with his endless source of energy and his dedication to using the law to protect the innocent, gave way to visions of him unable to do more than care for his most basic needs. Being an invalid suffering from blurred vision for the rest of his life was a high price to pay for losing his temper and threatening Dunn, but Sam shared responsibility for placing Ben in that position.

Ben had no one else to care for him. No family. Few friends, other than his clients. When Sam first arrived in Philadelphia, they had quickly become friends. Over the past two years, that friendship had grown into a bond of brotherhood that fueled Sam's loyalty and a burning desire for revenge, but he was very worried Dunn would not hesitate to order the job finished if he learned Ben had survived.

"Hire as many nurses as you need so he isn't left alone.

See that he has whatever he needs, but act with complete secrecy. If Dunn finds out his plan failed Ben won't be safe, so don't allow any visitors." He paused, thought through an idea, and decided it was necessary. "When Ben wakes up, write down everything he can remember. Have Ben sign it. Then you and Mrs. Koop can sign as witnesses, just in case . . ." His throat tightened and his vision blurred just thinking about the possibility Ben might not recover at all. "When I go back to Sunrise, I'll take him with me where I can keep an eye on him myself. Until then, you'll keep me advised?"

The doctor clapped his hand gently on Sam's shoulder. "Of course. In the meantime, young man, let's go downstairs and get those stitches out of your arm. I'll send Mrs. Koop back upstairs to sit with Ben, and we'll have a chat while I work. It'll give me a chance to douse that fire in your blood so you don't go off half-cocked and wind up next to Ben."

Sam frowned. "Dunn's gone too far this time. If anything happens to Ben . . ."

"Ben will be fine. And you'll find a way to handle Dunn in all due time," he insisted as he ushered Sam from the room.

"Time." Sam snapped to a halt and checked his pocket-watch. "It's after four. Let's see how fast you can work out those stitches. I have to get to the bank and keep another appointment at seven."

An appointment he looked forward to keeping now more than ever.

Unlike Ben, who had been lured from the safety of his home with a summons from an alleged new client, Sam had reason to be suspicious about the message he had received. At seven tonight, he would know whether his suspicions were valid or not.

If they were, Dunn would get a double message Sam was more than willing to deliver. If not, he had to warn Violet there was no time to wait. She and her sister had to leave immediately.

Chapter Fifteen

❧

After Flynn picked up his bank draft, Sam went directly to Fair Mount. A precisely seven o'clock, he was ready and waiting at the fountain pictured in the puzzle piece.

Sprays of mist escaping from the water flowing from the statue in the center kept strollers to the far side of the circular stone path around the perimeter of the fountain. The sun held a feeble grasp on the day and streaked the sky with strands of golden rope growing thinner by the hour. Wheels moaned with the weight of the water being pumped up to the reservoir, but Sam's heart pounded so loudly the sound amounted to nothing more than an indistinct hum.

From his seat on the bench nestled a few yards from the fountain, he had an unobstructed view of the entire area. A cliff of rocks framed by massive trees protected his back. Sheer force of will kept him calm, but he was poised to defend himself, despite being hampered by the still-healing wound on his arm.

By seven-fifteen, his head had started to ache with tension that tied a band around his forehead and stiffened his neck. With no sign of Violet, each passing minute only reinforced his suspicions. On edge, he paid close attention to the young woman who had strolled around the fountain twice. When she went to pass by again, she turned and headed directly toward him.

The word "stunning" did her no justice, even when she drew close enough to see she was a fallen, and probably quite expensive, angel of the night. With painted lips and cheeks, and eyes dramatically framed in kohl, she had copper hair and a body curved abundantly to inspire a man's most implausible fantasies and chase all other thoughts from his mind. He rose as she approached.

"Mr. Glennings? I'm Darla. A mutual friend thought you might enjoy a stroll. Shall we?"

Sam offered his arm and escorted the tempting bait while silently applauding Dunn. He was clever. He had known exactly how to flush Ben out into the night and must have thought Sam would find the alluring lady irresistible.

"You obviously know where we're going," he murmured.

She smiled and patted his arm. "It isn't far." She led him around the fountain once before guiding him toward a path that led along the Schuykill River and away from the other strollers.

The foliage grew denser. The air became heavy and still. His pulse began to race, and his muscles grew taut when they approached a curve in the path that gave no view of the other side. He strained his ears, but heard no unnatural sounds, no hint of whether or not disaster lay waiting.

Determination and a natural instinct for survival kept him alert and on guard. When they rounded the curve, he rocked to a halt and stared at the mountain of a man blocking the path. Sam swallowed hard. Apparently, Dunn had decided against participating. Even so, he might have had a chance to defend himself against a couple of thugs, but Miles could crush him with a single blow.

Darla let go of his arm and rushed ahead. "Delivered him safe and sound, darlin'," she gushed. Sam sucked in his breath, locked his knees, and balled his hands into fists. He might go down, but not easily.

Miles took a single stride that planted him just out of reach. "Head about ten yards into the woods until you find a clearing. She's waiting there. I'll be back in an hour."

Nearly stupefied, Sam cocked his head to the side to make sure he had heard right.

Miles gave him a shove. "Go on, man. She's back there all alone!"

Sam grabbed hold of a tree branch to keep from hitting the ground. He waited until he got his bearings back, but not his wits, before charging through the woods. Heavy undergrowth slowed his progress. Panting heavily, he used his arms to protect his upper body from low-hanging branches and squinted to find his way in the dimming light.

Being thrown off guard, once by Darla and then by Captain Miles, might be precisely the plan. Rather than tear through the woods like a crazed animal, he might be best served to let caution guide him.

He would be completely surprised to find Violet exactly where Miles said she would be. Just in case she wasn't, Sam would rely on skills he had learned hunting with his father long ago. He moved downwind as silently as he could.

Violet sat waiting on an outcropping of rock at the edge of the clearing near a copse of trees. She had every faith in Captain Miles's loyalty to Rosemary, if not to her. She had made a decision that weighed heavily on her mind, but her heart knew the trust she placed in Sam, again, was not misguided.

When she thought heard someone approaching through the woods, she shifted her body toward the sound to be able to see more clearly and have time to slip down and away in case someone other than Sam appeared.

When the sound stopped, she strained forward, listening and watching intently. Twilight shadows hampered her vision. She worried her bottom lip. Had it been Sam or just a pair of squirrels dashing through the trees in a frenzied courting ritual?

"Violet?"

Her heart jumped to her throat. She spun about on her seat so fast she lost her balance.

Strong arms held her in place. A weak smile offered an instant apology.

"Sam! You frightened me half to death!"

"I'm sorry. I wasn't sure you were alone."

The warm sensations dancing the length of her arms frightened her, too. "I'm steady now," she offered.

His gaze deeply troubled, he dropped down beside her. "Ben was attacked last night by a couple of hired ruffians. He's been hurt pretty badly."

She touched his arm. "I'm sorry."

He nodded and took a deep breath. "Apparently, your father was there, too."

Her grip tightened. Her pulse slowed to a dull thud that carried dread through her entire body. "M-my father?"

" 'Kill him.' That's what he ordered his hired thugs to do. To beat Ben to death. They almost succeeded," he murmured, deep pain etching his features.

Horrified by what her father had done, she dropped her hand away. "Are you certain it was my father?"

"Ben was able to tell Dr. Morgan what happened before lapsing into unconsciousness."

She blinked back tears. "You shouldn't have come tonight. It's . . . it's too dangerous now for you to be involved."

"I am involved, whether you like it or not. Ben is my friend as well as my lawyer," he argued. "I only found out about the attempt on his life after I got your summons to meet you here tonight. I wasn't sure if you'd really sent it after I learned Captain Miles had paid the boy to deliver it. After what happened to Ben, I thought I was being pulled into a trap."

"That's even more reason for you to stay away," she argued.

He squared his jaw and his eyes flashed with determination. "I was worried about you. I was afraid your father had found out about my inquiry and the true purpose for Ben's visit. Since you're here and unharmed, I think it's safe to assume he hasn't, but it's far too dangerous for you or your sister to stay at home any longer."

Violet briefly closed her eyes to clear her mind of visions of her father's wrath if he were to find out what she had already done. She dared not imagine what he would do if she failed to get the proof she needed to stop him before he ordered anyone else killed. "I'm sure he would have done something or said something by now if he knew," she murmured. "Have you had any success locating the books for the packet line?"

"Nothing so far. What about Miles? How did you enlist him to help you?"

She let out a sigh and condensed the events as they had unfolded at the country estate. "Rosemary is back in the tower, of course, and I'm staying with her, as I usually do. Everything is working out exactly as Father planned, as least on the surface. Rosemary is barely controllable, but once you get the proof—"

"I can't promise I'll have it in time. I'm not sure I can count on anything anymore. Nothing is clear—except for one thing. You and your sister have to leave now. Sign away what's left of your inheritance to your father and let Captain Miles sail away with both of you. Your father will have everything he wants, but that's a small price to pay for your freedom and your safety. You can always present the proof to the courts later when we find it."

She swallowed hard and battled tears. "No. Father wants more than money. He wants what we can't give him."

Sam rubbed his brow as if he could rub the confusion from his face as well as his mind. "What more could he possibly want?"

"Respectability. Even status. I've only begun to understand it myself," she ventured. "The money is important, but he's had the benefit of most of it for years. He's also had a difficult time. I've seen how people look at him. They don't admire him. They pity him. Or see him as a charlatan. He raised every eyebrow in the city when he married my mother. After she died, he was saddled with two young daughters and very short pursestrings, since my grandfather's fortune passed to us."

"He made choices that had unforeseen consequences. That's life," he spat. "No one forced him to marry your mother or stoop low enough to defraud his own daughters."

"No. But not all men can weather disappointment or climb out of the valley of despair with their character intact. Whatever he's become is his own fault. I don't condone it any more than I could ever forgive him, but understanding him gives me the advantage. And the courage to confront him with proof of what he's done to us because I know he won't be swayed by money alone."

She bowed her head and took a deep breath before continuing. "He wants the world to see him as a devoted father and a man of character. One who arranged a fortuitous marriage for a daughter no rational man would consider for a wife. One who grieves for the other daughter, so badly distracted she must spend the rest of her days in an asylum. The fortune-hunter-without-a-fortune will become a model of respectability and decency. If we disappear, he'll have no choice but to find us. If we sign over our fortunes to him, he could never live down society's disdain for a man whose fortune came at the expense of his own daughters."

The confusion in Sam's gaze finally gave way to understanding. "He'd look more than incompetent or irresponsible. He'd be contemptible."

"Exactly. Which is why I have to wait and trust you'll find the second set of books for the packet line. Once I can prove he's guilty of fraud," she explained, "I can offer him a private settlement. In exchange for nullifying the marriage contract and freely relinquishing any interest in our inheritance, he can escape notoriety and prison and keep his share of the businesses he started in order to defraud us. No one will ever learn how pitifully small the inheritance is now because Rosemary and I will be gone from the city."

"Blackmail?"

Her spine stiffened. "I don't have a choice."

"From what Ben told me, the funds available to you would scarcely satisfy your father."

She tilted up her chin. "He doesn't have the house or the

country estate. He'll want both, but I doubt he'll argue for the jewels that belonged to my grandmother." She scooted down from the rock, turned her back to him, and lifted her skirts. Working quickly, she untied the knot holding a velvet pouch that hung from a ribbon tied at her waist and removed the pouch.

After readjusting her skirts, she turned around and handed him the pouch. "My grandmother's jewelry and my brooch," she explained when he raised a brow. "Are they worth the price of a ship?"

He loosened the drawstring and let the contents spill into the palms of his hands.

Rubies and pearls lay intertwined like a gemstone rope wrapped around a spray of violets too stubborn to wilt. The rose brooch that belonged to Rosemary was the only piece Violet had held back.

"I'm not an expert, but I should think so."

"Will you sell them for me?"

He furrowed his brow. "I can try, but—"

"If you fail to find the proof in time, Captain Miles will need a ship for himself and Rosemary."

"He has a ship!"

"If he breaks the marriage contract with my name on it, his ship reverts back to my father."

Sam shoved the jewels back into the pouch, drew it closed, and handed it back to her. "You're talking in riddles. First you want to wait, against my advice, assured I'll find the proof you need to outwit your father. In the next breath, you ask me to help you with a plan to let Rosemary escape if I fail. What about you?"

"I'll survive until you do find the proof," she insisted in a steady voice, despite the fact that her soul was trembling. "Father won't argue with a slight alteration to his plans, especially when Captain Miles offers to pay for the ship and marry Rosemary, too. The world would only see exactly what he wanted it to see. One daughter happily married; the other stunned into perpetual distraction. Only the names have changed. Only the names," she repeated in a whisper she scarcely heard herself.

He slid from his seat and grabbed her by both arms. "No. You can't do this. You can't expect me to help you. I understand your loyalty to your sister, but it's wrong. It's . . . it's misguided. It's . . . it's . . ."

She saw the word hanging from his lips. "It's mad?"

He dropped his hold on her. "I didn't say that."

She pressed the pouch back into his hands. "Help me, Sam. You're the only one who can do this without arousing my father's suspicion. You're the only one I can trust. Please."

With their hands entwined, she gazed deep into his eyes. Beyond her control, desperate need became longing that wrapped around her heart. The pulse in his fingertips quickened, and her heart skipped a beat. She caught her breath and held it, daring to hope he would be the one man who could see beyond her reputation, accept her as a woman with a logical, sane mind, and agree her plan had merit. She had no right to expect him to respect her judgment, but she needed to know he trusted her as much as she trusted him.

As though touched by her unspoken plea to be accepted as an equal in their endeavors, he squeezed her hand, and she let out a soft sigh.

His gaze softened, and he hid the pouch in his pocket. "I'll take the jewels and sell them, but don't do anything else until you hear from me," he cautioned. "We'll meet here, again, at the same time in six days. If I have no luck by then, we'll work something else out. In the meantime, you need to be very, very careful. If you have any fear your father is about to harm either you or your sister, you have to promise to leave immediately."

Her heart swelled with joy and relief, but Captain Miles arrived before she could no more than agree to his terms. "Be careful," she whispered. And with every step that carried her away from Sam and toward Captain Miles, she prayed Sam would find those books. If he didn't, Providence would have to give her the strength to protect her sister one last time and wait for Sam to rescue her.

One last time.

Chapter Sixteen

Either Violet Dunn was completely mad or she was the most rational, if not stubborn, woman Sam had ever met. Next to his sister, of course.

Long after Violet left so abruptly with Captain Miles, Sam remained in the clearing, swinging on an emotional pendulum that carried him from stunned disbelief past sheer amazement to outright admiration and back again. To keep some sense of equilibrium, he remained seated on the rock and kept his gaze focused on the steady sickle of moon overhead in a turbulent sky that mirrored his own state of mind.

If he had any hope of understanding Violet, he had to clear his mind of every preconceived notion he had ever had about her and of the many forms of madness he had encountered in his life. He opened the lid on a cache of memories stored in the back of his mind and set free a host of images and events from his past.

Polly's image emerged first. Visions of her radiant beauty lasted only long enough to remind him why he had been so blinded to the demons hiding just below the surface. In the space of a single heartbeat, her image changed, and he saw her sitting in the courtroom, her face horrid and demented, her voice screeching a confession that had shocked the courtroom as the demons of mania claimed final victory over the last vestiges of her sanity.

In trying to juxtapose the two images of the woman who had been his wife, he spared no compassion for himself. He had let lust rule his body and overwhelm his senses. Pride had silenced the whispers of doubt in his heart and twisted her clinging adoration and cloying weaknesses into expressions of love instead of obsession he now knew no man could never satisfy.

He let the images of Polly fade away, and he recalled instead the gossip he had heard about Violet Dunn. He saw her warm brown eyes glistening with unshed tears, but she held her head high. The tales of repeated bouts of deep melancholia through the years that had required extensive confinements, and the labels that had been given to her illness, such as distraction, insanity, lunacy, or madness.

Mania was not one of them, and based on his own observations of her, he could no longer accept any of the others as valid, either.

With a sigh, he ordered gossip back where it belonged, safely stored away, but kept her image in the forefront of his mind by fingering the brooch he now held in his fist.

If past accounts about her were true, events he had witnessed with his own eyes should have triggered a relapse into melancholia deep enough to last a lifetime. If learning about her father's betrayal was not enough, adding a harrowing attack on her virtue, if not her life, the death of an old friend, and an arranged marriage to a man who had subsequently fallen in love with her sister should have done it. Considering all she had endured these past few weeks, he was surprised Violet had the mental strength to open her eyes to face another day, let alone face it with the strength she had demonstrated to him.

He tightened his fist and the edges of the brooch dug into his flesh. With all that had happened, she had not faltered in her resolve to outwit her father and protect her sister. Instead, she had rebounded, over and over again, as if she gained strength and renewed determination from each difficult experience, using logic and insightful analysis to shape her reactions instead of retreating into a shell.

And it was her selfless heart that guided every plan she had developed to outmaneuver her father.

The only evidence of irrational behavior he had witnessed had come tonight when she placed her absolute trust in Sam. Her faith in his ability to deliver the proof she needed had never wavered. She refused to give in to fear or doubt, even when he warned her it was no longer safe for her to remain at home after what her father had ordered done to Ben.

To compound any easy understanding of the workings of her mind, she trusted Sam with her very life by devising a plan of escape for her sister that would put Violet at the mercy of her father until Sam found the second set of books for the packet line.

Wasn't it irrational to be that trusting and that selfless? Or a mark of character in a woman whose loyalty and devotion superseded other extraordinary qualities that made her remarkable?

Like Jane?

His sister had kept silent after finding out Polly had been having an affair with her husband to protect Sam from being hurt. She had stoically tolerated condemnation from the townspeople and relied on justice and truth to reveal her innocence. And she had risked her life by refusing to let Daniel introduce the affair in court until he had proof Polly was responsible for murder, primarily out of fear she might one day harm Sam.

Stoic. Tolerant. Trusting. Protective. Devoted. All qualities that made Jane such a remarkable woman.

Like Violet?

She appeared to be every bit as rational as Jane, and stubbornly protected her sister just as Jane had protected him. Was Violet also guilty of being overprotective? The answer was obvious to him when he compared his relationship to Jane with Rosemary's relationship to Violet, but his comparison had one flaw: If Rosemary's battle with melancholia was indeed real, she might not be able to protect herself, as Sam could have done.

To his mind, that made Violet all the more noble.

And he loved her.

Stunned, he rejected the very notion he had fallen in love with Violet, but to any and all objections his rational mind could offer, his heart echoed back a rejoinder.

She's not born to the country. She was bred in the city.

Not by choice. By chance.

She's an heiress.

Not by choice. By accident of birth.

She's betrothed to another.

Not by choice. By cruel design.

She's mad! Distracted!

By choice. Judge her mind by the tender beauty of her heart.

His exasperated mind admitted defeat, and his heart beat with joy when he surrendered to the amazing truth: He had fallen in love with the woman he would have least likely chosen for himself.

And the most incredible.

He squeezed the brooch harder and knew the mantle of trust he now wore was but a burden of love that doubled the weight of the guilt he had been carrying for the past few weeks. If he had any chance of winning her heart, he had to have the books for the packet line to prove himself worthy of her.

While daunted, he could think no further than completing the task set before him to win her heart. He refused to consider what he would do if he failed.

Before he did anything else, however, he needed to see Ben. By now, he should be conscious and able to tell Sam exactly what had happened and how to contact Ludlam. With that in mind, he worked his way out of the woods and headed back into the heart of the city.

Unable to sleep, Violet slipped down to the second floor of the tower and set the candle she carried with her on top of her worktable. She had not had time or inclination to work on her hobby for weeks. She did have one lithograph depicting a world map already colored with waterpaints and decided she might try to finish the puzzle as a wedding present for Rosemary.

She worked quietly to avoid waking her sister and moved the candle to the center of the table. After preparing the paste and securing the proper brush, she found the thin sheet of cut and sanded mahogany already sized for this particular lithograph. She brushed a light coat of paste onto the mahogany and repeated the process on the reverse side of the lithograph before pressing the two together.

Still standing, she leaned her weight forward to smooth out the air bubbles with the heel of her hands. Her fingers brushed over the raised printing and the rhythm of her work freed her mind to ponder the troubles that had kept her from finding sleep.

Although she had previously managed to convince Dr. Poole to let her oversee Rosemary's care, she had not been home tonight when he stopped unexpectedly to visit his patient. He administered the medication Violet had been dumping into the chamber pot. As a result, Rosemary would probably sleep for a good twelve hours and that would give Violet a rest from constantly reassuring her sister she would soon be free.

Violet had not told either Captain Miles or Rosemary about selling the jewelry to fund their escape, if necessary, for two reasons. Most importantly, they might not need to run away if Sam got the proof they needed in time. After learning her father had tried to have Ben killed, she knew it was more imperative than ever before to keep Captain Miles from simply spiriting Rosemary away and undoing everything Violet had planned to protect them all.

But it was Sam who garnered most of her thoughts as she pressed a stubborn bubble of air toward a corner edge. As much as she wanted to trust him, she could not silence a small echo of doubt that niggled at her faith in him. After years of being manipulated by her father and the doctors in his employ, she had never trusted anyone but Elijah. Now that he was gone, she had no one else, and she could not outwit her father alone. Unfortunately, she had a tendency to over-analyze every encounter she had with other people instead of listening to her instincts because she was afraid she would be betrayed, and she had her father to thank for that, too.

If Sam decided to sell the jewelry and keep the money for himself, there was nothing she could do to stop him. He could just walk away and decide he could go home knowing he had not deliberately put her and her sister at financial risk and keep the jewelry as a gift from a woman reputed to be too distracted to be able to accuse him of anything.

She wiped away the extra paste that oozed out beyond the edges of the lithograph and fought against her own thoughts. However much she might be confused by others, she refused to let doubt undermine her faith in Sam. "He's a good man. He wouldn't do anything to hurt me," she murmured aloud to silence her fears.

She not only believed what she said, she felt it in every bone of her body. Just saying his name made and her heart beat a little faster.

He was a man unlike any she had ever known. With strong ties to his family, he had rebuilt his life after a tragedy that would have destroyed most men. He was loyal and had strong character, or he would not be so concerned about his role, albeit an innocent one, in placing her and Rosemary in financial jeopardy. He had courage enough to confront her father and refuse to be intimidated by him. He had even come to their meeting tonight, even though he feared it might be a trap, just to be sure she was unharmed and to warn her to leave.

And he had . . . such an engaging smile and tender touch. His arms were strong, but gentle . . .

She bunched the cloth in her fist and forced his handsome image from her mind. She might not be able to stop doubt from trying to erode her trust in him, but she could not let her growing attraction to him confuse foolish dreams with harsh reality.

Once he had given her the proof she needed, he would

leave for Sunrise, and he had no room in his life there, or anywhere else, for a tainted woman like herself.

I'm not just a visitor," Sam repeated, although with his jaw set and his teeth clenched, he might very well be mistaken for an ogre who would bully his way past the rotund sentry disguised as a nurse.

She blocked the doorway to Ben's room with her body, crossed her arms over her chest, and glowered. "Dr. Morgan said no visitors. That means no colleagues. No friends."

He hissed. "Then I'm not his friend. I'm his brother."

She pursed her lips. "He's got none. Now if you'll excuse me, I have a patient to tend to," she snapped, slamming the door and bolting it from the inside.

Outmaneuvered, but not defeated, Sam looked around the hallway for something to use to create a diversion, found nothing suitable, and quickly removed both of his boots. He tossed them down the stairs, satisfied by the noise they made when they tumbled toe over heel down the steps. He had his back to the wall before the door opened. When the nurse rushed outside to investigate, he slipped inside the room and bolted the door.

Several candles lit the room. Ben lay very still on the bed. With his eyes closed, he was asleep and apparently oblivious to the commotion. A tray with a bowl of broth sat on a bed-side table at the head of the bed along with an array of salves and bottles of medicine.

"Let me in! You can't go in there!"

When the nurse started pounding and shoving at the door, Ben cracked one swollen eye open to a slit and his lips shaped a lopsided grin. "Wondered . . . how . . . you'd get . . . past her," he managed to grit through obvious pain.

In spite of himself, Sam chuckled. "You heard?"

A nod. A painful wince. "Good . . . enter . . . tainment."

Sam smacked his palm onto the door, silencing the human battering ram on the other side. "I'll stay with Ben while you go downstairs to see Mrs. Koop, which is what I asked you to do in the first place. Tell her Sam Glennings is with Ben. She'll know who I am."

She gave the door a final shove that sounded more like a kick and stomped down the stairs.

When Ben closed his eyes and sighed, Sam touched the rim of the bowl of broth. It was warm to the touch. "Looks like you were about to enjoy a late supper. Let's see what I can do to help."

Both blackened eyes opened at once, and Ben swallowed hard.

Sam cocked his head. "What? I can't feed you a little broth?"

When Ben's gaze hardened, Sam shrugged, pulled up a chair, and sat down. "Have it your way. I won't stay long. I just needed to see how you were doing and to ask if you were up to talking about what happened."

Ben nodded. "My temper. My . . . fault. Not yours."

Sam put his hand on Ben's shoulder, and his heart swelled with grief. Ben was in no condition to talk for more than a few moments. Any questions Sam had about the attempt on Ben's life would have to wait until he was stronger."

Ben laid his bruised hand atop Sam's. "Be . . . careful. Dunn is . . . dangerous."

"Just tell me how to contact Ludlam."

"He'll . . . come when he's . . . done," Ben murmured. When his eyes slid closed and his hand went slack, Sam laid Ben's hand on top of the covers. As much as he wanted to learn the details surrounding the ambush, he was content to let that matter wait and trusted Dr. Morgan to put Ben's account down in a written statement when his patient was up to the task of recalling everything that had happened.

If Ben was right about Ludlam, Sam could do nothing more than wait to be contacted, which meant he should probably go home and turn Ben back over to his nurse.

Sam rose and had unbolted the door when Ben called after him in a strained whisper. "What did you . . . throw down the . . . steps?"

"My boots. I'll get them on the way out. You just mend.

We'll talk about my plans for you later. I'll stop back tomorrow."

"Don't forget."

"No," Sam assured him. "I won't forget."

Not tomorrow. Not ever, he silently vowed as he slipped out of the door.

From the top of the stairs, he could not see his boots anywhere. Since he was wearing only socks, he held onto the banister to keep from slipping on the bare wooden steps. He was at the foot of the stairs when he encountered the nurse. "Ben's resting, but he wouldn't let me give him the broth. I trust Mrs. Koop resolved your concerns."

She scowled, stepped back to let him pass, and started up the steps without a backward glance.

He scanned the foyer. Still no sign of his boots. "Would you have any idea where I can find my boots?" he called up the steps.

She never lost a stride, and she did not look back at him, either. "Check the street. Might have some luck there."

"I'll be back tomorrow," he warned before stepping outside. Fortunately, it was not winter, and he did not have to worry about his feet freezing while he searched the street for his boots in the dark. Rather quickly, he found one lying next to the curb and put it on.

Walking a bit lopsided, he traversed back and forth across the street with his head bent low to search for his other boot. When he finally spied it lying several feet away, he rushed forward to fetch it, but stepped on a large shard of glass with his stocking foot before he reached the boot.

"Blast!" He hopped about on one foot, yanked the offending hank of glass out of the bottom of his foot, and felt the blood ooze into his hand. "Blasted fool," he grumbled, angry more at himself than the nurse. He could only imagine what Ben would say when Sam tried to tell him he had been cut again by glass lying in the street. He was half-tempted to keep the piece of glass as proof.

He shoved his bleeding foot into his boot, but the moment he put weight on his foot, pain shot straight up the full length of his leg. Certain he had another piece of glass still in his foot, he hobbled toward home by using only the heel of his foot for support to keep from pushing the glass further into his flesh.

Now would be a perfect time for one of Dunn's hirelings to waylay him. He watched his back as best he could, and sighed with relief when he reached his own town house where he would finally feel secure, if only from his own sense of paranoia.

Completely exhausted from favoring his aching foot, he let himself in, pocketed his key, and entered the darkened foyer.

Before he tended to his foot, he wanted to make sure the pouch of jewelry was locked away. He made his way in the dark to the study, being careful not to step on any carpet, and stepped inside. There was no way he could fumble about in the dark to open the safe so he went to his desk to light a candle.

He struck a match, but before it lit, a whoosh of warm air blew it out and a deep voice issued a caution.

"Pull the drapes first. We've got some problems to resolve. In private."

Chapter Seventeen

❦

Shocked, Sam moved back a step, putting his full weight onto his injured foot, stumbled, and fought to keep his balance. He hoped the voice belonged to Ludlam. He should be here only if he had finished his investigation, which would be well ahead of the time Sam expected it.

Unless the voice belonged to Dunn. Outrage that the man would have the audacity to set a trap for Sam in his own house tempered his fear. In a matter of seconds, his body tensed, waiting for an attack to come from behind as well as ahead.

"Relax, Sam. It's Robert Ludlam. After what happened to Ben, I didn't want to surprise you outside."

Sam let out a hiss that did not settle the pounding of his heart or ease the throbbing in his foot. "No, you waited inside where I certainly expected to be alone."

"Sorry. I would have called out, but your footsteps sounded odd. If you'd pull the drapes, we might get to business," he prompted. "I've got a few leads to follow on the men Dunn hired to kill Ben."

"Right." Sam worked a knot out of his back as he limped toward the window. In the distance, a figure silhouetted on the second floor of the tower caught his heart in mid-beat and held it. He kept Violet's image in sight until he closed the drape. Before he even had a chance to turn around, light filled the room.

The smile on Ludlam's fleshy face when their gazes met only made the weariness in his eyes more pronounced. A three-day stubble on his ample chin, shoulders slumped beneath rumpled clothing, and red-rimmed eyes testified to the lack of sleep. He stood up from his seat behind the desk and extended his hand.

As Sam hobbled toward him, the investigator lowered his gaze. The smile on his lips turned into a concerned frown as he rushed from behind the desk. "What happened? You'd better sit quick before you drip blood from one end of the carpet to the other," he warned.

Sam looked down, saw the blood oozing from his boot and looked around to see bloody footsteps trailing across the carpet. When Ludlam pulled a chair forward, Sam dropped into the seat. "Just a typical night," he muttered. "The sooner I get out of this city, the happier I'm going to be. I cut my foot on some broken glass in the street," he added, to erase the confusion on Ludlam's face.

"Must really have been something to cut through the sole of your boot. Looks like you need a doctor more than you need to talk to me right now."

Sam attempted to remove his boot, but his foot must have swollen up and he gave up rather than risk causing further damage. "I didn't have my boot on. Do me a favor and don't ask me why. Explaining this once to Dr. Morgan will be more than enough."

When Ludlam started toward the door, Sam called out a protest. "Where are you going? I need to know what you've been able to find out about—"

"I'll be right back with Dr. Morgan. What I have to say will have to wait until then. Don't move that foot any more than you have to," Ludlam advised and then disappeared out the door.

Sam sagged in his seat and closed his eyes. He had no idea what Ludlam was going to tell him he had found through his investigation, but did not have any doubt he had to leave

Philadelphia soon. If not, his entire body might be criss-crossed with scars.

If he survived at all.

*B*eads of perspiration dripped down Sam's brow. He wiped them away with the back of his hand and finally drew in a deep gulp of air. After holding his breath practically the whole time Dr. Morgan had cut out a chunk of embedded glass and stitched up the lacerations, Sam was light-headed and weak from pain.

His ruined boot lay in several pieces on the carpet. A thick bandage wrapped around his foot covered the unsightly row of stitches.

Dr. Morgan handed him an old pair of crutches. "Good thing I brought these along. You won't be walking on your own for a couple of weeks. I'll have a talk with Miss Byrd—"

"It wasn't her fault," he countered, defending the nurse who had tossed his boots into the street. "Where's that chunk of glass you dug out?"

The doctor chuckled and handed it to him. "Souvenir?"

"Proof. For Ben. When did Ludlam say he'd be back?"

The investigator entered the room and answered for himself. "I'm here. Never did have a good stomach for watching what the good doctor does. Looks like you're all fixed up now." He spied the crutches and grinned. "Looks like you've got a set of wooden legs, too."

"That he does. Seems to me," the doctor warned with a chuckle, "you'd better keep off the streets after dark or you just might wind up next to Ben."

Sam gripped both crutches and scowled. "I'm glad you both find this so entertaining."

"Sorry, son. I was just trying to lighten the mood and get you to relax a little after what I had to put you through."

When Sam's stomach growled an unexpected response, he could not help but chuckle, too. "Missed dinner. Supper, too," he explained. "Mrs. Blake should have left plenty in the kitchen if anyone else . . ."

The doctor held up his hands. "No, I'm fine."

Ludlam's eyes lit up. "I'll fix a couple of trays for us," he offered and quickly left.

With his mind freed from trying to block out the pain he had endured earlier, Sam took this as an opportunity to speak to Dr. Morgan. "I know you've had a long day," he began, "but I was wondering if you'd be able to answer a few questions I have."

The doctor smiled as he packed up his bag. "Well, it can't be about stitching up lacerations. You're becoming an expert. Can I assume this is about Violet Dunn?"

Sam's eyes opened wide. There was nothing he had hidden from Dr. Morgan about the past, but he had never revealed his interest in Violet. "How did you know that?"

"Ben mumbled her name along with yours when I was setting his arm."

"Have you ever treated her or anyone else for melancholia?"

The older man paused, then snapped his bag shut. "As far as I know, Dr. Poole has been her physician for over ten years. As for other patients with melancholia, I've had only a few. From what I've learned, though, most recover. They might never have another episode, or they may battle the illness periodically over the years. If they do, some eventually sink into such a state they literally lose the will to live. If they don't waste away, they end the struggle and take their own lives. It's always hard to predict the outcome. In either case, they're mentally distracted, but not lunatics. Calling them mad is cruel, as well, but most people label all sorts of mental illnesses as madness out of ignorance or fear."

"Then these patients aren't usually violent. In your experience, that is." Sam murmured his deepest fears out loud, but his heart beat with the answer before Dr. Morgan could respond.

"Violence requires emotional feelings, like anger or disappointment. It's a passionate will for life itself that's either missing or overly controlled in patients suffering from melancholia."

Sam swallowed hard. Violet's passion for life and survival, her deep concern for her sister, as well as herself, made her the least likely candidate for melancholia he could imagine. He had never seen her become angry or violent, either. Even when confronted with difficult, even life-threatening situations, she responded with calm reason and determination, not despair or anger.

Indeed, her passion for life might very well be why she had been able to survive her controlling father all these years.

"She's not like Polly, Sam. Mania is a completely different disorder. There's no known cure, as you know."

"Only too well," Sam whispered. Images of Polly suffering alone, imprisoned in a body controlled by a demented mind, inspired only pity, but he had no regret for formally ending their marriage. Even if she were to be cured one day, he could never forgive or forget what she had done. Neither would the courts.

"Supper for two!" Ludlam carried a tray in each hand and set them onto the desk. "Cold sliced beef, fresh bread, pickled corn relish, and fresh buttermilk."

Dr. Morgan picked up his bag. "That's my cue to leave. Make sure you soak that foot. If it starts to redden, send for me. Otherwise, we'll give it a good ten days or so before I see how you're healing."

Sam ignored the dinner tray. "I'll be in Sunrise by then, but I'll get Dr. Birchfield to take out the stitches. I'll probably see you often enough at Ben's to let you know if I have any problems before I leave."

Dr. Morgan nodded and let himself out.

Using the crutches, Sam maneuvered himself to the desk, as ravenous for the information Ludlam would give him as for nourishment. Exhausted, he plopped into a chair and set the crutches on the floor. Out of the corner of his eye, he caught a glance of his frock coat and remembered the pouch of jewelry still in his pocket. He did not have the energy left to pick up a fork, let alone get up again to retrieve the pouch. "Help me out, will you? Inside the front pocket of my frock coat, there's a small pouch. Would you bring it here? I need to get it into the safe."

Without bothering to respond, the investigator secured the pouch and handed it to Sam. "Anything else you need before I tackle my supper?"

Acting on a sudden impulse, Sam chose this opportunity to resolve at least one problem before facing any consequences of the information he was about to receive. Ludlam's contacts and experience as a once-convicted pickpocket would serve Violet's interests much better and guarantee a fairer price than Sam might get. Faster, too, since Sam would need time to get used to walking with crutches.

"As a matter of fact . . . there is," he admitted. He dumped the contents of the pouch between the two trays, but separated the violet brooch and held it back. "Since I'm a bit handicapped now, can you sell these for me? They're fairly valuable. Family heirlooms, in fact. You have more experience with jewels than I do," he suggested.

His eyes sparkling with interest, Ludlam selected the pearl choker first. He held it for a moment by the clasp, inspected it closer to the light, then let it pool into his palm, which he used as some sort of scale. Deep in concentration, his expression was serious, but unreadable. He laid the choker aside and repeated the same process with the shimmering ruby necklace.

Sam watched every move Ludlam made and studied his eyes for some hint of his assessment, but again had no idea of the man's thoughts. When he deliberately dropped the necklace to the wooden floor behind the desk, Sam nearly leaped out of his chair.

Before he could yell a protest, Ludlam stood up and leaned his weight atop one of the stones with the heel of his foot. After hearing sharp crackles, Sam leaned over and stared aghast at the red crystals on the floor that looked as if they had been snatched from a summer sunset. "What the blazes——"

"Paste. Excellent quality, though," Ludlam explained as he retrieved the necklace and tossed it onto the desk. "Might have been tempted to snatch it myself in the old days. Thought I might be losing my eye for the genuine. Guess not."

"Paste? That's ridiculous," Sam argued. "These belonged to Violet's grandmother!"

"Maybe the settings did," he countered. "If they're that old, my guess is the original rubies were replaced with paste. As for the pearls, they're easy enough to duplicate with fakes. Care to let me see the piece you held back?"

Stunned, Sam handed it to the investigator before he knew what he was doing. "I was hoping not to sell it with the others."

Within moments, Ludlam handed it back to him. "That one's real, as far as I can tell, but far less valuable than the other pieces would have been if they'd been genuine."

Sam's relief was short-lived. Deflated, he took the brooch back and sank back into his chair. If Dunn had stooped this low, he might have thought of a way to get title to the mansion and summer estate, too, which would obliterate Violet's contingency plan. As a result, Sam was the only one who could prevent total disaster with the information Ludlam had obtained.

After a difficult day, the night was proving far worse by the minute. Hunger to know whether Ludlam had been successful claimed any appetite he had for food. "You can save me some time if you'd tell me what you learned from your investigation. No unnecessary details. Just the bare facts."

His expression grim, the investigator sat down again and held his gaze steady. "There's no second set of books for the packet line. No evidence of fraud. The losses sustained are valid. The problems you're facing are in your own books as well as your conscience."

Chapter Eighteen

A chilling tingle in his spine told Sam he did not want to hear the rest or ask why Ludlam had studied his books as well as Dunn's. His conscience required he listen. "Go on."

"Examine your books separately, and you'll come away as clean as Dunn, if not more competent. Set them side by side and compare entries by dates, you'll see you hit him hard and fast when he had a run of bad luck."

The hackles on the back of Sam's neck rose, and his pride demanded a rebuttal. "That's business. If one man wins, obviously another has to lose."

"You'll get no argument from me—not when it's fair competition."

"Are you suggesting it wasn't?"

Ludlam sighed, and his gaze softened. "Look, Sam, I know you and your family. You're good people. Honest to a fault, maybe, but you deserve the truth. I can get almost anything I need for an investigation. There isn't a lock made I can't pick, but I can pick a man's brains even better than I used to pick pockets. When I sit in a tavern near the docks, I learn as much there as I can from a set of books. Maybe more."

He paused, but he never let go of Sam's gaze. "I can't prove what I heard yet, but my gut tells me it's true. Although Dunn could have prevented some of the major losses by being more competent, his run of bad luck wasn't natural. It was man-made, and there's only one firm that profited the most."

"Mine," Sam murmured with dread pooling in the pit of his stomach.

"Unfortunately, yes. The food that sickened the crews on two ships and held them up at sea until the cargo rotted didn't spoil all by itself any more than the two fires that destroyed Dunn's warehouses after his insurance lapsed were an accident. Somebody tainted the crew's rations and set those fires."

"Flynn." The man's name leaped from Sam's lips before his entire body went numb. Whether Flynn had acted alone or with Sam's knowledge did not matter. Conscience dictated Sam hold himself responsible as the principal owner of Glennings Enterprises. The confrontation he had had earlier with Flynn over the mere suggestion of using arson and a fraudulent claim to avoid taking a loss erased any doubt Ludlam was wrong.

Sam should have known or at least suspected Flynn was up to no good, but Sam had only seen the man's ambition. He had not looked closely enough to see his greed. "It's my fault, in the end," he admitted.

"Maybe. Maybe not. Let me see what else I can find out about Flynn. If there's enough proof, you can take that to the authorities—"

"Flynn's gone. I fired him this afternoon, and he sailed at midnight. He said he wanted a clean break with his past. All I know is he's headed west."

"Mighty big place to find a man trying to hide. It doesn't make you look any better, either, by selling the firm so soon. Flip the same coin over, and it does make a difference. The packet line's already been sold. It doesn't exist anymore on the books. Fact of the matter is, you can go back to Sunrise and let it all lie knowing you didn't order or sanction what Flynn did."

"No I can't. Without suffering those losses, the packet line wouldn't have nearly folded or been sold for a fraction of its value. Whatever fortune I've acquired is ill-gotten and tainted now."

And whatever chance he had to win Violet's heart was forever doomed.

He gripped the sides of his chair and wondered why his heart was still beating when it had broken in two. If he had proven his competition had been fair and her father deliberately exaggerated the losses to cover up fraud, Sam might have had a chance of one day claiming Violet's respect and love.

He had no chance now. If not by intent, by association and incompetence, he stood guilty of acts as ruthless and unconscionable as her father had committed. If ambition had blinded Sam, greed had blinded Flynn, but the end result was the same.

He had no right, ever, to claim her respect, and a far better man deserved to win her heart.

Honor demanded he set matters right. Love demanded he tell her the truth. And he would have a lifetime to suffer the loss when she turned her back and shut him out of her life.

"Will you help me? I have to clear this up, and I won't be able to do it easily using crutches."

Ludlam smiled and pulled his dinner tray closer. "I'm ready to help as soon as I eat. I expected you'd want to do right."

Nauseated with self-disgust, Sam shoved his dinner tray farther away. "And I only have a week to figure out how to do that."

Ludlam held his fork midway between the plate and his mouth for a moment, then set it down. "Less than that, my friend, assuming you intend to solve Violet Dunn's problems as well as your own."

"Less than a week?"

"The wedding's been moved up to the day after tomorrow."

Stunned, Sam dismissed Ludlam's claim as ludicrous. "That's impossible. I just saw Violet and Captain Miles a few hours ago. She told me—"

"Apparently, she doesn't know."

Exasperated by the investigator's uncanny ability to learn

so much in so little time, Sam snorted. "But you do? Another bit of tavern gossip at the docks?"

"Ships need supplies, don't they? I talked to the *Carousel*'s ship master myself just before I headed over here. The ship sails at midnight the day after tomorrow. Orders to load the ship with supplies came from Dunn himself. You've got yourself forty-eight hours—at the most."

"I can't possibly—"

"Sure you can. You're a smart man. You'll think of something, and I'll be your legs, so to speak." He plopped a forkful of beef into his mouth, chewed it up, and pushed Sam's dinner tray back at him. "Eat up, son. You're gonna need some fuel to keep you going."

Sam picked up a fork and toyed with the mound of corn relish on his plate. "I don't suppose you have any idea what to do first?" he asked, after forcing himself to try a bit of beef.

"Matter of fact, I do. How does murder strike you?"

The beef lodged halfway down Sam's throat. When he finally coughed it up, he gasped for air. "Murder? Did you say *murder*?"

"Why not? This investigation's already revealed nearly every other crime. Arson, fraud, sabotage, assault, not to mention unethical doctors. Murder is one of the few that's missing, and I can't think of a more deserving victim than Charles Dunn."

"I said I wanted to set things straight, but I have no intention of putting a hangman's noose around my neck and thrilling a crowd of spectators!"

Ludlam grinned from ear to ear. "Public executions stopped a couple of years ago, but now that I've got your undivided attention, you might start talking. Tell me everything that's happened to you since you first met Violet Dunn. Don't leave anything out. Not a single detail. Sometimes it helps to look back before you leap forward. We'll figure out something together."

Sam stabbed a hunk of beef. "Murder," he muttered. Engulfed in an aura bordering on sheer madness, he recounted the events of the past few weeks, day by day, incident by incident, holding nothing back except his ill-fated love for Violet.

The investigator listened attentively. Occasionally, he stopped Sam in mid-sentence to pose a question, but offered no comment or judgment.

"That's everything up until I arrived home tonight," Sam concluded. The chaos in his mind was now ordered. His mind raced back and forth, posing a solution against something he remembered and weighing the outcome. Finally, there remained only one possible solution to solving the problem of meeting his responsibilities, freeing Violet from her father's control, and helping Rosemary, too.

If he thought about it all too long, he would probably realize he had close to no chance of succeeding. It was risky to everyone involved, but especially to Ben, who would be completely vulnerable should anyone connect him to Sam's plan. It was costly. Sam would end up with almost less than what he'd had in his pockets when he first arrived in Philadelphia.

And it was sheer madness to think he might succeed.

He could not tell Violet what he was about to do. She would immediately reject his plan. But when she did find out what he had done, she might never forgive him. And deservedly so.

Squires, the buyer for his business, would play an integral role. Once he agreed, Miles would be recruited easily enough, and he would take care of Rosemary. Dunn would fully pay for his sins, although Flynn never would, since Sam had already given him the opportunity to flee. Ben's help was also questionable. If he refused, Sam would simply have to honor his friend's decision not to participate and accept failure.

As far as he could foresee, he was the only one who would be held accountable. Giving up his honor, more so than giving up his life, would be suitable justice, and if he did succeed, he would not even have the right to stand in his sister's shadow when all he ever wanted was to be able to stand tall and proud in his own right.

But as long as Violet escaped unharmed, he was willing to make any sacrifice.

He cleared his throat and set his dinner tray aside. "We don't have much time, and I'll definitely need your help."

"I knew you'd figure out something. Where do we start?"

Sam could not keep his heart from thudding against the wall of his chest, if not his conscience. He looked directly at Ludlam, held his gaze steady, and tossed his own suggestion right back at him. " 'How does murder strike you?' "

Chapter Nineteen

❧

As long as Violet kept her hands busy finishing Rosemary's wedding puzzle, she had less chance of spending every waking moment worrying if Sam would be successful.

She should have worn gloves to protect her hands, but she needed to be sure she had sanded each puzzle piece smooth. Even though she had worn an apron to protect her gown, a sudden breeze wafted in from the open window above her worktable and blew sawdust into her face. She slammed her eyes shut just in time to avoid being temporarily blinded, but she tasted the dust on her lips just before a sneezing fit overwhelmed her.

She did not have to look into a mirror to know she probably wore a fine coating of dust on her hair, too. She was brushing her face clean with the hem of her petticoat before attempting to open her eyes when she heard a knock at the tower door.

"Miss Violet? Your father sent me to fetch you right away."

"Of all times, why now?" she grumbled, although she did not blame Bridget for interrupting at such an inopportune time. Cautiously, she batted her eyes open. Although her vision was clear, she was in no condition to see her father without first changing her gown. "Tell Father I'll be downstairs as soon as I've freshened up," she offered as soon as she managed to get the door open.

Bridget shook her head. "He wants you to go to your bedchamber."

"He's waiting for me there?"

"No, miss. He's in the study. Mrs. Dunsmore is in your bedchamber. She brought your wedding gown and wants to make sure it fits properly."

Violet rolled her eyes. The last thing she wanted to do was try on a gown she had no intention of wearing. "Tell Mrs. Dunsmore I'll be right there."

While the maid went to relay the message, Violet smoothed her hair to remove any wood dust. Before she left the tower, she went up to the third floor and found Rosemary curled asleep on the window seat. Again. Hoping she could get through the fitting and return before her sister awoke, she hurried to her bedchamber on the third floor of the main house.

Mrs. Dunsmore greeted her with a nervous smile. "Why there's the bride! Come. Let's see how lovely you'll look in the gown for your captain. He's rather an intimidating man, but I dare say he'll be speechless when he sees you in this gown," she gushed as she closed the door behind Violet.

"Speechless, indeed," she responded. She wondered to herself just how shocked her father would be when he realized he had no choice but to allow Captain Miles to marry Rosemary instead of his eldest daughter.

After removing her apron and day gown, she tolerated the fussing and primping from Mrs. Dunsmore, who insisted Violet could not look at herself in the mirror until everything was in place. She felt rather foolish, if not woozy, standing on a stool in the middle of the room and reached out to hold on to the bedpost for support.

"Oh, my. Oh, my! You look stunning. You can turn around now and take a good long look in the mirror. The gown suits you perfectly!"

Violet turned around slowly, took one look at her reflection, and nearly gasped. The pale gray gown fairly shimmered with a life of its own. Soft folds of French lace in pale rose were gathered at her throat and fanned into an elaborate bib decorated with flowers made of pearls that cascaded like a waterfall down one side of her skirts.

Tears welled and blurred her vision. She had never thought herself beautiful, yet she *felt* beautiful wearing this gown. Her father's cutting words when he compared her to Sam's former wife echoed back to haunt her again, and she blinked back her tears. Maybe if Sam could see her in this gown, he might be attracted to her long enough to realize her past was as much of an illusion as the gown that made her appear almost beautiful.

She sighed. That was as likely to happen as finding her long-deceased grandfather had risen from the grave to stop the wedding.

Mrs. Dunsmore helped her down from the stool and her face crumpled into a frown. "Oh, dear!"

"What's wrong?"

"The hem is too long. It shouldn't drag on the floor, just barely skim it. Thank goodness there's still time, although I'll have to get to work on it right away. I'm so sorry, Miss Dunn. Your father will be very angry with me for not having the gown done perfectly for you today."

"Father won't be angry, and neither am I," she said reassuringly. "We have days left until the wedding. I'm sure you'll—"

"But the wedding is tomorrow night!"

Violet felt the blood drain from her face. "Tomorrow night? You must be mistaken."

"Your father told me so himself when he called at the shop yesterday to make sure I'd have the gown ready in time. And now I've got to take it back with me, I'm afraid, but I promise I'll have it ready first thing in the morning if it means I stay up all night."

Numb from head to toe, Violet barely felt the gown and petticoats being removed. She stood there, by sheer strength of will, dressed only in her shift, long after Mrs. Dunsmore left. Every instinct she possessed screamed for her to go running downstairs to confront her father for not having the decency to tell her himself. From her own experience now, she had a rare glimpse of the shock Rosemary must have felt when the dressmaker told her Violet was getting married.

She did not, however, intend to respond hysterically as her sister had done. Violet could not afford any unusual display of emotion that could alert her father she was not willing to go through with this marriage he had arranged for her.

She also needed the time to face the possibility she might be marrying Captain Miles, after all, if she failed to contact Sam and let him know what had happened. She had once thought exchanging vows with a virtual stranger would be a terrible fate, but marrying a man who had fallen in love with her sister was beyond all comprehension.

Her trust in Sam was firm, but he could not have any way of knowing the wedding date had been pushed forward. Even if he did, he would not be able to stop her father by tomorrow night unless . . . unless he had already found the proof she needed. If he had, he would already have contacted her.

She sucked in her breath and realized her father had won. There was little she could do to stop him or to help Rosemary escape, either, since Sam had the jewelry now. If Violet had not given it to him, she might have been able to give it to Captain Miles and let him take Rosemary along with the jewels.

Maybe . . . it was not too late.

She still had tonight and all day tomorrow. If she had to, she could wait until dark, slip out to get the funds from Sam or the jewels, if he had not already sold them, and get Sam's help to alert Captain Miles.

She dressed again and brushed her hair. Her father no doubt expected a reaction from her for having changed the date for the wedding. She could not disappoint him, but first she had to make sure Rosemary was still sleeping.

She dismissed as unfounded and illogical the fear that her father might have told Rosemary about the wedding being changed for tomorrow. He appeared quite content with her apparent lapse into melancholia again and had no reason to want to shock her further.

Since there was no third-floor access to the tower, she had to go down to the second floor again. When she finally reached the tower, she opened the door. Immediately, an odd sense of foreboding overwhelmed her. Fighting against rising fear that made her heart pound, she forced herself to climb the circular staircase slowly instead of rushing and tripping on her skirts. When she reached the sleeping chamber, she found it empty.

Her heart pounded even harder. This time, she did rush, straight up the stairs to the treatment room on the fourth floor. It was empty, as well, and now her heart felt as if it were ready to leap right out of her chest.

Hoping she was overreacting because of the unexpected change in the wedding date, she stopped to catch her breath and calm down. Rosemary had probably just awakened and gone back to her bedchamber in the main house, but Violet had to get her back into the tower before their father found out.

She gathered up her skirts again and went back down the staircase.

Dr. Poole was waiting for her below.

She immediately feigned a bright smile, but held on to the edge of her worktable to keep her knees from buckling. Desperate to keep him from realizing Rosemary had left the tower, she held her place and blocked the staircase. "Dr. Poole. I didn't expect to see you today."

He smiled sadly, but as usual, his smile never touched his eyes. "Your father thought perhaps I should talk to you."

Relieved he had not come to see Rosemary after all, Violet felt her heart begin to beat more normally. "I'm fine. If Father was concerned I might be upset about moving the date of the wedding—"

"No. Not at all. Unless that bothers you. Would you like to talk about it?"

She gripped the table edge so hard now it dug into her palms. "No. Plans change, but that's part of life, isn't it?"

"Accepting change as inevitable or unavoidable is good. You've come very far, Violet. But I do have some rather disturbing news about your sister to share with you. I pray you can accept it well, but I'm here to help you. As always."

She froze in place, overwhelmed by cold so severe it emanated from deep within her own soul. She felt a bitter cold freeze her spirit, her body, even her tears as they formed. "Rosemary," she groaned. She managed only her sister's name before her lips went numb.

"I'm afraid she wasn't responding well to my treatment. You were with her so you know how deeply affected she's been by your forthcoming marriage. I've done all I can do. Dr. Arenz will be treating her now in his facility outside the city where she'll have the finest of care."

Father had Rosemary committed to an asylum?

The very thought jolted her heart back to life. Outrage melted the ice in her veins, boiled over the glacier of her self-control, and exploded into white-hot fury that incinerated the hopes and dreams she had carefully tended in the garden of her heart.

Envisioning Rosemary at the mercy of strangers inspired pure terror and unleashed fear that Rosemary would surely choose to end her life rather than endure the torture of spending the rest of her life in an asylum.

Violet bolted past Dr. Poole and rushed downstairs. Crying uncontrollably, she charged into her father's study without stopping to knock and stormed his desk.

"Liar!" She pounded on his desk with one fist. "You promised me you wouldn't send Rosemary away! You promised! How could you do this to her? What beats in your chest? It can't be a heart because you have none!"

He never flinched or blinked an eye. He did, however, reach out and grab her wrist. "Control yourself, Violet."

Panting for breath, she yanked away from him and wiped the flesh where he had touched her. "Don't. Don't ever touch me again."

He cocked a brow. "You're hysterical. Calm down before Dr. Poole decides you need to be sedated until the wedding."

"Perhaps you should send for Dr. . . . Dr. Arenz, instead. How much did you have to pay him? More than Dr. Poole? Just what is the price of a doctor's ethics?"

He leaned back in his chair and folded his arms over his chest. "Go on. Rant if you must, although I find your hysteria rather unbecoming."

"I will rant! I have every right to be angry! You're a coward and a rook and a miserable excuse for a man—"

"I'm your father!" He leaned forward, raised himself out of his seat, and glowered.

Shocked into silence by the sheer power in his gaze, she caught her breath. Trembling, she wrapped her arms at her waist and cowered at what she saw in the depths of his eyes.

Hatred, pure unadulterated hatred.

It slithered through his gaze, and she watched in horrified fascination as it snaked out to her, then turned back and retreated into her father. Despite her horror, she had a rare glimpse into his very soul, where she saw hatred wrap around a fear he had hidden away from the world.

He hated her.

He hated her sister.

But he hated himself even more.

Why?

The answer lay in the bud of his fear, which unfolded into a blossom of awesome simplicity. Finally, after all these years, she understood what drove him to become the cold, unfeeling monster he was.

"You're afraid," she whispered. "Every time you look at me or at Rosemary, you're frightened. I never realized . . . how much you fear for yourself. It isn't money you want or even respectability. It's peace of mind, something you can't have unless we're both completely gone from your life."

She choked back tears. "You're so afraid, you let your fear eat away at whatever goodness you once possessed and left room for evil to invade your soul. You're afraid it wasn't our mother who passed her madness to us, aren't you? You think . . . you fear . . . it was *you*."

She clapped her hand over her mouth and backed away

from him, one shaky step at a time. When she reached the hall and stood just beyond the doorway, she stopped to wipe away the tears from her cheeks. From the corner of her eye, she saw Dr. Poole standing by the front door, blocking any chance at escape.

"You think you don't have to be afraid anymore now that Rosemary is gone and I'll be leaving with Captain Miles tomorrow. But I want you to remember this: Every time you look into a mirror, you'll see nothing has changed. You'll still be the same man you are today, every day of your life. You'll always wonder, was it me? Was I the one who was responsible for my daughters' madness? And one day you'll know the answer is yes, but there won't be anyone who cares because you destroyed the only two people in the world who would have loved you anyway, just as we loved our mother."

He blanched. "You're talking nonsense. You're distraught and overwrought, which is why I won't bother to dignify your ramblings with more than this: Your mother was a madwoman," he countered. "She didn't deserve my love, and she didn't deserve yours. Only pity."

"Then you shall have it instead. I don't love you, Father. I don't even hate you, but I do pity you."

"Keep your pity for yourself," he spat as he walked around the desk and approached her. "After tomorrow, you'll have none to spare for me. And should you decide to test my will, remember that what I've arranged for Rosemary, I can easily arrange for you."

He stopped just beyond her reach. "All the doors have been locked from the outside. You'll spend the night in the tower. Until then, feel free to gather up whatever you want to take with you into your new life that hasn't been packed already and delivered to the *Carousel*. The rest will be discarded, along with your sister's possessions. I want no reminders that you or your sister ever existed."

Too numb to be hurt by his cruelty, she threw caution over her shoulder. "What about Grandmother's jewelry? Don't you want that, too? You've taken everything else."

He snorted. "Keep it. I replaced the stones years ago.

They're as worthless as you are," he taunted and quietly closed the door in her face.

Everything Violet valued had been packed into a small travel valise. Her tools and lithographs for making puzzles. Her pitiful little sack of coins. Her sister's rose brooch. She even had room to spare after deciding to take the puzzle she had finished as a wedding gift for Rosemary.

Her most precious possession, her daybook with her only mementos of her mother, was the only thing missing.

Now confined to the tower, Violet removed the daybook from its hiding place for the last time. With no fear her father might intrude, she settled herself on the chaise. Awash with memories of her mother, she held her treasure to her breast.

Inside the daybook, a variety of dried flowers from the garden, with their names and meanings scrawled in childish letters, filled only the first half of the book. Each blossom, picked by either Violet or Rosemary and identified by their mother, testified to happy moments they had spent together.

Before mental illness forever claimed their mother.

After witnessing Rosemary's lifelong battle with melancholia, she understood why her mother had ended her life, even though that meant she would leave her two young daughters behind. She pictured her mother as she had been on those special days spent in the garden, vibrant and full of life. She had the sense her mother might have been very much like Rosemary, with a spirit meant to be free, yet destined always to be controlled and broken to fit a mold she could not tolerate. First by her father. Then by her husband. And always, a series of doctors with treatments preordained to fail.

Her mother had had no one to protect her or to understand her needs, but she had made sure Rosemary would never be alone by instilling in Violet a strong sense of responsibility she would be strong enough, in mind and in body, to fulfill.

Unconditional love and devotion to her sister was her mother's only legacy, and Violet prayed with all her heart she would not let her down, especially now, when her success depended on her faith and trust in Sam.

She had used the daybook to help Rosemary, but she needed to peruse it now for herself, if only to renew her strength and keep despair at bay. She opened the daybook. The dandelion brought a smile to her lips, but she searched past the others until she found the last one, her namesake, the violet. Remembrance and loyalty. She traced its meaning with her fingertips and knew instinctively her mother had chosen her name carefully.

The stiff, unused pages that remained were silent witnesses to the memories she and her mother might have created, but they also represented hope. As if guided by her mother's spirit, she thumbed through each empty page, knowing one day she would have a daughter of her own. Together, they would gather new flowers and shape new memories to join the old ones.

When she reached the final page, her eyes widened with disbelief. Her heart started to race. When tears blurred her vision, she blinked them away and stared at something she had never known existed before this very moment.

A single heart fashioned from forget-me-nots was in the center of the page. Inside, a sprig of violets rested alongside a tiny pink rosebud. Below, her mother had written a short message:

> *Remember to love one another as I*
> *have loved you. Forgive me.*
> *Mama*

"Mama," she whispered, bowed her head, and wept. For herself, for having missed this final goodbye from her mother for so many years. For Rosemary, who had been taken away without ever seeing this for herself. For her mother, a woman who had somehow known she would not be able to defeat the illness that ultimately claimed her life, yet was strong enough to create a lasting memento of her love for her daughters.

And through her tears, she vowed to remain strong and to honor her mother's memory by keeping faith . . . in herself and in Sam.

Chapter Twenty

❧

As unlikely as it might seem, Sam needed to rely on every one of his talents and skills for business to bring his plan to fruition. Yet like all the deals he had brokered, he would not know until the final moment whether he would win his bid or lose to his competitor, Charles Dunn.

Sam's profit could not be deposited in a bank since justice was a vaporous, though priceless, commodity. Saving Violet from her father, even at the cost of his honor, would be the greatest share of his reward.

In the hour just before dawn, he lay awake in his bed, unable to put the long day's events to rest. He had not returned from his post outside her home until he had finally felt secure she would be safe until morning. He had yet to decide whether he had actually seen a light on the third floor of the tower or if it had been just a trick played by a very weary mind and tired eyes.

He could not imagine the depth of despair consuming her every thought, and prayed she would be as strong now as she had been every day since they had met.

All the players in his desperate game to outwit Dunn were now safely in place or had served their purpose. Squires, an integral component, had not balked at moving up the date of the purchase of Glennings Enterprises, especially after Sam had adjusted his price to take the spoiled inventory and warehouse repairs into account. Ludlam had proven his worth, as well as his talent and belief in justice, more than once today, as had others.

Above all, Ben had not only shared his legal expertise, but had proven the bonds of brotherhood they shared to be as strong as if they had been forged by blood instead of by choice. If Sam ever doubted his belief that justice merited self-sacrifice and always prevailed over avarice, he had only to look as far as the next bedchamber, where Ben was now resting, to know it was true.

Despite the fresh bandage and the pillow propped underneath, he felt a damp area where blood or fluids continued to ooze from his foot. He was still wobbly on the crutches and had put full pressure on his injured foot more than once today and winced from the pain. Hopefully, he would be better at hiding his discomfort later today when it counted the most.

When the dull ache in his foot finally subsided to the same soft rhythm as his heartbeat, he finally managed to slip into sleep. His hand never relaxed the hold he had on Violet's brooch, as if his spirit knew he would have a difficult time relinquishing it in the morning.

As promised, Mrs. Dunsmore returned by mid-morning with Violet's wedding gown. Also as promised, Violet had been allowed to leave the tower, but she was confined to her bedchamber. Below, servants bustled about preparing for the limited number of guests who would be attending the short ceremony scheduled to be held at nine o'clock tonight in the second-floor ballroom.

Once again, Violet stepped down from the stool wearing a gown far too beautiful to be part of such mockery, her thoughts and prayers locked on Rosemary.

Mrs. Dunsmore twittered about her. After adjusting the folds of the skirts, she stepped back and smiled. "It's perfect. Turn around now and take a look at yourself in the mirror."

Violet exhaled slowly. "I'm sure it's fine and every bit as lovely as before. Thank you for being so prompt this morning.

Perhaps you could help me to take it off now so Bridget can press the wrinkles out of the sleeves."

The smile on the older woman's face faded immediately. "Of course."

Endless minutes later, Violet finally slipped a robe over her shift. Sam had less than twelve hours left, but with every passing hour, she grew more convinced he would not be able to stop the wedding any more than he would be able to undo what her father had already done to Rosemary. Anxious to spend the rest of the day alone, she waited while Mrs. Dunsmore gathered up her sewing notions and packed them back into a small satchel.

The minute the dressmaker opened the satchel, her smile returned brighter than before. "I almost forgot! I have a package for you."

She retrieved what appeared to be a small box wrapped in gold velvet held in place by a silver ribbon and handed it to Violet. "It's a secret surprise," she whispered, as if someone downstairs might possibly overhear her.

Completely surprised, Violet had to take several shaky breaths to find her voice. She felt certain Sam had sent her the package and prayed the box contained good news. "A surprise? From whom?"

Mrs. Dunsmore stepped closer, and Violet was almost afraid the woman intended to whisper in her ear. Instead, the woman clapped her hands. "Even your father doesn't know. That's how Captain Miles wanted it. It's his wedding gift to you. He's such an incredibly romantic man. I simply feel awful for thinking he was an intimidating man."

Disappointment quickly washed away Violet's hopes. "Oh, it's from Captain Miles."

"He came to my shop quite early this morning and asked me to help surprise you."

Violet quickly recovered a frown before it gave away her true feelings. "Well, I am surprised. Thank you for helping him."

When she did not open the package, the dressmaker did not press the issue. She finished packing up her satchel and left. Even as her footsteps echoed down the hall, Violet bolted her door. She untied the ribbon and quickly had the box open. She gasped with one look at what lay inside. "My brooch? How did he get my brooch?"

When she lifted the brooch out of the box, she saw a very tiny puzzle piece lying inside. Actually, it was not a full piece. He had cut off the corner of a piece she recognized as part of the puzzle Sam had purchased at the stationery store.

Praying harder than she ever had in her whole life, she flipped the piece over with the tip of her finger. Tears of joy blurred her vision, and she had to read the message twice to make sure she was not rewriting the words with her heart. Trembling, she lifted the puzzle piece out of the box and held it to her heart, where his message had already been indelibly etched:

Trust me.
S.

"Oh, I will," she whispered. "I will."

Complete trust was an amazing thing.

At mid-afternoon, Violet had taken a short nap and had had no difficulty falling asleep. She even had had enough of an appetite to finish a light supper after affixing her signature below Captain Miles's to the marriage certificate that would be formally witnessed and signed by the minister at the con- clusion of the ceremony.

She had bathed leisurely and fixed her own hair by fash- ioning a simple braid she wrapped around her head with sure hands. The first hint of doubt appeared when Bridget helped Violet into her wedding dress, but it was only eight o'clock. Sam still had a full hour to stop the ceremony.

She dismissed the maid and paced back and forth across her chamber. She could hear the voices of guests gathered on the floor below and walked in rhythm to the melodies pro- vided by a single harpist. With the oppressive heat, all the windows were open, and she could smell the aromas of the after-ceremony dinner still cooking in the kitchen.

Where was Sam? Why hadn't he come yet?

By eight-thirty, she had paced through every conceivable reason for his delay, but none were good enough to keep doubt from sprouting wings and perching on her shoulder. To keep her mind and hands busy, she packed and repacked her travel bag, making sure her brooch and Sam's message were both stored at the bottom.

When her father came to her door ten minutes before nine o'clock, she knew from the satisfied look on his face Sam had yet to arrive. "You look . . . passably well," he remarked, "although you don't add the same beauty to a gown as your mother once did."

She ignored his belittling comment, but accepted his arm. He escorted her to the top of the stairs where he paused. "The Reverend Whelan sent his apologies along with a new associate who will be performing the ceremony, but we have to wait for Captain Miles to return. It seems he forgot to bring your wedding ring, but he should be back so the ceremony can begin precisely at nine."

A bud of renewed hope blossomed in her heart, which now raced a little faster. Was Sam going to arrive in Captain Miles's place and confront her father in front of his guests? Did he plan it that way deliberately, knowing her father would lose the respectability he cherished to immediate scandal? Or had Sam been forced by circumstances beyond his control to make his move at the last possible moment?

Minutes later, a servant she did not recognize appeared at the bottom of the stairs and motioned to her father. She wasted no time wondering who the maid might be. Her father must have added several to the permanent staff for tonight's event. Unless Sam had sent the maid, in which case her father would be very surprised when Sam, not Captain Miles, stood waiting for both of them in the ballroom.

Listening to a hauntingly beautiful melody, she descended the steps with her father. To her right, she could see the tables blazing with candles and laden with food in the room behind the ballroom. Straight ahead, long-time servants gathered on either side of the door leading to the ballroom, but she would not be able to see the minister or Sam until she actually entered the room and passed by her father's guests.

Fear made her stumble twice before trust steadied her progress toward her destiny. Once inside, she kept her gaze averted from the forty or so guests. When her father guided her to stop in front of the fireplace, which was filled with flowers instead of logs, she did not have to see the face on the giant who stood waiting to claim her as his wife.

She knew Captain Miles by size alone.

The music ended. All conversation ceased. The young minister smiled a welcome and adjusted his spectacles. When her father stepped aside after handing her to her betrothed, only a man as strong as Captain Miles could keep her upright by simply holding on to her arm.

Tears blurred her vision. Her heart pounded weakly, still clinging to hope. When he bent his head toward her, she flinched.

"You made me a promise. I expect you to keep it," he whispered.

Promise? Her mind was too awash with fear and confusion to understand the words she heard the minister say. She recalled the promise she had made to Captain Miles. *Nothing will ever make my mind snap. Nothing!*

She trembled. Hard. And vowed to keep her promise if only to live a very long life so she would be able to remind Captain Miles that *he* had failed to keep his promise to keep Rosemary safe from all harm, even at the cost of his own life.

"Miss Dunn?"

She snapped back to attention.

The minister smiled. "Do you vow to keep your promises?"

"I do so promise," she murmured, confident she was the only one in the room who knew exactly what she meant. Lost in her own thoughts, she paid scant attention during the rest of the ceremony until Captain Miles put the ring on her finger.

The simple band of gold hung loosely on her finger. It was too large for her, but was probably just right for Rosemary. Had she misjudged her new husband? Had he really intended to marry Rosemary, only to meet failure because she had been sent away before he had a chance to steal her away? Is that why he had given her a ring clearly meant for another?

Before she could even ponder an answer to the litany of questions in her mind, the minister pronounced them husband and wife. After Captain Miles pressed a kiss to her forehead, the guests clapped their approval. Her heart skipped a beat, and she held her breath until, amazingly, it began beating again; she had feared it might completely wither and die from disappointment.

When her father motioned for her and her husband to assemble in a receiving line, Captain Miles asserted his new authority over her. "I'm afraid we don't have time. My wife and I have a ship waiting. You'll excuse us if we don't stay to celebrate your victory."

The minister sputtered and mopped his brow. "At least wait until the witnesses sign the marriage certificate."

"Give it to Mr. Dunn. He'll appreciate it more than I do," her husband snapped. Without waiting for the minister or her father to respond, Captain Miles escorted her away from the stupefied minister and guests shocked into mortified silence. He guided her through the hall and down the steps so quickly she was too busy trying to keep up with his strides to argue.

At the front door, he paused less than a second to take her small travel bag from a servant, opened the door himself, and led her outside. A coach large enough to seat six people comfortably waited at the curb to take them to the *Carousel*. Given his size, she was not surprised. She was curious to see that the curtains on the windows were all down when it was so unbearably warm, and she found it odd the driver did not come down from his seat to help her into the coach.

Captain Miles opened the coach door, lifted her inside, and followed her into the darkened interior less than a heartbeat later. She held on to the seat when the coach lurched forward and huddled in cushions that practically swallowed her up like the lining of a coffin. The interior was just as dark, and the air stifling. She found the experience almost as unsettling as her new married state, but flinched when he made a request that sounded more like a command.

"The ring. May I have it back, please?"

If there had been any light inside the coach, he would have seen her mouth agape. "You want my ring? That's all you have to say about what just happened? The ring stays on my finger until I get some answers. It belongs to me, much to my dismay."

"No, Violet. It doesn't," he murmured. "I'm afraid your father was so busy insisting on the loophole you feared so much, he forgot a very important legal technicality."

"T-technicality?" she repeated, too shocked to do more than mimic his words.

He sighed. "Actually, there are two. Legally, a man can have only one wife at a time, which would make me a bigamist and render our marriage null and void. But in addition, the man who performed the ceremony is not an ordained minister. He's one of my crew."

Stunned, she scarcely had time to blink before a rustle of skirts that definitely did not belong to Violet sent her heart into a breakneck gallop. She did not recognize a very feminine giggle that followed, but the woman's voice coming from next to Captain Miles was only too familiar.

"It's me. Rosemary. And that's my ring you're wearing. Won't you please let me have it back?"

Chapter Twenty-one

❧

It's you! It's really you!" Violet kept crying the same words, over and over again, while hugging her sister for all she was worth.

A bump in the roadway rocked the coach and nearly pitched both of them to the floor. The minute Violet let go of her, Rosemary scooted away and jumped onto her husband's lap. "I told you it was me," Rosemary protested. "Now can I please have my ring back?"

Captain Miles chuckled, and the sound boomed off the sides of the coach. "Don't be so anxious, little bird. Your sister's not going to keep your ring."

Violet held her hand down and let the band slip free. She groped toward the shadowy figures, but it was Captain Miles's large hand she met when she held out the ring.

He took the ring and, seconds later, Rosemary cooed. "I just love the feel of it on my finger. It makes everything real instead of just a dream."

Violet could not get a single question out before her mind skipped to the next. "How did you . . . When did you . . . Where—"

"We'll explain everything later," she gushed. Right now, we need to get to the ship. We're all sailing at midnight. On the *Rainbow.* That's the new name for the ship. My captain renamed it just for me. Isn't he romantic?"

Romance aside, Violet grew nauseous just thinking about setting foot on a ship and did not care what name it carried. "I can't go with you. What about Sam? I need to see him. And what about Father? Once he finds out you've escaped, he'll send someone to find you. This isn't going to work. Don't you know that?"

"Yes it is. And Sam's coming with us. At least we hope he'll be back in time," Rosemary argued.

A premonition formed in Violet's mind. She pictured Sam confronting her father and chills raced down her spine. "Back? Back from where? And why would Sam be going with us . . . with you? He's supposed to be going back home, not traveling halfway around the world and back."

"Don't worry. Sam has it all figured out. All I know is he got me out of that awful place where Father sent me and had my captain waiting for me. Sam even arranged for a minister in New Jersey to marry us last night so I wouldn't be a soiled bride if we waited till morning."

"Rosemary!" Violet yelped. She could feel a blush on her face that nearly singed her brows along with her eyelashes.

"Oh, Violet. Don't be such a . . . such a spinster about it. You'll find out one day the marriage bed is such a grand adventure—"

"Ah—ahem!" The captain cleared his throat. "I think your sister means to say Sam and I were very concerned about protecting your sister's . . . welfare."

"Then you both should have thought of that when you came up with this plan," Violet argued. "It won't work."

Rosemary sighed. "Oh, diddle! You're not worried about Father at all. You're just worried about how you're going to be seasick."

"I am not."

"Oh, yes you are. You don't want Sam to see you all weak and green around the edges. You're afraid he won't think you're pretty anymore."

"And just why do you think I care what Sam Glennings thinks?" she retorted, grateful the dark hid her face from her sister's scrutiny.

"Because you've fallen in love with him, that's why."

"That's ridiculous. I just met him a few weeks ago."

"Now who's being ridiculous? I fell in love with my captain the minute we met. You've known Sam a lot longer. I think he's fallen in love with you, too."

Violet shook her head, but had no voice to argue with Rosemary again or the strength to convince her she was wrong. Violet and Rosemary were as distinct in their temperament and personality as they were physically. Rosemary had been impetuous since the day she was born, while Violet approached life, as well as her responsibilities, with careful planning and logic. It only made sense that when each of them fell in love, they would choose very different men and take different paths to reach the same goal, which was happiness with the man of their dreams.

The instant physical attraction between Rosemary and Captain Miles was only part of the amazing miracle that had bound their hearts together in love that was born the moment their eyes first met. Falling headfirst into love at first sight suited Rosemary's nature, but Violet was far too practical and analytical to ever fall in love that quickly.

Rosemary was wrong. Violet could not possibly love Sam.

Her heart trembled.

Her spirit rebelled.

But her mind finally surrendered to the stunning truth: She did love Sam. Beyond all hope. Beyond all reason.

But Sam could never love her in return. She knew that with every beat of her heart. Perhaps that was why she had hidden from the truth Rosemary forced her to acknowledge now—to keep her heart from being broken when he turned away from her.

Whether it was a matter of weeks, months, or years, Sam would never be able to give love a chance to grow between them. After a very sorry first meeting, his perception of her might have changed but he only saw her as an obligation. Nothing more.

Even if he did have some feelings for her, she could not blame him for ignoring them. Madness had claimed his first wife, a woman who nearly destroyed his sister, as well. He would never take the risk of marrying a woman like Violet, no matter how different her alleged mental distraction might be from Polly's.

"I don't love him, Rosemary," she whispered. The lie made her heart tremble, but it was necessary. Rosemary was likely to play matchmaker unless Violet could convince her she was wrong. "I respect him for helping us, and I'm very grateful to him, but I could never fall in love with him like . . . like you did with your captain."

That much was true. Aside from her initial physical attraction to Sam, her feelings for him had not been instantaneous. Her affection for him had evolved slowly and grown from seeds of respect and admiration before it flowered into the full blossom of love—one that was so very different from the affection Rosemary had for her new husband.

Violet did not love Sam for the protection he offered her or because he could give her a life of adventure. She loved him because he was a man of rare character who recognized and respected her needs as well as his own. His plans to spend his life simply in a small town, surrounded by family, when he could have stayed here in business and built an even larger fortune, spoke to values that made him all the more remarkable.

And all the more deserving of a woman who would bring him joy instead of daily reminders of his first wife.

When the coach ground to a halt, Captain Miles pulled the curtain aside and peeked out. "That's enough said on any subject," he warned. "We're at the docks now, and we're about to board the ship. I'll take you both below deck so I can concentrate on my duties. You can continue your conversation there."

Violet sank back against the cushions. Her stomach began to roll, and she closed her eyes. Whatever her feelings for Sam, the barriers between them would never be resolved. She had no choice but to set aside her love for him and keep it safely hidden in the garden of her heart.

She had a lifetime to learn how to do that.

In the meantime, her greatest challenge was figuring out

how she was going to board the ship and get below deck before she got so terribly sick she embarrassed herself in front of the seasoned crew, her new brother-in-law, and her very unpredictable sister.

From across the street, Sam and Ludlam waited until the coach headed for the *Carousel* was out of sight before making any move toward the mansion. Lively music and gay conversation filtered outside from the second floor as Sam worked his way closer on his crutches, but he was in no festive mood.

When he reached the marble steps at the front door, he rested only enough weight on the heel of his injured foot to keep his balance and handed his crutches to Ludlam. "Don't lose them. I'll be needing them later for sure."

"If you don't use them now, you'll wind up crippling yourself and needing them for the rest of your life. I still don't see why you have to charge in there without using your crutches."

"I'm not charging anywhere. I'm walking," he insisted. "I can't appear to be weak in any way. Just get yourself to the rear gate and have that wagon ready. If I'm not there in an hour, get to the ship and see that Violet sails with it. And make sure you explain everything to her before she leaves."

Ludlam tightened his expression. "I'll be there. If you're not at the gate in half an hour, I'm coming in to get you. Don't get into a heated debate. Don't give Dunn a chance to react. Just hit him fast and hard, then get out. I'll have the entrance door to the tower unlocked from the outside."

Sam nodded and swallowed the lump lodged in his throat. He and Ludlam had planned tonight's assault in exacting detail, but there was always an element of the unknown that could alter the outcome they hoped to achieve.

Once the investigator disappeared into the shadows, Sam hobbled his way up the steps and used the brass knocker to announce his arrival. Seconds later, when a servant opened the door, Sam stood straight and tall with his weight distributed evenly on both feet.

Ignoring pain ricocheting from his foot, up his leg, and back again, he stepped into the foyer. "I have business with Mr. Dunn. Kindly inform him Sam Glennings is here. I'll wait for him in the study."

The maid stared at him with her mouth agape for several seconds, then quickly recovered. "Mr. Dunn is entertaining wedding guests. I shouldn't think now is a good time to conduct business. Perhaps tomorrow might be better, if I may suggest so, Mr. . . ."

"Glennings. Sam Glennings. My business with Mr. Dunn is quite urgent, but please tell him so discreetly. I wouldn't want to spoil the festivities for his guests any more than I'd want to face him tomorrow and tell him disaster could have been avoided if I'd been permitted to see him tonight."

She hesitated and moistened her lips. "Follow me. I'll show you to the study and inform Mr. Dunn you wish to speak to him. Discreetly," she added in a tone just shy of berating him for insinuating she would interrupt her employer any other way.

Since he walked behind the maid, he could favor his foot on the short walk to the study. Still, by the time the maid lit a series of candles and closed the door behind her, he was drenched with perspiration and his foot screamed with pain. He took advantage of his privacy and hobbled his way to Dunn's desk. He used the desk as a crutch of sorts, worked his way around it, and dropped into Dunn's chair.

Deep gulps of air helped to settle his pounding heartbeat. He gripped the sides of the chair, crossed his ankles, and propped his bad foot atop the other. Luckily, pain had numbed his foot. For the moment.

Since the well of the desk was enclosed at the front, which faced the room, Dunn would have no idea Sam did not have both feet planted firmly on the floor. He should be quite surprised to find Sam sitting behind the desk, and that would give Sam added authority.

He set aside the papers lying atop the desk and laid out

the ones he had brought with him. While he waited for Dunn to arrive, Sam mentally reviewed his plans for their confrontation. He could find no gaping flaws. Although he could not predict Dunn's reaction with clear certainty, he knew enough about him to be fairly confident Dunn would fight Sam to his last breath.

He tightened his hold on the chair. He might not escape unscathed, if at all, but there was nothing Dunn or anyone else could do to him to equal the pain of knowing he had no hope of ever claiming Violet as his own. He would, however, emerge the victor tonight, if only to have the opportunity to tell her the truth himself instead of Ludlam.

When footsteps heavy with irritation grew closer and closer to the study, Sam straightened his back. Before the door burst open, he had his hands folded calmly on top of the papers on the desk.

Dunn tromped into the room like a challenging bull. He took one look at Sam sitting behind the desk and charged toward the desk. "You audacious bastard. Get from behind my desk!"

"Close the door. Sit down. And keep your mouth shut. You're here to listen—"

"Get out," Dunn spat as he rocked to a halt in front of the desk. "There's nothing you have to say I care to hear."

Sam smiled sardonically. "Not even how I can prove you ordered the murder of Ben Hastings?"

Chapter Twenty-two

✥

Dunn squared his shoulders, and his expression hardened. "You're as arrogant as you are wrong. I haven't ordered anyone to be killed," he gritted.

Sam rose from his seat, slowly, until they were eye to eye, and he matched his opponent's will with a stronger one of his own. Neither man had reached the pinnacle of success in the cutthroat world of business without the ability to hide their feelings behind a mask of power they wore to intimidate and defeat weaker men.

The contest between them was equal. The stakes were high for both. The air was fraught with tension thick enough to deflect the sharpest sword ever forged. Both men stood at attention, shoulders squared, gazes steady.

And the first man who dared as much as a blink would fall victim to the other, slain by the weakness and fear that lurked in his own heart.

Behind a shield of righteousness, Sam held his gaze steady and seized the initiative to force Dunn to retreat. "On your desk, I have a witnessed deathbed statement from Ben Hastings that gives every detail of his clandestine meeting with you that quotes your direct order to your hirelings: 'Kill him.' You may not have delivered the blows, but you're the man the authorities will ultimately hold responsible."

He paused for effect, but when he found no hint of fear

in Dunn's eyes, he struck another blow. "In addition to a certificate certifying to the cause of Ben's death as the direct result of a brutal beating, I have confessions of one Aloysius Lamant and Clyde Burns for you to read, as well. They were the thugs you hired to kill Ben, in case you've forgotten their names. They were quite able to remember yours. You should have found a larger rock under which they could hide, but I've taken care of that now myself," he challenged.

Still no reaction.

It was time to add the final and hopefully fatal blow to the supreme arrogance that kept Dunn holding firm against the damning evidence Sam had already listed. "Before he died, Ben told me where he had hidden the evidence he collected against you, proving you've defrauded your daughters out of their inheritance. The documents are all here for you to peruse."

Although Sam's heart was literally lurching against the wall of his chest, he kept his breathing as steady as his gaze and waited. Endlessly. Until Dunn finally blinked.

And then Sam knew he had won the first skirmish.

"You're bluffing," Dunn charged as he glanced down at the documents littering the top of his desk. "They're probably all forgeries. Total fakes."

Sam tightened his lips to hold back a smile, ready to end the war and emerge the victor. He placed both palms on the desk and leaned forward. "Am I, Dunn? Are you absolutely certain you can dismiss all the evidence Ben and I so carefully collected? Sit down and take a good look at it. You'll change your mind."

The only visible evidence of Dunn's fear was a small tic in his cheek—before he lowered himself into the chair in front of the desk.

Sam waited until the air once more was fraught with tension before resuming his own seat. "Ben Hastings was my lawyer, but he was also my friend," he taunted. "While I have a strong desire to see justice done, I'm realistic enough to know one man's misfortune can also be another man's treasure."

Dunn cocked a brow. "You'd use a friend's death to your own advantage? You really are a ruthless, unfeeling bastard, aren't you?"

"No more ruthless or unfeeling than a man who would use a ship as a dowry for one daughter or confine another to an asylum when she doesn't belong there. Or steal their fortune. Should I go back further, perhaps, and discuss Dr. Poole and his years of deliberate misdiagnosis for your oldest daughter? You're a fool if you discount a single piece of the evidence lying before you, but I give you my word—"

Dunn chortled. "Your word? There is no honor among scoundrels or thieves."

Sam hissed. "But there is. I assure you, everything here is quite valid."

Dunn snickered. "And I'm just to take your word. Is that it? That's highly unlikely, even when I've yet to hear your demands."

Sam lifted his gaze as if deep in thought, then let out a deep, exaggerated sigh. He reached into his pocket and withdrew a document he laid onto the desk. He was taking a significant risk, one he had yet to quantify, but he could not take a greater risk and lose Dunn's cooperation when complete victory was so near. "I have here a signed, witnessed statement I'll leave with you. In that statement, I freely admit my firm is accountable for the fires at your warehouses and so forth. It's yours. Peruse it now or at your pleasure, but it's all there, including dates, amounts of the losses sustained by the Montgomery Packet Line, and an estimate of the sale value of the firm had those losses been covered."

Dunn grabbed the document and quickly skimmed it. "You're insane! Do you know what I can do with this?" he spat. "I can have you arrested and sent to prison!"

"Exactly my point," Sam countered. "I have certain demands I expect you to meet. In return, I'll forget everything I know about your illegal activities, including your responsibility for Ben's death, and take him home with me to be buried. If I don't keep my word, you can take that document to the authorities."

"Even so, you're taking less of a risk than I am. Murder is a far cry from criminal sabotage."

"And I'm younger than you are. I have many more years to spend in prison than you have left to live if you're convicted. With your wealth and connections, I doubt you'll hang. I see the trade as equal."

Sam held his breath and felt the pounding of his heart. Dunn seemed to mull everything over for an eternity before he stored the document in his coat. "You mentioned demands?"

Sam finally took in much-needed air and collected his documents. "Actually, they're quite simple. Listen carefully. First, you sell everything you own in your own name, including stock certificates and other investments. Added to a fair settlement I'll provide for your percentage of the profits you should have earned from the sale of the packet line, you should do quite nicely if you alter your lifestyle a bit. You have two weeks to settle your affairs here, including closing up the town house and the country estate—after you have every bar removed from the windows on the tower."

Dunn's body stiffened.

"Second, you will assign guardianship for Rosemary, along with trustee status, to me to oversee her inheritance. Violet's share will be made available to her immediately. I have funds equal to the profits the trust fund should have earned already placed in accounts for both of them. Third, you're not to have future contact with your daughters. Ever."

Hatred blazed in Dunn's eyes, but he remained silent. Sam's heart was beating so fast he thought it might burst, but he was not finished with Dunn yet. "If you even think to violate as much as the spirit of my demands, think again. The investigator who helped to collect the evidence against you will be here watching you so closely he'll know if you sneeze in the middle of the night. He's also greedy enough to have accepted my generous offer to follow you to wherever you decide to make your new home. He'll make sure you honor my demands. He'll even make certain whatever endeavors you develop will be honest ones, long after I'm gone from this earth."

Dunn stared at him as if he had grown a second set of eyes. "You're not merely insane, you're a raving lunatic! By the time you fund this . . . this blackmail, you'll have no profit at all. There's no point to your demands!"

Sam sucked in his breath and held it until his heartbeat dropped from a heavy pounding to a dull thud. "The point, Dunn, is that before I go home to Sunrise, I want some semblance of justice for two vulnerable young women and a man who was brutally murdered. As rare or unbelievable as you might find it to be," he cautioned, "there is conscience, if not 'honor,' to be found among some 'scoundrels and thieves.'"

Dunn flinched. "Even if I admit that I believe your arguments and accept your demands," he countered, "why would you be so willing to let me escape virtually unpunished?"

Sam finally allowed a smile. "Will you? Knowing you're watched, day and night, your every move carefully documented and analyzed? The way I view it, you'll be in a prison of sorts. There won't be any bars on windows or locks on doors, but you'll never truly be free. Not as long as you draw a single breath."

Ignoring Dunn's obvious struggle to choose between admitting defeat and accepting Sam's demands or challenging Sam and risking public scandal, two equally disturbing options, Sam checked his pocketwatch. Ludlam would be charging inside in less than five minutes. Sam set the watch on top of the desk and looked up at Dunn. "It's your choice. Which prison will it be? You have precisely ten seconds to make up your mind."

There might not be pot of gold aboard the *Rainbow*, but there was an abundant supply of chamber pots.

Now sequestered in a very tiny, airless cabin below deck, Violet retched a second time and crawled back into her bunk. Even with the ship still tied to the dock, her sensitivity to the slightest motion of the water unleashed overwhelming nausea.

Her head felt as if it were spinning round and round like a painted horse forever bolted to a perpetually spinning carousel.

"So much for changing the name of the ship," she grumbled and tried to forget she was aboard a ship by pulling the covers over her head to block out the light from a single candle. It helped a little, but did not obliterate the sound of an army of footsteps and sharply issued commands overhead. She did not move a muscle when Rosemary returned with yet another chamber pot.

"Oh, dear! You were right. You are terribly sick. I'll empty this right away and come back to take care of you."

"I'm not sick. I'm dying. Please leave the new pot and let me die in peace." She heard Rosemary approach and groaned. "Please. Just leave me alone."

When Rosemary lifted back the blanket, Violet opened her eyes just a slit. "Go away."

An impish grin. Blue eyes sparkling with mischief. "I don't think you're green yet," she teased.

"Well, I feel green. And purple. And blue. And every other color of this awful *Rainbow.* Do you have to hover like an annoying moth trying to get to the flame of a candle? Go back to your cabin and find something to do besides—".

"Take care of you?" Rosemary smiled and smoothed the hair away from Violet's face. "You always took care of me. You never left me, even when you should have. Why would I leave you now?"

Violet tasted her own salty tears. "I don't like having you see me like this. I don't like being sick or feeling so weak I'm afraid I might not have the strength to lift my head. Not wanting to draw the next breath scares me even more," she admitted. "And this is just ordinary seasickness!"

Tears ran down Rosemary's cheeks. "That's what it was like for me when I was melancholy. All those feelings of being helpless were so overwhelming, I didn't know if I could survive. I didn't even care enough to try, but you never allowed me to give up. You shared your strength when I had none. You showed me compassion and gave me the courage to fight my way back. Every single time. Come with us, Violet. Please. This seasickness won't last forever."

Violet reached out from beneath the covers and took her sister's hand. Letting go of her sister hurt more than she could have imagined. "It's time, little sister, for you to spread your wings and leave the nest. You have a loving life with your captain now. I know I won't ever have to worry about you, but I'm going to miss you so very much."

Rosemary squeezed her hand and smiled through her tears. "I told Sam I didn't think you'd come, but you know you'll always be in my heart wherever I go. What will you do if you don't sail with us? Where will you go?"

Violet groaned and closed her eyes until another wave of nausea passed. "I can't think about anything until I get off this ship, but at the moment, I don't have the strength to get out of this bunk. Are you sure Sam said he would be back before we sailed?"

"That's what he said."

"When he does, tell him he has to change his plans for me. He'll think of someplace for me to go, even if it's just long enough to get over being so sick."

Rosemary tucked the covers under Violet's chin. She left the bunk for a moment and returned with a basin of water and a fresh cloth. She bathed Violet's face and smiled. "Tell him you love him, Violet. I just know he loves you, too."

Violet caught her lower lip with her teeth and sighed, but she could not deny her love for him again without breaking her heart. "I do love him," she whispered, "but you don't understand. He can never love me. Not ever."

Rosemary smiled. "It's too late. He already does."

"No," she responded and moistened her lips. "He can't. Sam was married before . . . to a woman who was truly insane. Although he's divorced and free to marry again, he would never allow himself to love someone like . . . someone like me."

"But you're perfectly sane! You're not—"

"Mad?" She closed her eyes briefly. "People believe that I am and that's what matters most. Sam has put the past behind him. He'd be a fool to give his heart to anyone who would remind him of what happened with his first wife."

"Oh, I see." Rosemary sighed. "I suppose you're right. You're far too strong for such a weak man."

Violet nearly bolted upright, but lacked the strength. "Weak? Sam is the strongest, most determined, stubborn man I've ever known! After what happened to him, most men would have been crushed forever, but he . . . he—"

"He survived. Just like you've done," her sister admonished. "Which only proves my point. He not only could love you, he does love you. He's an uncommon man. Precisely the kind of man who could see you for the treasure you are."

Too sick to battle with her sister, Violet let the tears flow freely. "He deserves a true treasure, not a tainted one. It's hard enough for me to face the truth and accept it, but if I can do that, then you must, too. Please," she pleaded. "I can't ever hope Sam will love me, and you shouldn't, either."

Rosemary wiped away the tears cascading down Violet's face. "So you're going to give up? Surrender? Accept defeat? That doesn't sound like you at all. You've won too many battles with Father not to try to win Sam's love."

Violet sighed and closed her eyes. She did not fight release when heavy eyelids closed and fatigue began to claim consciousness. "Some battles are doomed before they've even begun," she managed before she slipped into sleep.

"Nothing stopped my captain, and nothing will stop Sam, either," her sister challenged, but Violet was already asleep and did not hear her sister's response.

If she had, she might have told Rosemary how very wrong she was.

Chapter Twenty-three

❧

$\mathcal{D}$unn hedged in his seat. "I'll need a month to settle my affairs."

Sam's heart leaped from his chest to his throat and back again. "Three weeks. That's the best I can do."

"Agreed."

After Dunn signed the required documents, he stood up, but did not extend his hand again after Sam handed him a bank draft. "I'm curious about something. Perhaps you'd care to enlighten me before you leave."

As magnanimous as he felt, Sam had little time to spare to satisfy Dunn's curiosity. He pocketed the signed document and rose to his feet, but held on to the edge of the desk for support. "I have another appointment tonight. Be quick."

"Why would you want to go back to some small, rural town few people have ever heard of? Why not stay and make yourself another fortune? You're talented enough, and God knows you're ruthless as sin. It wouldn't take long."

Sam tightened his hold on the desk. "Money is a poor, poor way to be rich. I think you just may get to learn that lesson now, too."

Dunn shook his head. "I was wrong about you, Glennings. You're neither a raving lunatic nor a ruthless bastard after all. You're worse. You're a fool." He turned on his heels and left the study without giving Sam a chance to reply.

Seconds later, the same maid he had met earlier appeared in the doorway. "Mr. Dunn said to see you to the door."

Gritting his teeth, Sam tried to walk normally, but ended up with a small limp. While the maid headed toward the front door, Sam turned and rushed through the family dining room to a door he hoped led to the first floor of the tower. When he opened the door, Ludlam was waiting inside. Sam greeted him with a pained smile. "He took the bait."

Grinning, he clapped Sam on the shoulder. "I knew you could do it. And with a minute to spare. Thought I'd give you that," he explained.

Weakened by excruciating pain, Sam grabbed hold of his accomplice. "I'll take your shoulder, too. Let's see if our next stop bears fruit as well."

With Ludlam's help, he managed to get outside and through the gardens to the rear gate without putting pressure on his injured foot. He held on to the frame of the opened fence while Ludlam secured the crutches. Straight ahead, the wagon waited, as expected. To his left, the stable held memories both frightening and treasured.

He would never forget the terror of the night Violet had been attacked, but when he one day went to his final reward, he would carry the memory of holding her in his arms, of feeling her heart beating against his chest, and her lips gently pressing against his throat.

Any hope he might one day embrace her as her lover, instead of her rescuer, had already been diminished. After he concluded his next meeting, hope would be as nonexistent as his honor. And hidden somewhere in the midst of the sheer madness that had engulfed his life, his own sense of honor waited anxiously to be appeased.

He turned and looked back at the darkened tower for one last look. More memories. More images. More pain. But never again would Violet or anyone else be hidden and barred from the world in that tower.

When he finally had the crutches back, he got himself situated into the back of the wagon while Ludlam untethered the horse. Once Ludlam was in the driver's seat, he turned his head and looked over his shoulder. "All set?"

Sam leaned against the side wall and extended both legs out straight. He held himself in place by grabbing a firm hold on either side with each hand. "We don't have much time to worry about ruts or holes. I'll be fine. You just get us there so we can conclude our business and get to that ship in time."

Ludlam grinned, turned away, and clicked the reins.

As the wagon traveled the grid of city streets, some lit, some cast in shadows, Sam bid Philadelphia a final farewell. He had arrived here two years ago with his heart full of anguish, but his mind had been stronger, full of dreams built on a foundation of talent, ambition, and determination. Every deal he brokered, every bid he won, had made every day more exciting than the day before.

The time away from Sunrise had given him an understanding of his failed marriage. Time had also gently eased away his anguish. All that remained from the scandal was the wisdom to know he had no share of the blame for Polly's mental disorder any more than he was responsible for her despicable deeds.

His heart had healed. His soul was at peace. His fortune had grown beyond imaginable proportions. Until he met Violet Dunn and found himself faced with reality instead of illusion.

He bowed his head and closed his eyes. The euphoria he had hoped to carry home when he returned to Sunrise had evaporated within weeks. Tainted, his fortune now belonged to others who deserved it more than he. His talent notwithstanding, his determination and ambition had blinded him to his responsibilities and troubled his soul more than ever before. The scars on his heart had ripped open again, only this time, when they eventually healed, they would be so thick he would never love again.

When the wagon slowed to a halt, he looked up and stared at a humble yet dignified dwelling on the west side of the city. Surrounded by stately trees gently rustling under a starlit sky, the single brick home beckoned him to do his duty.

He took a deep breath and slid forward until his legs dangled over the edge of the wagon. His foot immediately began to throb, but he grabbed hold of the crutches and had got to his feet by the time Ludlam arrived.

Concern etched his friend's features, and he held on to one of the crutches. "You don't have to do this, Sam. You've done enough. No one would blame you if you went home now. I certainly don't expect you to do this, and the good Lord knows justice doesn't demand it."

"But honor does," Sam replied. He laid his hand on Ludlam's shoulder. "Let's hope for the best, but whatever happens, I'll always be grateful for everything you've done. And make sure you keep a close eye on Dunn."

Ludlam winked. "It'll be my pleasure."

Sam thought he detected dampness in Ludlam's eyes and swallowed hard. Emotion choked his throat. "I'll be back," he murmured and set off on the walking path toward the front door.

Surprisingly steady on his crutches, he faced the coming moments with no small measure of dread. He had a healthy dose of fear, too, but not regret. He would enter this house with his name and honor intact; however, when he left, he would have only his honor, tarnished and battered, but still worthy of claiming as his own.

Ben's image gave him strength to walk forward, his sister's image gave him the courage to knock on the door, but it was Violet's image that gave him the determination to step inside.

The small parlor was unearthly silent. The air was humid with tension. The white-haired man sitting across from Sam read the documents again, but typically shuttered any reaction from his expression.

Beneath a craggy brow, eyes that had witnessed testimony to every form of human depravity studied copies of some of the very same documents Sam had given to Charles Dunn. Flesh wrinkled by time sagged over a thin face. Lips that had spoken for justice for a lifetime now moved silently as Borden read.

Judge Adam Borden.

Like any defendant, Sam waited nervously while the judge pondered the evidence. The verdict was not in doubt, only the sentence he would impose.

He looked up and cocked his head. "The case itself isn't unusual, unfortunately, but handling your plea here instead of in a courtroom is. Make no mistake, young man. It's only my deepest regard for Ben Hastings that inspired me to make an exception for you."

"Yes, sir. I know that, and I'm very grateful—"

The judge silenced him with a snap of his fingers. "Yes, yes. I'm sure you are. Defendants who plead guilty always are, even before I set the sentence."

Sam flinched. The old judge, set to retire from the bench next year, had not left his imperial demeanor at the court-house.

"Before I decide your punishment, I need to clarify a few concerns. And, mind you, I'll tolerate nothing less than the truth."

Sam dared not speak again until given permission.

"This Flynn fella. As far as you know, he's gone from Philadelphia. Do you have any idea where he went?"

"No, sir. Out west is all he told me. I did list the date somewhere in the documents. I suppose he could be traced—"

"Hardly," the judge spat. "The west swallows up all sorts of vermin. Good riddance and good fortune for us, but dam-nably unfortunate for anyone west of the Appalachians. Looks like you're left to pay for his sins as well as your own."

He set the papers on a side table and folded his hands on his lap. His penetrating gaze held Sam immobile. "Setting aside your incompetence as the owner and the obvious am-bition that blinded you to your duties, I'm tempted to think you're a decent man. Otherwise, you wouldn't be here."

Hope flared in Sam's heart.

"Unfortunately, our prisons are full of decent men who faltered on the path of righteousness."

Hope died. His heart fell to his feet and stayed there.

"Nevertheless," he continued, "not all men try to make restitution as you've done or step forward to plead guilty to crimes likely to have gone undiscovered." He paused. If possible, his gaze became more penetrating. "I accept your admission of guilt, and I'm satisfied by your efforts to rectify the wrong that's been done. I also endorse your decision to step forward and claim responsibility. That said, I'm willing to file the proper papers and settle this matter here instead of wasting courtroom time, not to mention expense. My sentence, I warn you, will be equally binding and recorded as official. Understood?"

A stiff nod was all Sam could manage. The lump in his throat was so big he could not draw in enough air to voice a single word.

"Then if you'll excuse me, I'll need a moment to compose a draft of my decision." He rose and left Sam sitting alone with only his hopes and fears for companionship. He tried to brace himself for the worst—a prison cell—yet prayed for mercy knowing full well he would be imprisoned by his own conscience for the rest of his life.

When the judge returned and took his seat, he had a single-page document in his hand that spelled out Sam's fate. Running his fingers over the words, he was satisfied that the ink had fully dried, and folded the document and handed it to Sam. "I made a copy for you. I assume you retained copies of the rest of the documents?"

Sam forced his hand to remain steady and held the judge's sentence tight in his fist. "Yes, I have."

Judge Borden leaned forward. "You are a man of rare conscience, Sam Glennings, which I suspect will remind you of what happened over the coming years and keep you from ever straying again. Since justice and reform are the ultimate goals of our judicial system, I see no value in ordering your imprisonment. Should I be wrong, you'd best not appear in *my* courtroom."

Relief shot Sam's heart back up from his feet to his chest where it belonged. "Thank you."

The judge scowled. "I'm not finished. I accepted your plea and suspended your sentence, but I do have conditions you must meet. First, you're not to own any sort of business enterprise for at least ten years. Agreed?"

"Yes, of course."

"Second, you may not invest in or own part of any business venture for the same period of time."

"Yes, sir."

"Understand," he cautioned, "should you violate these conditions, here or elsewhere, I'll rescind the suspension and you'll serve a full five years behind bars."

"Yes, sir. I understand."

"Good. Consider yourself lucky as well as blessed to have had Ben Hastings as your friend. He was a good man and an exceptional lawyer. I take it you've made all the arrangements to take him back to Sunrise?"

Sam checked his pocketwatch. "The ship sails in half an hour. With your permission, sir, I'd like to be aboard."

"Go on, then. Get yourself going. We're quite finished here."

Sam shoved the document into his pocket, scrambled to his feet, and maneuvered his way on crutches without any trouble at all. The judge watched from the open door as Sam easily handled the single step down to the walkway. Ludlam leaped down from his seat and met Sam at the back of the wagon. "Well?"

"Get me to the ship. I'm going home," he murmured, but he left his deeper thoughts unspoken. He had left Sunrise two years ago, scarred and embittered. He would return, scarred anew, as a confessed and convicted criminal. Before he did, he still had the most difficult task left to be done.

He had faced Dunn and the judge. Later, he would have to face his family, but he did not know how he would ever find the courage to face Violet and tell her what he had done.

Chapter Twenty-four

❧

When Sam arrived at the ship, he was in pain, physically exhausted, and stripped of his honor. Actually boarding the ship and getting below deck claimed whatever pride he had left.

Being carried across the deck by two burly seamen in full view of the others had been barely tolerable, although he dared not countermand Captain Miles's orders. Being held from above and grabbed from below to reach cabin level, like a sack of grain, had been thoroughly humiliating.

The only saving grace he could muster from the entire experience had been Captain Miles's reassurance all the others were safely aboard. Unfortunately, he had not had an opportunity to say goodbye to Ludlam.

Actually, he mused as they carried him to his cabin, the entire experience was good preparation for facing life as a convicted criminal and would help him to face the next few hours as he bared his soul and confessed his guilt to Violet. His love for her was safely hidden in his heart, the only part of his mind, body, or spirit waiting to be broken.

The two seamen deposited him into a chair and promptly left, but he heard their snickers as they proceeded back to the main deck.

Ludlam entered and approached Sam with his hand extended. "I had to sneak past the captain. They're ready to sail.

The ship's doctor is busy, but he'll be here in a bit, so you'll be in good hands till you get to Havre de Grace. After that, you're on your own. You take care of yourself and don't worry. I'll keep everything here under control."

Sam shook the investigator's hand. "Thank you. I couldn't have unraveled all of this or resolved it without your help."

Ludlam shrugged his shoulders. "Just followed your lead. You're a good man, Sam. Give my regards to Daniel and your sister when you get back to Sunrise. I know how glad Jane will be to have you back home for good, but she'll be just as proud when you tell her what you've done to set things right."

That said, he quickly exited the cabin, leaving Sam alone with his thoughts.

Telling Jane the truth did not inspire visions of pride. Only shame. He would shoulder that burden later. In Sunrise. Long after Violet sailed off into her new life knowing the man she had entrusted with her life deserved the same disdain she held for her father.

When the planking beneath his feet began to roll and pitch and the footsteps overhead creaked to life, he sighed with relief. Added to good wind in the sails, a strong river current would carry them all south to a busy port in Maryland, Havre de Grace, where he and Violet would part forever.

From there, she would leave with her sister for a new life. Sam would board a smaller ship bound up the Susquehanna for Columbia, a decent Pennsylvania port in its own right, yet home to more ghosts from his past. He had not returned to Polly's hometown since the trial. He had heard her father was no longer in business there and had moved his family away to escape the notoriety and shame of his daughter's deeds.

Sam would be able to arrive, rent a wagon, and leave for Sunrise without worry about encountering Polly's family. Memories of their whirlwind courtship and marriage had long lost their bite, leaving only vague impressions of hopes and dreams long put to rest as youthful mistakes and replaced by a yearning for love that would be pure and true to fill his scarred heart with joy.

He had found that love in Violet, only to discover he was no longer worthy of even saying her name and he had no right to ever claim her love.

Still, his traitorous heart hoped she would one day make room in her heart to forgive him and judge him by his efforts to make restitution and to help her escape, although he knew that day, if indeed it ever came, was far in the future.

Over an hour later, when he was on the verge of sinking deeper into the quicksand of anxiety and despair, a man with dark, compassionate eyes set in a weathered face appeared in the doorway. "Mr. Glennings? I'm Dr. Willis. Captain Miles suggested you might need my services. I would have been here earlier, but—"

"Come in. Please," Sam urged. "I can wait. I do have some concerns about Ben—"

"Let's take a look at that foot and get you patched up first. We'll talk later," he countered with a firm expression that invited no argument.

Sam actually had little feeling in his lacerated foot at this point. While he braced for a repeat of the ordeal he had endured when Dr. Morgan first stitched his foot back together, he had a host of questions begging for answers he hoped would be reassuring.

While efficient and expert, Dr. Willis was a good twenty years younger than Dr. Morgan and lacked both his humor and tolerance for conversation while he worked. While that spared Sam a well-deserved chastisement for not using the crutches at all times, he found it nearly impossible to wait to pose his questions.

By the time Dr. Willis finished with Sam, yet another boot lay in shreds and another bandage hid the new row of stitches that decorated the sole of his foot. When the doctor insisted Sam rest in his bunk for a while, he did not argue. He was feeling a bit light-headed and somewhat nauseous, although he had no worries he might be experiencing the onset of sea-sickness. He had not suffered any effects the few times he had sailed in the past and attributed his weakened state to having his foot tended again.

He sat with his back against the wall and both legs extended the length of the bunk, but refused the doctor's offer to help him undress. He waited impatiently while Willis cleared away evidence of his work.

"You shouldn't have any permanent damage, but don't try walking on that foot again for at least two weeks. I'll check you again before you debark at Havre de Grace. Which brings me to something concerning Miss Dunn that I discussed with Captain Miles before I came to see you."

Sam's body tensed from head to toe. "Violet? What's wrong? I saw her earlier. She appeared to be fine."

The doctor cocked his head and narrowed his gaze as if astounded anyone would challenge him. "Obviously you saw her before she boarded the ship and found it so debilitating."

Sam relaxed a bit. "We're barely under way. She's seasick? Already?"

"Violently. The crew has long conquered the malaise so I don't treat it often, but I've never seen anyone stricken so badly—or so quickly."

As much as Sam regretted that Violet's first hours of freedom would be spent sick in her bunk, he had no fear she would gradually adjust to the motion of the sea. "Poor Violet," he murmured.

"She'll need more than your pity, I'm afraid. The captain's wife tried to tend to her, but summoned me shortly after we set sail and left Philadelphia. Unless Miss Dunn improves dramatically in the next few hours, I'm afraid you'll have to take her with you when we reach Havre de Grace."

Wide-eyed, Sam tensed again. "You're putting her off the ship because she's seasick? She'll adjust in a matter of days, if not hours."

"She may not, which is precisely what I just discussed with the captain. She's dehydrating quickly and unable to take in liquids and that is a grave concern. If I allow her to remain on board and she continues to deteriorate when we're in the open sea and days from the closest port, she may die. I won't be held responsible for that."

Sam leaned forward. "Die? People don't die from seasickness."

"No," the doctor countered in a fierce voice. "They die from dehydration. Or the stress put on the heart from repeated, violent retching, although she's young enough so I don't think that's likely to happen. Unless you have medical training and fifteen years' experience at sea, you shouldn't argue with my diagnosis. And I'd think twice before countermanding an order from Captain Miles. He makes the final decisions on board ship, not the crew or any of the passengers."

Sam could scarcely believe this was happening. He should have expected something in his complicated plans to go awry, but it had never occurred to him that Violet would be unable to tolerate sea travel "Captain Miles ordered her off the ship?"

"Pending my final opinion? Yes." The doctor's grim expression softened. "He's agreed to do so when we reach port unless I advise him otherwise. He thought you should be prepared to make appropriate plans should that need arise."

Sam collapsed back against the wall. If Violet was as sick as Dr. Willis claimed her to be, Sam would not get to speak to her anytime soon.

The mere possibility she would worsen and he would have to take her with him was incomprehensible. Surely she would recover enough to convince Dr. Willis she could survive at sea.

She would. She had survived far too much in the past to let seasickness set her back now. She was physically fit, as his body was quick to remind him when he recalled how beautiful she had looked in the gown she wore when she left the mansion. She was strong-willed, a fighter, a woman who had conquered far worse ailments and unbelievable betrayal to emerge healthy in mind as well as body and spirit.

By the time they reached Havre de Grace, he had no doubt she would surprise Dr. Willis with her ability to rebound. Then the doctor would be forced to admit his concerns had been unwarranted, although well intentioned. Sam was equally certain Captain Miles would delay his departure until

Sam had had a chance to talk to Violet in private.

He tossed out the porthole the notion he might have to take Violet all the way back to Sunrise with him and turned to the doctor to pose the questions he had held back since first boarding the ship.

He could ill afford to antagonize the doctor, unless he wanted to relinquish any chance of getting answers to questions that had plagued him since he boarded the ship. "I'll abide by your decision, as well as the captain's orders concerning Miss Dunn," he murmured. "If she's too ill to continue the voyage, then I'll make arrangements for her care in Havre de Grace. How long do you think it would be before she would be able to travel again?"

"Let's wait and see. This may all be premature," the doctor answered, typically evasive, yet seemingly mollified by Sam's acquiescence.

Satisfied he had regained the doctor's good will, he pressed his more immediate concern. "What can you tell me about Ben? Was he brought aboard without any difficulty?"

"Mr. Hastings tolerated the transfer to the ship very well. He's resting comfortably in the next cabin, as a matter of fact. I assume you'd like to speak with him as soon as possible."

Sam finally had good cause to smile and a reason to look forward to the future. "Yes, Doctor, I would very much like to talk to my friend and let him know we're on our way home."

Chapter Twenty-five

❧

After a long night spent in a chair with his foot propped up on a stool next to Ben's bunk, Sam had to wait until long after dawn before Ben finally opened his eyes. "Lazarus has risen," he teased. "You still look dead, though. How do you feel?"

Ben turned his head, stared at Sam, and grinned. "I guess I'm feeling pretty well—for a dead man." He narrowed his gaze and the grin faded until the ends of his lips trembled with the effort to keep from frowning. "You still have two heads, both of which you need to have examined by Dr. Willis, by the way."

Sam chuckled, despite the disappointment that Ben's vision had not started to clear. "Only two? Maybe that's not a bad thing. I can probably use the dose of extra brain power."

Ben closed his eyes and sighed. "Sorry. I still get dizzy and light-headed pretty quickly if I try to force . . . Since you're here, I assume Dunn was the first man to back down and Judge Borden suspended your sentence."

"Correct on both points," Sam replied. He spent the better part of the next hour providing details to the events that had unfolded while Ben lay safely hidden on board the *Carousel.*

"We're actually sailing on the *Rainbow,*" Sam offered. "Captain Miles changed the name of the ship as a wedding gift to his bride. I don't suppose you've given any thought to a new name for yourself."

"The whole situation is so ludicrous my mind freezes up every time I think about it."

"You can't rush time, which is all you're going to need, besides Aunt Nester's home cooking and fresh country air, to get back to normal. In the meantime, you need a new name. I can't very well book passage for you in Havre de Grace under the old one without leaving evidence you really didn't suffer your demise. Once your associate files your will for probate and sends me my 'inheritance,' I'll need to put it into an account in your name. So pick a new one."

"I rather liked the old one," he grumbled.

"So will Dunn if he ever finds out you're alive. I doubt he'll believe you rose from the grave and neither will Judge Borden. Pick a new one for yourself, unless you want me to do it."

Ben cracked open one eye. "You still have two heads, but I don't trust either one of them to pick out a name for me. I'll think of something by myself, thank you."

Sam ignored him. "I like Washington. It's a strong name. It was good enough for the first president," he offered when Ben made a face.

"That was in the last century. I'm a more modern man than that."

"Like Jackson."

"Exactly."

"Then Jackson it is. Now for the first name."

"I didn't say I liked it. I said . . . Oh, forget it. If I can't use Hastings, then I suppose Jackson is as good as any other name."

When he paused and tried to moisten his lips, Sam held a cup of water to his lips. After drinking greedily, Ben dropped his head back to his pillow. "Thanks. Sea air makes me thirsty."

"And argumentative," Sam teased.

"I am not," he protested, but a yawn interrupted. "I just

don't want to get stuck with something I don't like for the rest of my life."

"You didn't pick out your first name. So while you're resting, I'll think of one and surprise you when you wake up. I'm kind of fond of Sam so maybe . . ."

Both eyes snapped open this time, and Ben glowered. "You will not name me Sam. I have a name I want. Creed."

Sam blinked twice and shook his head. "Creed?"

"Creed."

"That's not a name. It sounds more like a . . . a legal term, not a man's name. You'll never—"

"It was my father's name," he whispered, his mood sober instead of playful. "Because of my temper, I may never see normally again. I'll probably never practice law again. If I have to give up my name, too, then I'll take my father's given name and try to live up to his expectations a little better this time."

Sam swallowed hard. "It's a good name, Ben, as good as your chances of fully recovering."

Ben closed his eyes and yawned again. "Maybe. I think I'm going to get some more sleep. While I do, it's your turn to do some serious thinking about changing names before we land at Havre de Grace."

"I don't need a new name."

"Violet does. Ask her to marry you and take her home to Sunrise. If you don't, you'll live to regret it. And I'll be there to remind you," he warned.

Sam opened his mouth to argue, but chose to remain silent. He would live to regret many things. He already did, but he had no right to ask Violet to share his name or his life. Even if he did ask her to marry him, she would only say no. That was one painful memory he definitely could prevent from branding itself in his mind. He already had too many others.

By the time he thought of something else to occupy the conversation, Ben had fallen asleep. Before Sam realized what was happening, sleep had claimed him, too, but not before his heart trembled at the very ridiculous notion Violet might one day have said yes if he had not been such an incompetent fool.

*P*acing the cabin did not help. Neither did a colorful stream of expletives. Nothing Sam had done to diffuse his frustration had worked. He even had been desperate enough to think he could shove the noon sun straight back to dawn to get more time, but the sun was as uncooperative as Dr. Willis.

Within moments, Sam would be leaving the *Rainbow,* yet he had no idea whether Violet would be allowed to continue on the voyage or be set ashore. And he still had not been allowed to see her to explain all he had done before he left.

He answered the knock on his door expecting Dr. Willis. He found Rosemary instead. Her eyes were red. A sense of foreboding told him she did not carry good news about Violet, but he knew she had tremendous sway with the captain. If there was the slimmest hope Violet would recover at sea, Rosemary would not allow the doctor to convince Captain Miles to order her ashore. "Mrs. Miles?"

"May I come in?"

"Of course." He stepped aside carefully to keep his balance, but she sidestepped his crutches before he had to worry about catching them on her skirts.

"Dr. Willis asked me to leave while he examined my sister again. Since the captain is supervising the transfer of your trunks, as well as your friend's, I thought I'd visit with you instead of pacing outside her cabin door. Do you mind?"

He hid his disappointment with a gentle smile and pointed to the chair with the end of his crutch. "Please have a seat. Tell me how your sister is feeling."

She dropped into the chair and her entire body went limp. "Violet slept so well last night, I was certain she was finally improving. Then this morning..." She paused and wiped away a fresh batch of tears with her handkerchief. "She was so pale. And so weak. I tried to get her to take a little tea, but she barely had it down before I had to rush for the chamber pot. What am I going to do if Dr. Willis makes her leave? I tried talking to my captain, but he's being very stubborn. He won't listen to me, only to Dr. Willis."

Her bottom lip trembled. "If he makes her leave, will you stay with her? I can't bear to think of her sick and all alone in a strange city."

"You know I will," he murmured, "but you shouldn't underestimate Captain Miles. He knows how important it is for your sister to be with you. If there's any hope she'll recover within the next few days, he'll let her stay. If not, none of us really has any choice, do we?"

Her eyes welled with fresh tears. "I suppose not."

"Then we all have to be prepared to do what's best for Violet, don't we?" While he did not doubt Rosemary's concern was real, he trusted Dr. Willis and the captain to be more objective. Rosemary loved her sister, and it was not inconceivable she was overreacting to a mild setback or letting her fears obstruct her judgment. If she knew everything Sam had done, he knew she would reconsider entrusting her sister to his care now or ever.

She lowered her gaze and nodded. "I suppose you're right."

"Did Dr. Willis mention how long he might be?"

Her hands shook as she wiped the tears from her face. "He just said he wouldn't be long."

"And I kept my word," the doctor offered as he stepped into the cabin. He walked directly to Rosemary and put his hand on her shoulder. "Your sister is resting comfortably for the moment. I've examined her very thoroughly, and I want you to know my decision is based solely on your sister's best interests."

She started weeping before he could continue. "She has to leave, doesn't she?"

"I'm afraid so. The captain has already ordered her things transferred ashore. I told him I would speak to you. And Sam, of course, since he's going to be responsible for your sister's care."

Sam tightened his grip on his crutches. He had no choice, exactly as he had told Rosemary, but that did not make his responsibility to take Violet from the ship any easier to contemplate. "I'll see she has the finest of care in Havre de Grace and remain with her until she's able to decide what she'd like to do from there."

The doctor shook his head. "Delaying Mr. Hastings here for several days or weeks and then moving him later when Miss Dunn is finally settled may set back whatever progress he makes between now and then. Since you already have plans to continue immediately with Mr. Hastings, you'll simply have to take her along."

Sam was so shocked he nearly lost his balance. "You got the captain to order her set ashore, yet you're telling me to put her right back on another ship? That doesn't make any sense."

The doctor dropped his hand from Rosemary's shoulders and glared, exactly as he had done the last time Sam questioned his opinion. "As concerned as I am about Miss Dunn, Mr. Hastings's condition warrants greater attention. I've given her some medication that should help her sleep. I understand it's only a matter of a few hours to reach Columbia by ship. From there, you'll be traveling by wagon, is that right?"

"Yes, but—"

"Then that's what you'll have to do. I'm quite certain she'll sleep through the next few hours. Once she's on land, it will only be a matter of a day or so before she's quite restored."

Sam gritted his teeth. He had not come this far to turn his back on his duty to Ben now. His responsibility to Violet was just as strong, but his love for her gave him no other choice but to take her home.

To Sunrise.

* * *

Rosemary kept vigil at the porthole and watched until Sam and Violet were safely ashore. When she heard her husband give the order to prepare to set sail and return to sea, she turned back to face Dr. Willis and smiled. "Thank you for everything."

He did not return her smile. "I follow orders, ma'am."

"Yes, I know. Thanks to you, Violet will be feeling better very soon."

"She was improving a bit this morning, ma'am. She was looking forward to getting her feet back on land, although she didn't take to leaving on a stretcher very well until the captain spoke to her."

"The captain can be a very persuasive man."

"Yes, ma'am."

"He's actually quite remarkable."

"Yes, ma'am."

"And very romantic."

He blushed. "Yes, ma'am. With . . . with your permission, I'd like to get back to my post."

"Of course," she murmured. She turned back to the porthole for a final glimpse of her sister and the man she loved. Before her sister disappeared from view, she waved goodbye and dabbed her eyes with her handkerchief.

Violet obviously could not see her wave. She would not be able to hear Rosemary, either, but that did not stop her from getting the last word this time any more than it had before.

She laid her hand atop the rose brooch Violet had returned to her last night and pinned to the collar of her gown. "I told you nothing stopped my captain, but nothing stops the captain's wife, either. I've given you one last chance to speak to Sam from your heart, Violet. Now don't squander it," she warned.

Violet would probably be very angry with her when she realized Rosemary had stretched the truth by telling her Sam had insisted on taking Violet home with him. Very angry.

"Some things never change," she whispered before she giggled her way back to the top deck and her captain. She counted on Violet to undo Rosemary's mischief now just as she had always done before.

But this time only with her heart.

Chapter Twenty-six

❧

The moment the wagon dragged to a halt, Violet gritted her teeth and said a prayer for forgiveness. She did not remember anything about the short voyage to Columbia, but she had spent the last few hours on the road to Sunrise with nothing but revenge on her mind. As numerous as the host of stars overhead, her thoughts ranged from murder to a solid dressing-down, everything in between and back again.

Unfortunately, Rosemary would be oceans away for years and well beyond reach, but that did not matter. One day, Violet would find a way to make sure her sister never plied mischief again. Captain Miles deserved punishment equally well, but Dr. Willis escaped her wrath. She had misled enough doctors in the past to consider herself completely unworthy of chastising him for his part in Rosemary's little plan.

Although Sam had been kind and considerate, the expression in his eyes and the firm set of his jaw revealed his true feelings. He no more wanted to take Violet home to Sunrise than Ben Hastings wanted double vision. Duty and circumstances dictated this whole scenario, and Rosemary was responsible for every minute Violet would have to spend in Sunrise with a man who obviously did not want her here.

The townspeople would not want her here, either, if they were to hear of her medical history, and she had no desire to complicate Sam's life any more than she had already done.

He had refused to give her any more than a brief sketch of the events that had set her free and refused to discuss exactly what he had learned from the second set of books for the packet line.

While she had won the battle to keep her name and nurse Sam's friend during his recovery until she had decided where to settle, her heart had yet to win the battle raging within her mind.

Sam did not love her. He never could. Pure and simple. And that was no illusion.

When the wagon finally drew to a stop, he made quite a lot of noise trying to dismount from the driver's seat and get himself settled onto his crutches, but gentle light apparently pouring from the windows in Sam's home showed her Ben was still asleep. Feeling nothing more than weak, she leaned up from her makeshift bed and peered over the side of the wagon. With everything dark except the windows on the first floor, she cold not see much of the house to judge its size, but there was no mistaking the figure of an older woman sitting in a rocker on the front porch.

Violet's eyes widened when the woman spat into a spittoon before she rose and took small but feisty steps to greet Sam as he approached the porch. "I was gonna say it's good to see you lookin' so well, but from what I can see, you and the rest of your outfit didn't win the battle, let alone the war. Welcome home, Sam."

He chuckled. "It's good to see you haven't changed a bit, Aunt Nester."

She stepped down from the porch and looked up at him. "I'm still shrinkin', my bones are still creakin' louder than that front door of yours, and I'm still chewin' tobacco, which is to say I'm feelin' just fine now that you're home. Grateful, too. Without those crutches, you'd be swingin' me around like a sack of potatoes."

He leaned on one crutch and hugged her before giving her a big kiss on her weathered cheek. "Give me a few weeks. I'll be swinging you and Jane around in no time."

"Don't you dare," she argued. "She'll be here in the morning with Daniel, but she's carryin' special cargo now so you treat her tender. Speakin' of cargo, let's see what you brought home."

Violet gripped the side of the wagon and swallowed hard as the woman approached. Thin and short of stature, she had a face wrinkled by the years, but eyes filled with wisdom and a twinkle that hinted at a temperament as impish as Rosemary's. She poked her face closer as if to get a better look at Violet, and her breath smelled of tobacco. "I'm Aunt Nester."

"I'm Violet. Violet Dunn."

"You look mighty peaked. Don't like sea travel, or is it my nephew here that's got you lookin' as pale as a white pumpkin?"

"Actually, both," Violet admitted with a smile.

She smiled back. "He used to drive a wagon like he was in a chariot race. Guess that much hasn't changed." She paused and stared deeper into Violet's eyes, then nodded. "You'll do," she murmured and pointed to Ben. "What about this one?"

Sam answered quickly. "That's the friend I told you about. Creed Jackson. He needs a little time to mend after an accident so Violet will be staying to take care of him for a few weeks."

Aunt Nester looked at his crutches. "What about you?"

He raised up his injured foot. "Just some nasty stitches that should come out in a few weeks. After that, I can take care of him so Violet can be on her way."

She shook her head and sighed. "Well, let's get on with it and get you folks to bed. Knew I was right to pack a few things to bring with me after I got that telegram you sent askin' me to open the house."

"You're staying?"

The look on Sam's face was so comical, Violet had to put her hand to her lips to keep from laughing out loud.

Aunt Nester swatted his arm. "'Course I'm stayin'. This isn't the city. You're back home. Best keep that in mind. Folks here find out that pretty young thing is out here alone takin' care of two rutting young bulls, even for a single night, they'll run you both outta town and stone her in front of the church before they do. Besides, you can't expect her to be nursin' you both and running the household. Not alone."

"Rutting bulls?" he thundered, ignoring the fact he *had* overlooked the need for a housekeeper to help Violet. "Ben can't see straight enough to put food onto his own fork, and I can't mount the stairs without crawling!"

Violet cringed. Aunt Nester might be old, but she was far too quick to have missed Sam's blunder.

His aunt reached up and yanked his ear. "Good. Don't have an extra bedchamber for you anyway. You can sleep in the parlor. You can see about tuckin' your sleeping friend here into bed. I'll take Violet upstairs, and I'll talk to you later. Maybe by then you can decide what his name is."

Sam paled, leaned on one crutch, and wiped his brow. "You're as ornery as ever. I suppose you'll want to hear the whole story tonight, won't you?"

A chuckle that rumbled through her chest finally escaped her lips. "Lots of things here in Sunrise have changed, but I'm not one of them."

He nodded, but his lips never formed a smile when he directed his gaze at Violet. "If you're not too tired, I'd like to meet with you first before I talk to Aunt Nester."

$\mathcal{B}$en was safely tucked into a bed. Aunt Nester was also upstairs putting away her things. After a refreshing bath, Violet sat on a chair in the front parlor wearing a fresh gown. Sam sat opposite her with his crutches lying on the floor alongside a package of documents he had prepared for her.

No ghosts from his life with Polly lived in his home now, but the very energized spirits of all the mistakes he had made in Philadelphia had followed him home to witness his moment of truth. He had come back to Sunrise with his most difficult tasks yet to be accomplished.

It was now midnight, and he found it rather fitting to have one task completed before sunrise. By then he would have set everything right with Violet and there would be time enough in the days ahead for him to grieve for all he had lost.

Violet looked at him expectantly. Trust still glistened in the depths of her doe-brown eyes. Although pale, she did look vastly improved. Lips curved into a gentle smile that once spoke of trust and hope, but would soon twist into a frown. He held this image of her now for several more heartbeats before he attempted to speak.

Her smile deepened with concern. "Your eyes are troubled. Apparently, you're not looking forward to explaining who I really am to your aunt. Is that why you're speaking to me first?"

Pain sliced through his chest. "No. You have a right to hear what I have to say before anyone else. She decided she was too tired, anyway. I'll speak with her tomorrow when I meet with my sister and her husband." He reached down for the package and handed it to her.

She laid it on her lap and folded her hands on top. "These are the documents Ben brought to the house, aren't they?"

"And several more. I have an additional one I can show you. Unfortunately, I don't have a copy for you to keep."

She raised a brow. "Would that be the accounting for the second set of books?"

He swallowed hard. Although his heart was pounding, he managed to remain on the course he had set for himself. "There was no second set of books. The losses for the packet line we originally documented are valid. If you set them alongside an accounting for my firm, you'll see how closely my profits match your father's losses. He was guilty of many things, but he did not deliberately defraud the line and shouldn't be held responsible for most of the losses. That's my burden to carry. Only mine, which is why I've restored the funds the packet line should have earned and set them up in separate accounts for you and your sister."

Confusion and disbelief sparred in her eyes and turned them a deeper shade of brown. "So you feel guilty."

He nodded.

"That's why you set up the accounts for myself and Rosemary from your own profits when most men in business would have simply taken their fairly earned fortune and walked away. Uncommon and undeserved guilt."

Her gaze hardened. "I can understand why. You might have been content to compete and win against my father, but you couldn't accept knowing you earned a fortune at the cost of two poor mad sisters."

"That's not true!"

She held her gaze steady. "I saw it in your eyes the moment you heard my name. Pity. Disappointment. Perhaps even scorn. That's why you decided to help us. Because we were reportedly mad."

He closed his eyes briefly. "That's exactly what I felt, but that was before I knew you. I don't doubt Rosemary has had severe episodes of melancholia requiring treatment, but I suspect yours were deliberately feigned to protect her—from your father as well as herself."

She bowed her head and tightened her hold on the package. When she finally looked up at him, her eyes were moist, but clear. "Then you don't think I'm distracted?"

"I've never met a more rational, logical, competent woman in my life. Or one as brave. With or without my help, you would have survived whatever your father did and emerged stronger," he murmured. "My only reward now is that I helped you escape sooner rather than later." The words flowed straight from his heart. Love gripped his very soul and held it firm, as if preparing for the wondrous miracle he now beheld.

Love glistened in her eyes and reached out to his trembling heart, offering him a love greater than he had ever known. Or would ever know again.

And with every beat of his heart, he knew he had been wrong. His heart would not simply tear open or break in a few moments when he told her the full truth and she turned away from him. It would shatter, and every day for the rest of his life, he would be destined to remember he had hurt her most by not being a man of unblemished honor.

If only he could have known and claimed her love. If only for a moment. If only for a lifetime.

Before fear and indecision ran roughshod over his will and his duty, he dropped his gaze. After he took a deep breath for courage, he faced her again. "My competition with the Montgomery Packet Line was anything but fair. Every charge your father made, every claim he made that I was ruthless, was founded in truth. The losses were not due to a natural string of bad fortune. The fires at the warehouses were caused by arson, the crew's rations tainted by deliberate poison. I may not have ordered my associate to use criminal mischief, but as the principal owner of the firm, I am responsible. And I'm no better in the end . . . no, I'm far worse than your father."

Her eyes widened with disbelief, and her lips trembled with denial that came swiftly. "I don't believe you. I can't believe you'd allow anything—"

"You're wrong."

Her hands twisted the package. "My father has no conscience. He's never once taken responsibility for what he's done until you forced his hand. You're nothing like him. Nothing."

He took the document Judge Borden had given to him and held it out to her. When she refused to take it, he pressed it into her hand. "I am now a confessed and convicted criminal. If it weren't for Judge Borden's mercy, I'd be spending the next five years in a prison cell. I may not have a number tattooed on my arm, but my shame is no less than if I did. I was incompetent and irresponsible. Whether or not your father suffered as a consequence or 'two mad sisters' or Lucifer himself, make no mistake. I don't feel guilty. I *am* guilty. And simple justice demanded using my tainted fortune to set things right. Not pity or guilt. One day, I hope you can forgive me."

Her breath came in short gulps. Her shoulders trembled. Her eyes flickered with flames of horror that consumed the trust once burning within their depths until only the ashes remained. The image sucked his breath away and shattered his heart more than any words she was about to say.

Shocked and disappointed beyond belief, Violet felt a sharp pain in her chest. She prayed her racing heart would not burst, but she could not find any forgiveness in her heart for his betrayal. Sam was right. He was as devious as her father had been. She had spent her whole life being manipulated by her father; she refused to allow Sam to do that to her, too, and recognized him for what he truly was—a mere illusion of the man who had claimed her heart.

While her heart silently pleaded for her to reconsider, she refused to listen. She had not survived all these years by depending on ill-guided sentimentality. Calm thought and rational reasoning had always been her salvation, and she used them now to see through Sam's words to find the truth that shattered her affection for him. "I—I trusted you with my life. With my sister's life, and I believed you were being honest with me from the start. That's the pity," she murmured. "You knew all along what you had done. You misled me to gain my confidence so you could salve your conscience. You only helped Rosemary and me for one reason: to impress Judge Borden and sway his decision so you could avoid a prison cell. You punished my father, not for me or my sister, but to protect yourself. What you couldn't do fairly, you orchestrated by deceit. You've cost your friend his career and very nearly his life. For that," she whimpered, "there is no simple justice or forgiveness."

When she rose to her feet, the documents fell to the floor. She swayed, but when he reached out to help her, she flinched. "Don't. Please don't try to help me now or ever again. I told Ben the night he came to my home that I didn't need your help, that you'd done enough. Now I know why you were so persistent. I was just another part of your plan. Nothing more, but certainly nothing less. You never would have done a thing if you weren't afraid of my father. You're only lucky you found the proof of your guilt before he did."

Violet squared her shoulders, tilted up her chin, and prayed for just a little more courage. "Store your documents along with your earlier calculated compliments to me. They suit one another perfectly. If it weren't for Ben, I'd leave in the morning so I wouldn't have to see you again. I'll stay long enough for him to recover and care for his own needs; that shouldn't take longer than another three weeks. And then I'm leaving. When I do, I'm going to try very hard to forget you ever existed."

She managed her last words without hearing her voice break. She even managed to escape his presence and climb the stairs to her bedchamber without crumpling to the floor. But when she closed the door and extinguished the lamp to escape into darkness, she fell atop the bed and wept bitter tears.

Disappointment was an old, loyal friend. Deception had been her lifelong companion. Betrayal shouldered closer and nudged Sam's image next to her father's, where they now stood together in the shadow of her deep disdain.

But the grief of true heartbreak was so devastating, she thought she might die from the pain.

She had once thought it impossible to find a man who would not judge her by gossip or the past. How cruel of Fate to send him to her, to tempt her to give away her heart, only to find him to be a man like her father, without conscience or a soul.

She sobbed into her pillow as shudders wracked her body and grief claimed whatever happiness she had ever possessed. Over the years she had found an inexhaustible supply of courage and determination to face almost any obstacle, but they were useless to her now. There was no hope. No redemption. And there was no cure for a broken heart.

Only endless pain born in the echoes of midnight despair, and there was no healing that would come at dawn.

Not tomorrow.

Not ever.

Chapter Twenty-seven

❧

In a homestead nestled on the outskirts of a town set between verdant mountains, Violet felt as though she had been dropped into what could have been Paradise. Living with Sam under the same roof for two long weeks, however, had proven Paradise to be nothing more than yet another illusion.

As she had feared, no healing had come at dawn on any morning since her arrival. While her heart was heavy with disappointment, her will to put Sam out of her life as well as her heart was still strong. Images of Sam, as she had known him in Philadelphia, kept slipping out from behind her father's shadow to confuse her thoughts. Desperately clinging to life, her love for him nibbled at the certainty that the man she had come to trust and love had only been an illusion, too.

Maybe today would be different.

After taking a breakfast tray to Ben, she returned to the kitchen. Aunt Nester had already cleared away their dishes. A pile of very sorry-looking apples lay in the middle of the old kitchen table. After one whiff, Violet wrinkled her nose.

Aunt Nester caught her and grinned. "This is the last bushel down in the root cellar. Thought we might sort through and see what we can do with them."

"Some must be rotten," Violet commented by way of apology. She sat down on the bench next to Aunt Nester and began helping to separate the rotten from the good apples.

"All mixed together, too," the older woman offered. "Sorta like your feelin's for Sam."

Violet froze and dropped her gaze. Her first instincts about Aunt Nester's quick mind and knack for tackling problems head-on had proven to be right many times these past two weeks, but this was the first time she had even mentioned Sam and Violet in the same conversation.

"You could tell an old busybody to mind her business. Or you could wanna talk it through. Your choice, but I don't expect you'll unbutton your lips any more than Sam did when I offered to listen. Stubborn fool," she muttered.

When Violet flinched, Aunt Nester patted Violet's shoulder. "Not you. Him. Don't know you well enough yet to call you stubborn. You might be a little foolish, though."

Violet chanced a peek and found twinkling gray eyes waiting to catch her gaze. She smiled weakly. "Maybe I'm a little stubborn, too."

"Won't hurt you none to have a little of each. Let's work, child. It's good for the heart and necessary for the soul. Gives folks time to think out loud," she advised and turned her attention back to the apples.

Violet followed suit and soon found herself pouring out some of the troubles burdening her heart. "Sam was the one person in my life who never seemed to be anything but what he appeared to be: a good man with a conscience."

"You found out different?"

"Yes. No. I—I don't know. That's what's all mixed up. When he first told me everything he had done . . ." She paused, unsure Sam had told his family all or only part of his tale.

"You're not tellin' me anything I don't already know. Sam's got no secrets from his family. Heard what he done and how he fixed it with everyone, includin' the judge."

Satisfied she was not betraying Sam, although he probably deserved less consideration, Violet continued to talk as she worked. "Sam didn't set the fires or anything else. I realize that, but he should have known what his associate was doing.

He could have prevented it. He could have told me from the beginning—"

"If he knew."

Violet felt her cheeks warm. "If he knew. If he didn't . . ."

"Then that's a whole different ball of yarn."

"Yes, I suppose it would be, but everything is all twisted up and knotted in my mind. It doesn't matter. It's too late to try to untangle it all."

Aunt Nester let out a sigh. She folded her hands together and tapped one thumb against the other. "As I see it, it all boils down to one thing: trust. Without trust, you can't love."

"I don't love—"

"Now let me finish," she grumbled. "Jane knew there wouldn't be any love without trust. That's why she couldn't tell Sam that wife of his was having an affair. Maybe Jane could've saved a lotta heartache by telling him, but she knew he'd never love his wife the same way after he found out she'd been unfaithful to him. Got his heart broken real good at that trial. Never thought he'd love again after that. Till he brought you home."

Violet dropped her gaze. "He didn't have any choice. My sister was trying to play matchmaker and got the doctor to tell Sam I had to get off the ship and go home with him."

Aunt Nester frowned. "Sam wouldn't do anything he didn't want to do. Wouldn't let no doctor force him to, neither."

"He was only listening to his conscience," she argued.

"Thought he didn't have one, accordin' to you."

Violet blinked back disbelief, then realized she must not be making herself clear.

Aunt Nester paused to wipe apple juice from her fingers. "He could have settled you in Havre de Grace. He didn't. He brought you to Sunrise."

"He was worried about Ben, not me, and I was still too weak to travel by water and . . . and drowsy from the medication."

"Thought you said you weren't, when we talked last week."

"Sam didn't know that at the time."

"But you knew. Seems like he might have trusted you to tell him otherwise."

Their exchange of words had been so quick, Violet had barely had time to think before blurting out her objections. Or to face the truth. If she were honest, she would admit to herself she could have insisted on staying in Columbia, especially after she knew Sam had not offered to take her to Sunrise. Instead, she had let Rosemary's ploy to keep them together go unchallenged.

Guilt heated her cheeks up a notch.

Aunt Nester made a suggestion as she started sorting through the apples again. "You know, sometimes we think so hard and so long about our troubles, we don't have time to listen to our hearts. I think we've talked about Sam enough for one day, though. We got some decisions to make about these apples."

Relieved to have the subject altered, Violet gave Aunt Nester her full attention. She had a lot to learn about cooking and could ill afford missing a single step along the way.

"First thing we did was to separate the rotten apples, the ones good for the compost pile." She paused, and her eyes got all dreamy. "Reminds me of when I was old enough to want to be courted. Some beaus I just set aside right off."

She blinked and turned her attention back to the apples. "Now let's look at the apples we got left. Some we can use, but not all, till we decide what's good for what. Some might be good eating right outta your hand. Most got enough sweet flesh to make a fine pie if you peel 'em and scrape off a few bruises. The rest you slice up, cut out the worms, and make applesauce."

She grinned. "You know, apples are just like men. Some are good for lovin' late at night, but not much more."

"Aunt Nester!" Violet clapped her hand over her lips.

The older woman scowled. "Well, it's true. Now let me finish 'fore I forget what my mama told me a long time ago. Let's see . . . Yes, now I remember. She said some men are good at makin' you smile, even when you wanna cry. Some will work hard and provide well. A few got a plain loyal soul and a conscience they listen to. Trick is to find one man who can do all them things and still make your heart flip-flop every time he looks at you. And that's the apple you pick, accordin' to my mama. And you don't diddle around, 'cause if you do, somebody else will snatch up that apple instead of you."

As if to prove her point, Aunt Nester sorted through the bruised and withered apples, found a plump one, and set it right in front of Violet.

Violet stared at the apple and frowned. "That one's pretty badly bruised."

"Watch." Aunt Nester used a small paring knife to peel off the skin. Pockets of light brown marred the juicy white flesh. Within seconds, she had scraped them away. "Now it's good to eat. Most of us get a bit bruised tryin' to get through life, Violet. Don't know a soul who doesn't, but it's the heart and soul that really matters. To find that, you gotta stop thinkin' and cut right through what you see on the outside with your heart."

She took the knife and quartered the apple to reveal a healthy core protecting small, perfectly formed seeds. She used the tip of the knife to free them before pushing them toward herself. One she nudged toward Violet. "We're Sam's closest family. Me. Jane and Daniel. We know Sam's heart, and we love him, bruises and all, which is what family is expected to do. A good man like Sam makes it easy, though. Might just take an exceptional young woman to love him as much as we do, to trust her heart and let the first seed of love grow knowin' nothin' in life is perfect. It's the effort that counts most."

She paused and felt through her apron pocket. "Must have left my tobacco upstairs. I'll be right back," she promised and left Violet alone to contemplate her words.

Violet stared at the seed, tempted and torn between facing life with Sam or without him. She put her finger on top of the tiny seed. Deep in thought, she absently traced the top of the table. Scarred and knicked, it must have served this family for several generations, but the wood itself was still sturdy and strong.

Was Aunt Nester right? Had Violet been so shocked and so hurt by Sam's stunning revelations, she had let her mind rule over her heart? If she had, was it too late to set things right?

One by one, she brought the images of the people she had known or loved or who were involved in her life these past few difficult weeks to her mind's eye. She used her heart to understand them and refused to let her mind shape a single illusion. Her father, a man filled with fear that he allowed to destroy his soul. Dr. Poole, a weak, greedy man. Captain Miles? A protective titan. Ben, a champion of the spirit of the law. Rosemary had an impish heart, but a good one.

Violet's heart swelled, and her throat choked with emotion, but she forced herself to continue and consider the few people she had met here in Sunrise. Jane's image stood intertwined with Daniel's. Their love for one another created an aura that showed how strongly their hearts and spirits were united. Little Olivia was the most precious and innocent of all. Aunt Nester? She was country-rough, but her heart was smooth as silk.

Finally, when all the others faded away, Sam stood alone. A man of character and conscience, he wore the mantle of shame willingly.

For simple justice.

For her.

She bowed her head and let the tears wash away the illusion of Sam that had nearly claimed her love for him. She spent more tears regretting the hurtful things she had said to him, and even more for the future they might have had together if she had only trusted her heart as much as she had once trusted Sam.

When she heard Aunt Nester returning to the kitchen, she wiped away her tears and started peeling one of the apples.

Aunt Nester was muttering to herself as she entered the kitchen shaking her tattered pouch. "It's the darnedest thing."

Violet kept her hands working and her face averted. "Oh?"

"Since Sam was going into town to see Doc Birchfield to get those stitches out, I asked him to stop and get me some tobacco. Thought I still had enough to last till he got back, but the old pouch is plumb empty," she grumbled and shoved it into her apron pocket.

"He left hours ago. I'm sure he'll be back soon."

"Doubt it. He said he was stoppin' in to visit little Olivia. I think he mentioned takin' time to see the Reverend Reilly, too. Sure hope he stopped at Foster's first. New shipment due in yesterday. 'Course, the store might be clear run outta tobacco anyway, what with all the rafters here durin' tradin' season."

Violet had not been to town yet. Sam had insisted it was too crowded with outsiders now for her to venture there alone, and he was not about to escort her on crutches. The prospect of having an opportunity to repay Aunt Nester for her friendship and wisdom set aside any concerns Violet had for her own safety.

She laid down the apple she was peeling and set it alongside her knife. "I'll go to Foster's for you."

Aunt Nester scowled. "That'd get you and me in a whole heap of trouble with Sam, not to mention Aaron Foster. He's—"

"Can't be any worse than the trouble I've got," Violet suggested with a weak smile. She rose and rinsed her hands at the sink. "I have to freshen up a bit before I go."

She was nearly to the door when Aunt Nester called her back. When Violet turned around, the old woman's eyes were twinkling with mischief, reminding her of Rosemary.

"You got a good walk to get to town, but if you follow the main road, you can't miss it. Try stoppin' first at Jane's house. You'll see Daniel's shingle hangin' out front. Sam's probably still there, and you can ask him first about my tobacco. Save you a trip into Foster's by yourself, but if you have to, tell Foster to put it in the book for me."

Violet grinned. "I will. Don't worry. I'll be fine." She turned and hurried to her chamber. Once she redid her hair, she donned a straw bonnet to protect her face from the sun.

She did not bother trying to pinch a little color into her cheeks. The hot, long walk would have them rosy by the time she got to town, if the spirit of adventure pounding through her body did not do it first.

Before she left her chamber, she gathered up a few things, stored them in her small travel bag, and left the house by the front door. She was at the bottom of the front steps when she heard Aunt Nester's voice.

"You try rushin' like that all the way to Sunrise, you'll swoon on the main road and get run over by one of Peterson's wagons from the mill."

Violet swung around and found Aunt Nester sitting in the rocker on the front porch with her spittoon close by. "I thought you might be finishing up the apples."

She shrugged shoulders rounded with age. "Just restin' a spell here first. Go on, before I think twice about sendin' you off by yourself. I'll just be sittin' here worryin' and waitin' for my tobacco. Awful habit, but I'm too old to change now."

Violet's eyes misted. "I wouldn't change a thing about you. Not one," she insisted before she hurried on her way. She had no intention of going farther than Foster's, but she could not tell Aunt Nester she did not want to risk seeing Sam at Jane's home.

Not now.

Not until she had figured out a way to face the fact she had had one chance at true love and had thrown it away.

Chapter Twenty-eight

❧

$\mathcal{N}$o crutches. No more stitches. Sam had no more patience for an ornery, meddling aunt, either.

He returned from a prolonged visit to the site where his late brother-in-law, Hiram Foster, had been found dead to face the ghosts of his past life in Sunrise one last time. He rode up to the house determined to convince Aunt Nester to leave him alone instead of pestering him with questions about why he did not stop wallowing in self-pity and try talking to Violet again.

He could not talk Violet into believing he had no knowledge of how guilty his firm had been when he first approached her offering to help. He had destroyed her trust in him as well as the love he so desperately wanted to claim.

When he spied his aunt rocking on the porch, he rode straight ahead and did not bother to dismount. Violet must be either upstairs tending to Ben or in the kitchen attempting to avoid making another disastrous meal, so this was a perfect time to approach Aunt Nester.

She squinted and spat tobacco juice into the spittoon. "Guess you saw Doc Birchfield. How's the foot?"

He leaned back in the saddle and tipped back his hat. "Good as ever."

"Guess you talked to Peterson at the mill."

"Actually, no. I needed some time alone to make some

decisions," he admitted. He would not risk telling her where he had been to do his thinking. All that mattered now was finding the right words to tell her forcefully, but respectfully, to stop meddling in his affairs.

She grinned, revealing stained teeth. " 'Bout time. Hope you came to your senses. Suppose you need to see Violet. She's not here. She went to town about an hour ago."

He sat up and tightened his hold on the reins. "Alone?"

"Well, I can't walk that far," she grumbled.

"It's too hot for her to walk that far, too, and the town's crowded with riffraff. You should have stopped her."

She stopped rocking and leaned forward in her seat. "Seems to me that's your business, not mine. You told me to stop meddlin' often enough. Change your mind?"

"Now? When she's heading for nothing but trouble? Now is when you finally decide to stop meddling?" He wiped his brow and let out an exasperated sigh. When he saw the pained expression on her face, he felt a huge tug on his conscience. "I'm sorry. I'm just hot and thirsty and—"

"And snappy. Go get yourself a tall glass of cider and cool off. She'll be back soon. You can talk to her then," she muttered. She set her rocker into motion and laid her head against the back of the chair.

"I'd rather make sure she didn't swoon on the road along the way there or back. If she didn't, I may as well find her and bring her home. Do you know where she wanted to go in town?"

" 'Course I do. Least I'm pretty sure I heard her right. Might have to admit I'm losin' some of my hearing, but you'd best not tell Libby or Penelope. They've been grumblin' a lot about that lately."

He narrowed his gaze and tightened his jaw. "Where did she go?"

"I know she took the main road 'cause I told her to follow it to town."

He gritted his teeth. "And once she got there?"

She still had not bothered to sit up and look at him.

If she had, she would probably knock him off his horse

after seeing the frustration he knew etched his face.

"Not sure where else, but I think she went to Foster's."

"Foster's?" he thundered. "Of all places in town, why would she go there? And if you knew that's where she was going, you should have locked her in her room to make sure she didn't go!"

His aunt bolted up straight in her seat and braced both feet on the porch floor. "You should be happy I'm not meddlin' anymore. Besides, where else can she go to buy a ticket for the stage?"

"The stage? She's not supposed to leave for another week," he protested.

"Don't know about that. Took her travel bag with her, but polite soul that I am, I didn't ask her what was in it. Couldn't be much, though," she added with a grin. "I'm pretty sure she'll be back in a bit."

He yanked his hat down on his head, turned the horse around, and started off at a canter toward town. Of all the changes in Sunrise, having a stagecoach stop in town no longer appeared to be an advantage. If Violet had decided to leave, she probably only packed up her documents, the bank draft he had given to her, and her few precious coins. But she had no idea how vitriolic Hiram's brother would be when she tried to buy a ticket for the stage.

It only came through once a week, but he had no idea if the stage would arrive today or not and suspected Aunt Nester might have done a little meddling, notwithstanding her claims otherwise.

"Stubborn, stubborn, stubborn," he gritted. Violet must really hate the sight of him not to even want his help getting into town. Like it or not, she would take his help coming home if he had to hogtie her to the saddle and hold her in front of him all the way home.

He grinned at the image that inspired and spurred the horse to go a little faster down the main road to Sunrise.

*　　*　　*

After a frightfully long walk, Violet entered Foster's General Store. Hot, winded, and temporarily sun-blinded, she was in a cranky mood.

When her vision cleared, she found the interior more rustic than the specialized shops in Philadelphia and the array of goods simply amazing. Bulky farm implements hung on the walls. Delicate trinkets filled a glass display case. Everything in between was either stored on ceiling-high shelves or on wooden counters running the length of the store.

She also found a dozen pairs of curious eyes staring at her, and the drone of animated conversation eased to a hum of whispers. Although her heart was racing, she greeted them with a smile. She switched her travel bag from one hand to another and wiped her sweaty palm on her skirts.

An older man, obviously the shopkeeper, Aaron Foster, stood behind the counter where he must have been serving a pair of odd-matched women standing only a few feet away. As round as he was tall, he was sweating profusely and his hair lay in damp strands that he pushed away from his face. His expression was anything but kindly.

Awkward silence descended until the tall candlestick of a woman standing next to a woman that looked like an inverted sugarloaf spoke up. "You must be Violet. I'm Libby Holtzman. Nester is such a dear friend of ours. She told us all about you."

The sugarloaf nodded. "Welcome to Sunrise, Violet. I'm Penelope Washburn." Her lips curled up. "It's little wonder Sam's kept you out to the homestead all to himself. Nester didn't tell us you were such a fetching young woman. I'm so glad he's finally brought you to town so we could meet you."

Violet was in no state to receive compliments any more than she wanted to explain anything other than the purpose for her visit. She nodded, and the women parted as she approached the counter, but she spoke directly to the shopkeeper. "Aunt Nester used up all her tobacco. I'd like some for her, please. And a new pouch, as well."

He studied her so heatedly she expected to actually melt. "A nurse? That's what you're claimin' to be?"

She clenched her teeth. It was clear she was not going to easily escape the attention she had drawn to herself by coming to town, but she did not want to antagonize the man who had what she wanted to purchase. "Only for another week. Mr. Jackson won't be needing my care beyond that so I'll be leaving."

Satisfaction lit his gaze. "Good. Last time Glennings brought a woman back to Sunrise, it cost my brother his life."

She flinched, but held her gaze steady.

"Now Aaron, you can't keep blaming Sam," the candlestick admonished above the hum of new whispers.

He scowled back at her. "I sure as Hades can't blame anyone else, now can I? He nearly cost his own sister her life, too. That's why he left in the first place. Thought he'd have better sense than to come back. Some folks here haven't forgotten the scandal he brought here, neither. At least he knows better than to come in here himself and sent her instead." He paused and glared at Violet. "You want that tobacco or not? No credit. Cash or barter."

Shocked by the bitterness in his words, Violet silenced her heart that pleaded for her to defend Sam. "Yes, I do."

She set her travel bag on the floor to retrieve the dissected picture puzzle she had made for Rosemary. In the chaos of leaving the ship, she had neglected to give it to her sister and hoped it would serve her purpose now. She laid the gleaming mahogany box onto the counter and held her precious coins in reserve in case he did not want the puzzle.

"Will you take this in trade for the tobacco? And the new pouch, as well," she added confidently. Although bartering for goods was a new experience, she rather liked the concept. Even if Ben did not need her care longer than another week, she could easily finish another two or three puzzles. If she could get the wood. She could use her coins to purchase it, assuming Aunt Nester could tell her how to find the local sawmill.

She practically held her breath as he inspected the puzzle and tried not to think about the townspeople who were watching her as well as him. When he finished, he shrugged his shoulders. "Quality piece, but I don't get much call for something so expensive." When he shook his head, her heart sank. "Won't get near what it's worth in the city. Might take six months to find a buyer. I'll give you the tobacco. Pouch would be more."

The candlestick gasped. "Don't you cheat that girl! Let her have the pouch, too."

Her companion leaned over the counter, crushing her ample bosom against the top in the process. "And credit, too. At least a dollar."

He scowled so deeply his brows knitted together into a solid worm of hair. "One plug of tobacco. One pouch. That's my best offer."

"Then I accept," she gushed, relieved not to have to part with any of her coins. "You don't have to bother wrapping them. I'll just put them into my bag."

He carried her puzzle with him when he turned to secure her purchases, and the two women edged so close she felt sandwiched. The candlestick sighed. "He's still smoldering with anger he directs at Sam or anyone close to him."

Her companion shook her head. "That doesn't give him the right to cheat you out of what's fair. That puzzle's worth twice what he offered you."

"Maybe more," her friend suggested.

Neither woman seemed to care that the shopkeeper could overhear them, or that other customers had entered the shop. "I have no reason not to trust Mr. Foster to be fair with me. He's a businessman. I can't expect him to base his decisions or his business affairs on what I may need or want any more than I can expect to see what's really in his mind," she said in a loud clear voice, attempting to dissuade the notion she was other than pleased with her trade.

Voices from the small crowd of people chimed in with responses she could not help but hear.

"She's a fool for sure."

"Gotta be, 'less she's just set on gettin' what she wants."

"Or plumb distracted. Nobody can be that trustin'."

She cringed, but held her tongue. When the shopkeeper

returned, he slid the items across the counter. Smiling tightly as she tried to keep from lashing out at her detractors, she packed her purchases into her travel bag. "Thank you," she murmured.

He hesitated, then grabbed a handful of colorful hair ribbons from the shelf behind him. "Got these in from New York. Guess I should toss in a few. Just to be fair."

She closed her fist around the ribbons and gave him a genuine smile this time, but his offer only inspired renewed comment, this time only from men. "She's still touched in the head," someone muttered.

A sardonic chuckle. "Maybe old Foster here is, too, if he thinks Glenning didn't bring her here for himself. Might be tastin' those sweet lips already."

Another snide laugh. "Old Nester can't stay awake twenty-four hours a day. Sam's no fool, and he sure ain't no angel, neither."

"Man would have to be made of stone not to want that one."

Humiliated and angry, she swung about and faced the crowd. Her heart pounded in her chest, and she blurted out her feelings without stopping to think or to pay attention to yet another late-arriving observer. "Maybe I am distracted. Some people might even tell you I am for certain, but I can't change what they think about me any more than I can change what Mr. Foster thinks of Sam. Or any of you, for that matter. I just have to trust people will judge me by how I act or how I treat them."

Chest heaving, she drew in a deep breath. She let the words she had tried so hard to deny with her mind flow from her heart, guided by Aunt Nester's simple wisdom. "I will tell you this. Sam Glennings is a good and honorable man. He isn't without his faults. None of us are. But he has the courage to take responsibility for anything he's done and the wisdom to forgive himself for everything else. Maybe . . . maybe we would all be richer if we had the heart to do the same."

Her words echoed in the store and shattered whatever misguided illusions she once held as a shield around her heart.

She swirled about and marched to the door, blinded by tears.

The man who blocked her way was no illusion.

Yet it was definitely an illusion to think he had not heard every word she had said.

Sam stood tall again without his crutches, but she quickly averted her gaze. Before he could tell everyone what a complete hypocrite she was, defending him in public while condemning him in private, she stepped around him and hurried out of the store.

Her coins jingled in her bag. She needed them now more than ever. Sam would just have to find someone else to care for Ben. She had to get the next stage out of Sunrise.

Desperate to find out how to secure a ticket, she charged across the planked sidewalk and down the steps. She headed down the middle of the street so she could find the stagecoach office, certain Sam might try to stop her only long enough to say a few choice words she most surely did not want to hear.

Chapter Twenty-nine

◆≻

For several incredible heartbeats, Sam was so stunned by everything he had seen Violet do and every word he had heard her say, he could not move a muscle if he tried.

His chest tightened with emotion, and his mind blocked out every word she had said save one: *if*.

She had said *if* she had courage or wisdom she could forgive him.

If?

He was distracted himself if he wasted as much as one more heartbeat and doubted that she had both. And he was a raving lunatic if he did not run after her and convince her she was both courageous and wise.

And that he loved her.

If it meant he had to follow her all the way to eternity before she believed him, he would. And then he would simply have to convince her to marry him.

With all gazes glued to him in the general store, he turned around and ignored everyone but the woman he found marching down the middle of the street. He never lost a single stride as he pursued her. The townspeople had already witnessed the scandal surrounding the worst betrayal a man could suffer. If he made a complete fool of himself now and lost her because he was going to confront her in front of the entire town, his reputation had little to lose.

If he won her heart, which he swore to do with every step he took, the townspeople would consider the spectacle great entertainment and fodder for gossip that just might put the rest of his past to rest once and for all.

He stopped at the edge of the planked sidewalk.

"Violet!" he shouted and tore down the steps.

She kept walking and drivers of the wagons in the street were forced to avoid her. They pulled to the side and stopped to watch, their amazed gazes shifting from Violet to Sam and back again.

"Violet! Wait!" he ordered as he rushed down the street after her. When he heard a wagon approaching him from behind, he looked over his shoulder and grinned. "Help me out here, Louis. I need a little space."

His cousin chuckled and brought his wagon to a halt. "Glad to oblige. Got yourself a runaway filly?"

"Sure do. Thanks!" Sam hurried his steps and closed the distance between himself and Violet until he was only a few feet behind her.

She waved him back by swinging her travel bag behind her. "Don't you dare follow me!"

She sure sounded mad and flustered.

"Wait. We need to talk," he insisted. Out of the corner of his eye he saw shop doors open and people hustle outside to line the street as if they were late for a parade.

She walked even faster. Where did that woman get her spunk and energy?

"Stop, Violet. Now."

"Go away. I don't want to talk to you or see you again. Ever."

Panting, he still managed a hearty chuckle. "Yes you do. You love me as much as I love you. Admit it."

Right choice of words.

She snapped to a halt and swirled around, her image a blur of fury and skirts. No tears washed her cheeks, but her dark eyes definitely were blazing. With her chest heaving up and down and her face all rosy, she looked absolutely delicious. He stopped and folded his arms over his chest to keep from swinging her up into his arms and tasting those sweet lips he had longed to savor for weeks.

"Love you? You must be mistaken," she gushed. "How could you possibly think I—I love you?"

He grinned and rolled up the sleeve of his shirt. He held up his forearm to display his scar to her and waited till the gathered crowd had a good look. "I risked my life to save you."

The crowd applauded. Men whistled. Children cheered.

She tossed back her head. "Only because you were stubborn enough to stand out in the rain for three straight nights to speak to me when I told you I had no intention of doing any such thing."

He noted that the women nodded and smiled with approval, but his heart trembled when he saw his sister standing on the front porch of the home she shared with Daniel.

When Violet tilted her chin up a notch, he knocked it down again. "You were the one who slipped out at midnight to see me, just like you did the night you went to see Elijah Dennus."

Violet frowned. The women followed suit, but the men on either side of the street chuckled.

"Don't look like a fallen angel, does she?" a man shouted. "Maybe she's just—"

"She's my angel. Mine alone," Sam insisted. He did not want her reputation touched, only her heart.

She paled, but her eyes still glistened with anger. "I have no reason to love you at all. You're . . . you're mad!"

He held up his newly healed foot, but did not want to take his eyes off her to stoop and remove his boot. "I probably am mad. And utterly and completely distracted. By you. Didn't I nearly bleed to death and spend weeks on crutches because I—"

"Walked through city streets in your stocking feet?"

He flinched.

She smirked. "That had nothing to do with me, but Ben told me all about it. Next time don't try to bully a nurse taking care of a very ill patient. If you don't throw your boots down the steps to distract her, maybe she won't toss them into the street."

Hoots of laughter.

He fumbled with his shirtsleeve while trying to think of a retort. He latched onto one, but decided to end the show so he could finish what he had to say in private. "Give me the stage ticket, Violet. We'll talk about this at home."

Confusion rained across her features, and she shook her head. He waited with great anticipation for her to speak, standing tall, fighting for the woman he loved with his shoulders square and his head held high.

Steady, determined footsteps brought Violet closer to Sam. Too distraught to think, she let her heart guide her. She tossed the rainbow of hair ribbons at him and watched them fall to the ground at his feet. "How could you possibly think I could go home with a man who chased me down the main street of his hometown and made a spectacle of himself and me, in front of half the town?"

He flinched again, but when she did not see his determination falter, she set her travel bag to the ground and issued a challenge to force him to respond. "Tell me why you love me. Name the reasons. One for . . . one for every ribbon at your feet. If you can—"

"Then I get your stage ticket?"

She caught her breath. What on earth was he talking about?

He cocked his head, but waited for an answer without taunting her this time. She could not lie about having a stage ticket, but she could not let him off this easily, either. After completely humiliating her, he deserved nothing less.

"No, I'll . . . I'll marry you," she blurted, aghast at her inability to keep her heart from putting words into her mouth.

A riot of applause erupted, replete with clapping hands, hoots, whistles, and stomping feet.

When Sam looked at her, she felt a hot blush on her cheeks spread down her neck to her toes.

"One reason for every ribbon," he repeated. "That's all I need, and you'll marry me?"

She caught her lower lip. She could not very well take

back her challenge with all these witnesses, but there were at least eight ribbons lying in the dirt. She banked on him not making it past two. Maybe three. He would never get to all eight.

Her heart chuckled. *Yes he will.*

"Yes, I will," she responded, smugly challenging her heart with her mind.

He stooped down, picked up the ribbons, and brushed them clean. The crowd grew restless, and Violet thought her heart might burst with anticipation.

"Today. This afternoon," he murmured. "You'll marry me."

She lifted her chin. "I—I . . . well, yes."

He chose the yellow ribbon first and tied it around her wrist. "I love you because you have a loyal heart, even for fools like me who don't deserve your love," he whispered.

His touch sent tingles up her arm and down again, and his words confirmed that he had heard what she had said about him in the general store.

He tied the red ribbon around her other wrist. "I love you all the more because I know you love me, too." He put his finger to his lips to warn her not to argue. Then he took the green, blue, orange, and indigo ribbons and tied them end to end to make one long ribbon before he looped it around her waist and held it closed with a crude but effective bow.

His touch made her tremble.

"I love you because I envy your courage. I greet every new dawn with the hope you'll forgive me by sunset and pray I won't die for longing to hold you close as my helpmate and my champion, my love and my wife, for now and for always. You've had to be so strong for such a long time," he whispered. "Let me be strong for you. Let me take care of you. Let me stand by your side so we face the future. Together, as one."

Her heart nearly stopped beating. She could not breathe much past the lump in her throat. She could barely see through the tears that blurred her vision as his heart reached out to hers. His words and his love fulfilled the very dreams she had once thought to be impossible.

The crowd grew deathly still. Not even the horses dared to neigh, and children held on to their parents' hands like little statues. Violet thought her knees might buckle when he tied one end of the purple ribbon on the finger where once she had worn her sister's wedding ring.

"Violet is the color of forgiveness, given freely with trust." He paused and tugged on the ribbon until her hand pressed against his heart. "From this day forward, I vow my heart will beat with love that I will share only with you. I will cherish you, protect you, and care for you every day of my life—if you bless me with the gift of your love and marry me."

Overwhelmed with joy beyond any she had ever known, she listened to her heart and nodded her assent. When he swept her into his arms, she pressed frantic kisses to his throat, as if to prove he was not a dream. He was real. So very, very real. He was . . . simply and wonderfully, Sam. Her friend. Her ally. And her beloved.

When his lips joined with hers, sheer physical delight exploded through every one of her senses. If this was what happened with their first kiss, she could scarcely wait to get married and get home.

A cacophony of cheers, whistles, and wild applause erupted as the throng of bystanders rushed toward them.

"Hurry and find the preacher," she gushed. "I think Rosemary was right after all."

"Rosemary? Right about what?"

She whispered her answer into his ear. "The marriage bed. It will be the grandest adventure!"

He chuckled all the way to the church. With the entire town at their heels, he stopped several times to kiss her again and again, much to the boisterous delight of the parade of people behind them, and to whisper his own ideas about just how grand their adventure tonight would be.

And it was.

* * *

*L*ong after her new husband had fallen asleep, Violet waited for daybreak. She had no illusions or fears, only old dreams fulfilled and new ones forming with every beat of her heart—for herself and for Rosemary. The healing she had prayed to come with each new dawn finally filled her heart and soul.

Not with the first rays of a new dawn, but with the love of a man named Sam . . . in a little town called Sunrise.

Epilogue

❧

1838

Sam cupped his hand over Violet's face. "Now close your eyes. I'll lead you the rest of the way."

She kissed the heel of his hand, but did not hesitate to follow his request. She had not challenged him earlier when he asked her not to look through the windows of the train as they had approached this city en route to their final destination: New York City. Or not to peek through the curtains of the coach, either.

She trusted him implicitly. Even here.

The last stop on her journey to complete healing.

He dropped his hand to capture hers and entwined warm, strong fingers with her own, offering encouragement, but most of all, unconditional love. A gentle spring breeze carried a multitude of floral scents, but it was the soft cooing from inside the coach and Ben's frantic voice that garnered her attention.

"Don't be too long, Violet. I'm not sure I can keep these two bundles very happy."

She stifled a giggle and called back over her shoulder. "It's only a baby, and one at that."

"Well, I see two. One baby couldn't possibly produce all this . . . this dribble."

"He's teething again. Bounce Elijah on your knee. Gently," she admonished and added a silent prayer the specialist in New York would be able to restore or at least improve Ben's vision.

Sam squeezed her hand. "Are you ready?"

She moistened her lips. "Show me the way," she murmured. Her heart raced with blessed joy that kept her steps steady and helped to soften the memories of her past life.

Before Sam.

Before freedom.

Before Sunrise.

When she detected the strong scent of mint, she knew they had passed the herb garden, and her heart skipped a beat. When he tightened his hold, she thought they might be near their destination, and her heart started to race. But when he stopped and turned her toward him, her heart literally pounded with anticipation. He claimed her lips with a gentle kiss and pressed one to each of her closed eyelids. "It's time."

She nodded. Even though her father had met his final reward several months ago, she still felt his presence here. Nevertheless, she had wanted to see this very place with her own eyes before offering the property for sale. She feared nothing, not even the sight of barren earth, would be strong enough to forever replace the painful memories that burdened her spirit.

In the next heartbeat, he stole her breath away when he swung her off her feet. He finally set her down several strides later. She swayed a bit on the uneven ground until she opened her eyes and realized she was standing on the cultivated earth in a garden.

A very large garden where the tower had once stood, next to the city mansion where she had been born and raised.

At her feet, embracing violets of deep purple hugged the perimeter of the garden where once bricks and mortar had sat upon the foundation of the tower. In the center, where room above room had been home to pain, despair, and desperate dreams, stood a bare, arched trellis. Wild roses, promising to bloom in every shade of pink from pale to vivid, defied the gardener's best efforts and formed a maze of freeform glory that honored the essence of Rosemary's spirit.

Wide-eyed, she spun around to face him. "When I asked

you to have the tower removed before the house was sold, I had no idea you would . . ."

His grin. His dancing eyes. They stole her heart all over again.

"I thought you might be pleased," he teased as he handed her a small package.

Intrigued, she turned the package over in her hands. "What is it?"

"The original blueprints for the house," he murmured. "Ludlam managed to replace every existing copy with new ones that don't show the tower sketched next to the house or anywhere. We won't outlive everyone who knew about the tower, but our children will. One day, no one will know the tower ever stood here. And no one will know what happened inside its walls."

She kept her gaze on him and looked deep into a heart filled with the love, devotion, and breathtaking passion he had given to her these past several years. Before she could tell him what was in her heart, she thought she heard a familiar giggle behind her.

When she looked over her shoulder, her eyes widened, and her heart began to race. At the rear of the yard near the back gate stood a titan. In each arm, he held a darling little boy who held onto his daddy's beard with tightly closed fists. At his side, cradling an infant swaddled in a soft pink blanket, stood her sister, Rosemary.

With tears streaming down her cheeks, she turned back to her husband and cradled his face with her hands. "Have I told you today how much I love you?"

He grinned from ear to ear. "I think you need to tell me again before you have a long-awaited reunion with your sister." He pulled her into his arms and kissed her until she was breathless and quite anxious to continue the grandest adventure of all: loving Sam.